D1383919

Sweet Annie

Center Point
Large Print

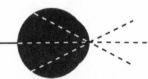

**This Large Print Book carries the
Seal of Approval of N.A.V.H.**

Sweet Annie

Cheryl St. John

CENTER POINT LARGE PRINT
THORNDIKE, MAINE

This Center Point Large Print edition
is published in the year 2015 by arrangement with
Harlequin Books S.A.

The text of this Large Print edition is unabridged.
In other aspects, this book may vary
from the original edition.
Printed in the United States of America
on permanent paper.
Set in 16-point Times New Roman type.

ISBN: 978-1-62899-626-5

Library of Congress Cataloging-in-Publication Data

St. John, Cheryl.
   Sweet Annie / Cheryl St. John. — Center Point Large Print edition.
       pages cm
   Summary: "Everyone treated Annie as a fragile doll because of her
deformed hip, except Luke Carpenter. The only times Annie felt like a
whole person was when she was with him because Luke challenged her
to do things others discouraged her from trying—even becoming his
wife"—Provided by publisher.
   ISBN 978-1-62899-626-5 (library binding : alk. paper)
   1. Large type books. I. Title.
   PS3569.T12424S44 2015
   813′.54—dc23
                                                      2015012335

Dedicated to my friend Anita Baker, who, though she hasn't walked since 1974, has run a good race, and fought a good fight. She has enriched the life of each person who knows her. I look forward to dancing together on streets of gold.

Sweet Annie

Prologue

Copper Creek, Colorado
1878

The expansive spring sky was that vibrant shade of purest blue that always made Annie's chest ache with an unexplainable sadness. The color stretched in all directions like a heavenly canopy dotted by only the merest whispers of fleecy white clouds. Surely, if a person stood on one of those snow-capped mountaintops in the distance, he could reach out and touch that mysterious and elusive glory.

Sounds of laughter and music slowly drew her attention back to earth, back to the grown-ups scattered on her parents' lush green lawn in chattering clusters. She observed the boisterous children who dashed about, playing games of tag and hide-and-seek.

Several were intent on an impassioned battle of croquet beneath the sun-filtering leaves of the ancient aspens. Annie watched with a familiar mixture of yearning and bereavement in her ten-year-old heart.

"Are you warm enough, darling?" Her mother's concerned voice wasn't enough to divert her attention from the game, but she nodded in reply.

"Would you like some more lemonade?"

"No, thank you. Can you push me a little closer to the players, Mama?"

"One of those wooden balls might fly up and strike you," her mother said in her most discouraging tone. "You're safer right here."

"I got out of my chair this morning, and I made it to my dressing table all by myself," she said, knowing the effort would displease her mother, but desperate to assure her she wasn't completely helpless. "I know I could stand under one of the trees there for a while. I could hold on to it. Please, Mama? Please let me?"

Mildred Sweetwater tucked the plush lap robe more tightly around Annie's legs. "I'll not have you upsetting yourself this way, child. You know you can't walk and play like other children. There are roots sticking above the ground, and you could trip and hurt yourself. No more foolish talk like that. You're safe in your chair. Hold your sweet new doll. There—isn't she the prettiest thing?" Mother glanced about and spotted Annie's brother. "Burdell, come and keep your sister company."

The boy obediently moved to stand beside Annie's wheelchair, and Mildred glided gracefully back into the crowd.

"You don't have to stand there, Burdy," she told him with a disgusted wave of her hand. "Go on and have fun with your friends."

No one but Annie could have called him by that nickname without getting a fist in the teeth. At sixteen he was already taller and broader than their father, and possessed a chip the size of Colorado on his shoulder. But he never treated Annie with anything less than devotion. "I don't mind," he replied. "I know it must be hard sittin' in that chair all the time. It's something you're going to have to accept. I wish it wasn't so."

Annie sighed, glad for his company and his loyalty, but resentful that he looked at her the same way their parents did. She glanced distractedly at the delicate Dresden doll in her lap—an addition to the ponderous collection that already ladened the window seat in her room.

He stayed beside her until she noticed his friends glancing their way, and she shooed him off to join them. The gangly boys tramped toward the creek, and she envied them their independence.

Sometime later, two riders approached the house. They tethered their horses near the gate and walked toward the festivities. One was Gilbert Chapman, a man she'd seen visit her parents before. The other was an unfamiliar lanky young man who looked younger than Burdell. Annie observed with interest as Mr. Chapman introduced the boy to her parents and a small gathering, then moved on to talk with someone else.

Left alone, the young man observed the croquet

game for a few minutes, then spotted her. Hands jammed in the pockets of his trousers, he ambled his way to where she sat. Compared to her brother's compact sturdiness, he seemed all legs and angles and booted feet. A breeze caught his shiny black hair and lifted the locks away from his forehead. "Hey," he said.

Annie looked up into eyes as bright and blue as the sky. "Hello. I haven't seen you before. What's your name?"

"Luke Carpenter. I'm visiting my Uncle Gil. What's yours?"

"Annie. This is my birthday party."

"Happy birthday. Pretty doll."

"Thanks. That your uncle's horse?"

"No, he's mine."

"What's his name?"

"Wrangler. He's a Swedish Warmblood. They were bred as cavalry horses originally. Part Spanish, part oriental."

"You sure know a lot about horses."

"Some."

"So, he's from Sweden?"

He chuckled, and a long dimple creased his lean cheek. "Nah. He's from Nebraska. Wanna see 'im up close?"

"Oh! Can I?"

"Sure. What's wrong with you?" he asked as he pushed her chair toward the gate. "I mean, why can't you walk?"

"I was born with a misproportioned limb," she said, knowing as she spoke them, even before he leaned forward to see her face and raised a brow, that her mother's fancy words sounded ridiculous. "A gimp leg," she clarified. Her mother would have a fit of apoplexy at the coarse term.

"Oh," he said simply.

"Mama and Papa have had me to all the best doctors in the East. There isn't an operation that can fix what's wrong. My bones aren't made right in my hip."

"Does it hurt?"

"No. I can walk a little, but it's clumsy and Mama says I shouldn't embarrass myself."

Her chair came to a stop a few feet from the horse. "Can you ride?"

She gaped up at him with surprise, and a hopefulness she hadn't dreamed sprang up so strong, her chest hurt. "I don't know. Is it dangerous?"

"No more dangerous than most things, I guess."

She stared up at the enormous shiny brown animal wistfully. Oh, what a birthday it would be if she could ride him! *Her,* lame Annie Sweetwater, on a horse. Oh, glory be! "Can I see if I can sit on him?"

He glanced back at the party; no one was paying them any attention. "Reckon so. How will we get you up there?"

She dumped the china doll alongside her cashmere lap blanket on the grass and struggled to her feet. Luke caught her arm to steady her.

"How do *you* get up?" Standing right beside the beast was more intimidating than just imagining. But she wanted to sit in that saddle badly—so badly she shoved aside the sudden qualm and paid close attention to his reply.

"I put one foot in the stirrup here, and throw the other leg over his back. Can you do that?"

"I don't think so." That was the leg that didn't allow her mobility.

"Maybe if I lift you so you can get your good leg in the stirrup, then I can help you get the other one over."

"Okay."

He picked her up much as Burdell and her father often did, then directed her foot to the stirrup. "Grab the horn and pull."

She got her foot secured, held on tightly, and he raised her body, indelicately pushing her bottom upward until she had her weight in the stirrup. Determined, Annie held on with all her inexpert strength.

Holding her weight above him was obviously a strain, but he seemed as stubborn as she, and after several awkward grunts and shoves, Annie found herself in the saddle. Her voluminous skirts and eyelet petticoats had bunched and rumpled, but he even helped her adjust them to cover most of her pantaloons and limbs modestly.

"Anything hurt?" he asked, panting as he

squinted up, the sun casting blue highlights through his now rumpled black hair.

"Nope." Oh, but the ground was so very far away and the view of the countryside from up here was positively elating! "I'm doing it!" she squealed. "I'm on the horse!"

"Move your foot now, so I can get on behind you."

Surprised, she obeyed, and he swung up easily to sit behind her. "Scared?" he asked.

"Oh, no! This is better than I ever imagined!"

"This is nothin'," he said, reaching rawboned arms around her to pick up the reins. "The best is coming." With a flexing movement of his legs and feet that she felt through her clothing, he urged the horse forward.

Startled, but delighted, Annie's heart raced. "Make him go faster!"

He kicked the animal into motion, and Annie gripped the saddle horn. After the first few jolting minutes, she adjusted her weight to the gait of the horse. Her home stood on a sparsely populated tree-lined street near the corner of town, and Luke headed Wrangler away, toward the open fields of grass and rabbit brush to the south.

The wind caressed Annie's cheeks and whipped through her hair, loosening the once faultless sausage curls and streaming the locks over her shoulders. The sky rushed forward to meet them, blue in all directions, breathtaking as far as her eyes could see. A liberating sense of freedom and exhilaration tuned her every sense and thought and feeling into this moment.

She'd never felt so light, so delicate and free from the chains that bound her to the earth; the restrictions of her body that tethered her to that chair were forgotten. Annie laughed and cried a shout of pure jubilation. Daringly, she released her hold on the leather and spread her arms wide open.

It was the best day of her life.

Riding was better than her most fanciful dreams—better than ice cream, better than birthdays and Christmas. The horse carried them along a creek lined with nodding daisies as far as the eye could see.

Eventually, Luke turned the horse's head, guiding him back the way they'd come, then slowed him to a walk as they got closer.

Annie's head was full to bursting with the pleasure of her first taste of freedom. "This was the best birthday present anyone could ever give me," she said over her shoulder. "Thank you, Luke Carpenter."

"Happy Birthday, Annie."

"How long are you staying with your uncle?" she asked, hopefully.

"I'm not sure. I might be coming to work for him."

The feel of the wind numbing her cheeks and

this smile of joy would always be on her face, she was sure. Excitement filled her to bursting.

Wrangler carried them down the dirt lane to her house, and as they neared, Annie caught site of the crowd, which had re-formed and now milled near the front gate. Her mother stood, lace handkerchief balled in a fist and pressed to her breast. At her side Annie's father wore a thunderous expression.

Panic exploded inside Annie. Dread washed over her, erasing her joy and lightheartedness like water thrown on a slate. Burdell broke through the crowd and pointed at Luke as they approached.

"Oh, Annie! Oh, my God, Annie!" her mother cried, and Annie's father steadied his wife for a moment, then passed her into a neighbor's hands and rushed forward.

"What is the meaning of this?" he demanded. "Annie, are you all right?"

"I'm fine, Papa," she said, sounding more breathless than she liked, terrified at the anger on his face. "Luke took me for a ride."

Her father reached up and plucked her from her seat on the horse. "My daughter has a delicate condition," he said to Luke. "Come down here, young man, and explain yourself. What have you done to her?"

Luke had barely lowered himself to the ground when Burdell lunged forward and shoved

17

his fist into Luke's face with a sickening crack.

"No!" Annie screamed, and struggled in her father's arms. "Papa, don't let Burdy hurt him! Luke gave me a ride on his horse!"

Several of Burdell's friends formed a circle around the now scuffling pair, blocking Annie's view, but the awful sounds were enough to make her stomach twist.

"Stop! Stop them, Papa!" She grabbed her father's arm. "He's my friend! He didn't know I couldn't go riding! It's my fault! Only my fault!"

Luke's uncle lunged into the scuffle, and a break appeared in the cluster of boys. Mr. Chapman pulled Luke away and held the boy's back against his chest, pinning him with both arms.

Luke's midnight black hair fell in his eyes, and a bright-red trickle ran from the corner of his mouth. His flannel shirt was torn and spotted with blood. He glared at Burdell, now held firmly by one of their older cousins and sporting a swelling right eye.

"I'm sorry about this, Eldon," Mr. Chapman said to her father, then, "Mrs. Sweetwater," glancing her way. "I'm sure my nephew didn't mean any harm."

"You keep that boy away from here." Her father pointed indignantly. "If she's been harmed in any way, I'm holding you responsible."

Annie wanted to turn everything back to before

this had happened. She wanted to say something that would convince them that Luke had only been treating her like a friend, but the sobs that racked her body prevented her from speech. How could things have changed from the wonder and perfection of only moments ago into this *nightmare?*

"I'm sending for the doctor," her father said, cradling her protectively in his arms.

Her mother dabbed at her cheeks with her handkerchief and fluttered over Annie helplessly. "He should look at her limb and listen to her heart."

"I'm f-fine," Annie said on a sob. "Have the doctor look at *h-him.*" She pointed to Luke, being led away by his uncle. The boy gave her a reassuring little nod and his battered mouth turned up at one corner with regret, but something more. *Respect.*

He was the only person who'd ever treated her as if she were as good as he was, and he was being punished for it. Tears welled and blurred her vision.

Annie covered her eyes with her hand, so she wouldn't have to see him taken away. Her father carried her toward the house, toward her room, toward her bed.

For the first time she didn't have to imagine what being a whole person was like. For the first time she knew exactly what she'd been missing.

Luke Carpenter had offered her a forbidden taste of life—the kind of life she craved and yearned for and dreamed of.

And then reality had snatched it away.

It was the worst day of her life.

Chapter One

Copper Creek, Colorado
1888

"I know this wagon isn't as fancy as your Papa's carriage," Annie's cousin Charmaine apologized for the second time. "But we are going to have ever so much fun at Lizzy's this afternoon."

"I'm looking forward to it," Annie said, arranging herself on the pad of blankets Charmaine had prepared in the wagon bed. "You know I don't get to do things like this when Mama and Papa are home."

"Lucky for us, your mother agreed to accompany Uncle Eldon to Denver this time."

"You ladies stay out of trouble." Annie's Uncle Mort lifted Annie's chair into the back of the wagon. It rolled toward her, and Annie set the brake.

Charmaine smoothed her russet-and-cream-printed broadcloth skirts and climbed up to the driver's seat with her father's assistance.

Annie observed her cousin as she sat and took up the reins. "Are you sure you know how to drive this thing?"

Charmaine frowned at her. "I'm positive. I've done it plenty of times, haven't I, Daddy?"

"She has," he assured Annie good-naturedly. Uncle Mort was her mother's brother, and neither her aunt nor her uncle were as strict or possessive as Annie's parents. The best times of her youth had been spent here on their ranch during the infrequent occasions that her parents had traveled together and entrusted her care to her aunt and uncle.

Not that they didn't respect her parents' wishes and enforce rules, such as no riding, but where there were no specific guidelines, they allowed Annie to make her own decisions. Like today's trip into town to visit Charmaine's school friends.

"Have fun, girls." Uncle Mort waved them off.

Annie held on to her hat and ignored the bumps to enjoy the ride. The sun warmed her through her clothing, and she inhaled air pungent with the scent of freshly turned earth in a nearby field.

"We're going to make boutonnieres for Lizzy's wedding," Charmaine called. "Lavender ribbon, with tiny paper flowers." Her cousin chattered on, and Annie surveyed the spring-dressed country-side. Purple aster blanketed the hillsides with brilliant color.

"I'm going to stop at the stable and ask some-one to drive us to Lizzy's, then take the rig back until we're ready," she called down. "That way we don't have to try to wheel you over the board-walks and stairs and the dirt street on the way."

Annie nodded her consent. Charmaine did like

to make things convenient, and Annie hated to be an encumbrance. Her cousin slowed the rig in the shade of a new building.

"So this is the new livery!" Annie said, shading her eyes and perusing the freshly painted building. "I heard the hammering and pounding from my room for weeks." The Sweetwater home was several streets away, but close enough for the sound to carry on a clear day. Annie's curiosity had been piqued, but to her frustration, her dinnertime queries had been ignored.

A tall, broad-shouldered young man stepped into the wide-open doorway, and the reason for her parents' stubborn refusal to discuss the new livery became unmistakably clear.

Sun glinted from hair as black as midnight. He wore a loose shirt, laced up the front, and trousers tucked into tall black boots. A healthy-looking male, tanned and confident in his surroundings.

Luke Carpenter.

Chaotic images tied to more chaotic feelings bombarded Annie's senses: Luke smiling his irrepressible smile and giving her a forbidden taste of freedom; Luke with blood spattered on his shirt, blood trickling from his lip, looking confused and humiliated; Luke noticing her in the mercantile and nodding her way before her father caught him; Luke riding that beautiful white-stockinged horse as though he and the animal were one.

Once, a few weeks after that horrible incident at her birthday party, he had leaped the hedge as she sat in her chair on the side lawn, enjoying the sun.

She'd inquired about his injuries, and he'd shrugged off the subject. And then Burdy had arrived home.

They'd crossed paths only briefly through the years—a banker's daughter moved in different circles than the ranchers—but Annie had seen him many times from a distance.

"Mornin', ladies." His voice, now a deep mellow tone, brought a tremulous flutter to her chest. He stepped toward the horse. "Put 'im up for you?"

"Actually, if it wouldn't be a bother, we'd like you to drive us to the Jamison home, then bring the rig back." Charmaine's voice had changed since Annie had last heard her speak sixty seconds ago. Where had that throaty breathlessness come from?

"No bother at all," Luke said, and leaped up onto the springed seat beside Charmaine. The wagon dipped with his weight and Annie's stomach did the same.

"You two ladies look mighty pretty today," he said, and cast an inscrutable look over his shoulder.

Annie blushed, thankful he had to turn back to navigate the street. She studied her hands against the blue-sprigged satin of her velvet-trimmed dress, then grabbed the side of the wagon when he clucked and the horse stepped forward.

"We're helping with the decorations for Lizzy's wedding," Charmaine said. Good Lord, was that a *Southern* accent? "The wedding is only two weeks away, you know."

"You'll both be going?"

"Oh, yes, we wouldn't miss it, would we, Annie?"

Luke nodded and listened to Charmaine's girlish chatter. Within minutes he drew the horse and wagon up before their destination. He helped her cousin down from the seat. Charmaine blushed and cast him a coquettish glance from beneath the brim of her bonnet.

Annie stood. Normally, she would have walked to the end of the bed and waited for her uncle's or cousin's help, but she didn't want Luke to notice her clumsiness, so, feeling painfully awkward, she stayed put.

He rounded the wagon and lowered the gate. She avoided looking at him as he lifted her chair effortlessly to the ground. He leaped onto the back of the wagon beside her, and her gaze flew upward.

His thin and lanky body had developed into an eye-pleasing study of muscle and grace. Broad shoulders blocked a good portion of the street behind him. Deliberately, she refocused her attention.

Eyes as blue as the boundless spring sky studied

her back. Her gaze lowered a notch, took in a fine straight nose, mobile lips curved into a smile, and a scar at the edge of his upper lip.

"Let me help you, Miss Sweetwater," he said politely in that disturbing voice.

Her face flamed, yet somehow she managed to speak. "Thank you."

He gathered her into his arms, just like her brother and father and uncle did all the time, but this was different. He was not a family member. He was a full-grown man—a strong, graceful stranger. Annie was self-conscious of her helplessness, ashamed to be such a burden and to have him see it.

She immediately circled her arms around his neck, feeling his hard body pressed along her side and hip, and studiously avoided the sun-kissed face so near hers.

With amazing agility, he crouched on the back of the wagon then lowered her to the ground. With a few powerful strides, he carried her around the back of the wagon. Annie felt like one of her Dresden dolls in his solid arms.

Hands fluttering between the handles and her stand-up collar, Charmaine stood waiting behind Annie's chair. Annie had never hated the conveyance as much as she did at that moment. She wanted Luke to carry her on past, carry her somewhere where there were no wheelchairs or limits or attentive caregivers.

But of course, he didn't. Luke placed her gently on the seat, disentangled his arm from her skirts and arranged them neatly across her knees.

"Thank you," Annie said, but she couldn't make herself meet his eyes again.

"My pleasure." He must have glanced at Charmaine. "What time would you like me to bring the rig back for you?"

"You'd better come by three, if that's convenient. My Mama expects me home to help with dinner."

"I'll see you then. Ladies."

Annie saw only his boots move away and then glanced up to watch him leap onto the wagon seat with an economy of motion.

"My, my, my . . ." Charmaine said breathlessly. "You know he built that stable and owns it himself," she offered.

Annie hadn't known that. "I don't hear news of Luke Carpenter."

"No, I guess you wouldn't." They both watched until the rig was around the corner and out of sight. "Word has it he saved on his own to build the place."

"He did?" Annie knew little of business or the cost of things.

"That's a big accomplishment. Most people would have taken a loan."

"Oh." She met Charmaine's eyes, comprehending the significance. A loan came from a bank, and her father owned the only bank in Copper Creek.

Sudden embarrassment at her father's unjustness flared hot in her cheeks.

"I barely remember that day of your birthday party," Charmaine said, apparently thinking back to where the trouble had started. She was almost two years younger than Annie. "How old were you?"

"Ten."

Charmaine pushed the chair toward Lizzy's house. "But you remember it well?"

Hardly a day went by that, while being tied to the earth in this chair, she didn't remember the day that she rode into the wind and tasted freedom for the first time—only to have it snatched away and scorned like it was something ugly.

She remembered all right. How could she ever forget? And how could she forget that Luke had been the one to suffer for it? In more ways than one, she knew now.

"I remember it very well."

Chapter Two

There were dumber things he could do than show up early and ask Annie Sweetwater and her cousin to join him for ice cream. Like lie down in the middle of Carver Street and wait for a buckboard to run him over. Or walk up behind that skittish sorrel he was boarding for Ike McPhillips and startle her good. The results would be the same.

Once Burdell Sweetwater found out Luke had so much as spoken to his sister, he'd march out of his fancy bank in his fancy clothes and run Luke over, kicking 'im a couple o' times for good measure.

Reckon it'd be worth it if she gave him one of those smiles.

Luke stood in the narrow sleeping room of his spartan quarters in the rear of the livery and adjusted the collar of his clean chambray shirt. He glanced at his appearance in the grainy mirror over his washstand, assured that his unruly hair had momentarily been tamed.

Leading Mort Renlow's freshly washed and curried mare into the center of the stable, he fastened the harnesses and hitched her to the wagon. Miss Renlow had told him three, but he would be at the Jamison place a good forty-five minutes early—enough time to buy the young ladies a treat.

A colorfully dressed gathering of young females graced the gingerbread-trimmed porch of the home; heads turned and voices hushed as he halted the horse and wagon and climbed to the ground.

Charmaine set aside a delicate cup and saucer, stood and came down a few steps to meet him. "Why, you're early, Mr. Carpenter."

"I was hopin' you and your cousin would join me for a dish of your favorite flavor at Miss Marples' Ice Cream Emporium."

Charmaine fluttered her eyelashes, and two dimples winked becomingly as she gave him a flirtatious smile. "Why, we'd be delighted to join you!"

A few girlish whispers echoed across the distance.

In the bevy of starched and ruffled girls, Annie Sweetwater was easy to spot. Not because of the chair in which she sat, because they were all sitting, whether on chairs or a swing or a cushion; not because she was dressed any differently, since her attire fit right in with all these frilly schoolgirls; not even because she was older, which she was. No, it was because something drew his gaze unerringly to hers and made his heart lift when he saw her.

She wasn't even smiling; in fact she wore an

expression of apprehension on her delicately featured, ivory-skinned face. He'd have been hard-pressed to think of a time when he'd wanted something more than he wanted Annie to show a little enthusiasm over his invitation. She fascinated him, and the desire to know her better clouded his thinking.

"Charmaine, Uncle Mort wants us home," she said, rolling her chair forward, past the now silent girls on the porch. She stopped at the top of the stairs.

"We have plenty of time, silly," Charmaine assured her.

"Yes," Luke agreed, not wanting to accept her excuse. "I'll return you in time to help with dinner." He moved up the stairs and Annie's eyes grew alarmingly wide. He paused, torn between wanting this and not willing to make her do anything she really didn't want to do. He knelt beside her chair and said so that only she could hear, "Only if you want to, Annie. It's okay if you don't."

She seemed to lose herself in his eyes for a moment, giving him precious time to examine her face up close: bright green-gray eyes, winged reddish brows, a delicately bowed upper lip and a charming smattering of nearly invisible freckles. Springy wisps of red-gold hair curled along her hairline and in front of her ears.

"I want to." It was a tentative whisper, as

though she were admitting something to herself, and the confession took his breath away.

"Here's your bonnet, Annie." One of the girls handed her the hat.

He recovered and managed a smile, then nodded to the watching girls and set the brake on Annie's chair. Annie placed the bonnet over her hair and tied the starched ribbons in a wide bow beneath her chin.

She raised a slender arm to his shoulder, and that measure of surrender, of trust, was like the kick he was expecting from her brother. How he hated that she had to entrust her care to others, but how he loved that at this moment he was the one blessed with the privilege.

She wasn't tiny, but neither was she heavy. Her pleasant tactile weight, her feminine softness, and the delicate scent of lilacs were reward for his persistence. He carried her down the path toward the street, wishing the distance was farther.

She peeked at him from beneath the floppy brim of her bonnet. He met her gaze, only inches from his.

"You have the bluest eyes," she said softly. "I've never forgotten."

His breath hitched in his chest. She'd remembered his eyes all this time? He couldn't help wondering what else she remembered—if she resented his intrusion in her life—if she'd been humiliated over the scene at her party? Afterward, he'd tried several times to get close enough to speak to her. He'd even taken another licking from Burdell. But nothing had daunted his unexplainable captivation with the girl.

Even now, after all these years, he wanted to take her for a ride—buy her ice cream—do anything that would bring joy to her expressive face.

He reached the wagon and lowered her to the pallet of blankets in the back. She arranged her skirts, deliberately avoiding looking at him. He returned for her chair and assisted Miss Renlow up to the wagon seat. With a giggle, Annie's cousin waved to her friends.

Miss Marples' wasn't very busy that afternoon, and the pudgy woman herself waited on them. After taking Charmaine's order, she asked, "And what will she have?" indicating Annie with a nod.

"Well, I don't know, why don't you ask her?" Luke replied. "She's in a wheelchair, but she's not deaf or stupid."

Miss Marples recovered quickly, her round cheeks pink. "No, of course not. Uh-what will you have?"

"I'd like a dish of peppermint ice cream, please," Annie replied, her own cheeks aflame. Being treated as though she were an idiot because she couldn't walk was one of the most irritating things about her life situation. And usually, her parents ordered for her, making the matter even worse.

No one had ever addressed the situation bluntly in her presence before, and secretly, she took delight in Luke's words.

Returning with their orders, Miss Marples fussed over them. Luke had asked for black walnuts for his vanilla ice cream, and she supplied him with a bowlful. He shared with the ladies.

"My Daddy says you're quite a businessman, Mr. Carpenter," Charmaine said, delicately nibbling a walnut meat. "He says that's a right fine livery you built there and that you know your horses."

"Your daddy would be the one to know," he replied, pleased with the compliment from a man he respected. "He takes good care of his animals and runs a fine ranch."

Charmaine giggled as though he'd complimented *her*. He couldn't help but smile at her obvious flirtation.

Annie, with cheeks as pink as the peppermint swirls in her ice cream, kept her gaze lowered to the frosty dish. She wasn't as flattered by his attentions as her cousin, and he wondered how to rectify that.

"Do you still live on your Uncle Gilbert's ranch?" Charmaine asked.

"No. I have a couple of rooms in the back of the livery for now."

"For now?"

"Eventually I'll build a house."

"In town?"

The silly girl was full of questions, while he was still trying to think of something to say to Annie. "Probably just outside town," he replied distractedly.

"Do you still have Wrangler?"

The softly spoken question came as a surprise. Even Charmaine turned to look at Annie.

Luke jumped on her first sign of interest and nodded in reply. "He's at Gil's."

"Do you still ride him?"

"Yes. He's fifteen now, but I still take him out for exercise."

Her lashes rose. She looked right at him. And smiled. Her gray eyes were filled with a passionate yearning he wanted to fulfil. If only he knew how. If only her family didn't think of him as the scourge of the earth.

Maybe he hadn't been born under the same affluent circumstances as the Sweetwaters, but he'd worked long and hard to save and start his own business. As soon as he rebuilt his savings, he would build a house—a home. One he could bring a wife to.

But money was only a secondary reason for her family to scorn him. He'd lost their favor the day he'd taken their little girl for a ride.

He had never decided if it had been worth it or not.

She didn't say she'd like to see his horse—or that she'd like to ride him again. Her disturbing eyes said the words for her. She lowered her lids as if to hide the longing reflected in their depths.

"I could bring him out to your cousin's," he offered.

Annie blanched at his suggestion. "Oh, no, you mustn't!"

"Wouldn't you like to see him?"

"Yes, but, I couldn't—I mean, you shouldn't—well, it's just not possible."

Annie folded her hands in her lap and looked down at them. She couldn't bear for him to endure any more harm because of her. That one time had been enough to give her nightmares for years. "No," she affirmed, with a certain shake of her head.

Luke's name had been an unmentionable profanity in her home for as long as she could remember. She didn't want to imagine what would happen if her family discovered she'd encouraged him.

The last bites of ice cream sat melting in the bottom of her bowl. Annie didn't look up to see Luke's expression.

After an awkward stretch of silence, Charmaine piped up, "Will you be at Lizzy and Guy's wedding, Mr. Carpenter?"

"I wouldn't miss the event of the season," he replied, his tone still good-natured. "We're having a little prewedding celebration at the Red Garter tonight, as a matter of fact."

"What do gentlemen do on those occasions, anyway?" she asked, curiously.

"Would your mother want you to know?" he asked.

Annie couldn't help looking up to catch the mischievous lift of his ebony brow.

"Probably not," Charmaine said with a matching grin. "Tell me anyway."

"We drink whiskey and smoke cigars and tease the groom mercilessly."

"That doesn't sound like much fun." Charmaine's forehead creased.

"I'd say it's as much fun as sipping punch and giving feminine presents is for you ladies."

"Now, that's a lot of fun."

"It wouldn't be fun for the men unless you spiked the punch and passed out stogies."

Charmaine laughed and Annie couldn't help joining her at the thought of their prissy girl-friends smoking smelly cigars.

"I'd better see you on your way now," Luke said, standing. "I promised that you'd be home in time to help with the meal."

"This was a delightful idea," Charmaine said. "Thank you for the invitation."

"My pleasure."

Annie made herself speak, but she kept her eyes averted. "Yes, Mr. Carpenter, thank you."

"You're welcome, Miss Sweetwater." He paid their bill, then took charge of her chair, wheeling her out the door.

She focused all her attention on not thinking that he'd be lifting her again—holding her close against his chest. She stood and took a step to hang on to the corner of the wagon while he helped Charmaine up to the seat.

"You're standing!" he said, returning to her. The surprise in his voice embarrassed her.

"I can stand," she replied.

He remained a few feet away. "Can you walk?"

She lifted her chin. "Yes."

"Well, come over here to me then." He reached a hand toward her.

His words froze her to the spot. Face burning, she shook her head. "Charmaine will help me up if you don't want to."

"I didn't say I didn't want to." Stepping forward, he swept her up so quickly, her breath caught. "I just wanted to see you walk."

"I'm not a side show," she said, bristling.

He climbed into the back of the wagon and knelt to lower her to the blankets. Without standing back up, he knelt before her, reaching out to catch her chin on his thumb, forcing her to meet his gaze. "I'm a friend, remember?"

Lord, those eyes were blue. And filled with compassion. She hated his pity. "My friends don't ask me to humiliate myself."

"Is that what I did?"

She nodded best she could with him holding her chin.

"I'm sorry then. I would never hurt you, Annie."

He wouldn't. Of that she was certain. And he was a friend—or he had been—for a wonderful fleeting afternoon long ago. "I know."

He released her and sat back on his haunches. "See you at the wedding."

She lowered her gaze to her gloved hands in her lap and nodded.

He jumped down from the tailgate, raised and latched it. "Afternoon, Miss Renlow," he called to Charmaine.

"Bye!" she called. "Thank you for the ice cream!"

At her urging, the horse pulled them away.

"Why are you so prickly around him, Annie?" she called over her shoulder.

Annie moved to sit behind her cousin. "I wasn't prickly."

"You were almost rude."

"I was not."

"Were so."

"You know how my parents feel about him."

"And I don't know why. He's charming."

"I know *you* think so. You're going to have bruises on your cheeks from pinching them every time he looked away. And where did that dreadful accent come from? You forgot it part of the time."

Charmaine groaned. "He probably thinks I'm an idiot."

"He wouldn't think that."

"No, he wouldn't, would he? We'll see him again at Lizzy's wedding—and at the reception. Maybe he'll ask me to dance!"

Annie's heart fluttered, then sank at the thought of seeing him again—of watching him dance with Charmaine. She cast the hurt firmly aside. Annie loved her cousin. Charmaine was a lovely young girl, and she deserved someone nice—someone handsome and thoughtful. As much as it disturbed her to think it, Luke and Charmaine would make a lovely couple. Both were strikingly attractive, both graceful and energetic and good with people.

She had no right to feel possessive about Luke Carpenter. Just because he'd been kind to her on more than one occasion didn't mean anything. Quite likely, he felt sorry for her.

And that thought broke her heart.

"Annie," Mildred Sweetwater said in her most discouraging tone.

Two weeks had passed and Annie was standing before her dressing table, a dozen ribbons scattered across the top, searching for just the right shade of blue.

"Oh, Mama! I need your help with some of these buttons." She turned and glanced over her shoulder at her lower back in the mirror.

"Your dressing table is made so you don't have to be bothered with getting out of your chair," her mother said, gliding forward.

"I can't do things from that chair," Annie complained. "And no one can see me in my own room."

"Make certain you stay seated throughout the wedding and the reception," her mother admonished her.

Annie sighed heavily at her reflection. "I always do."

Her mother buttoned her dress and kissed her cheek. "You're my good girl."

Annie handed her the ribbon she'd selected and seated herself in her chair.

Her mother wound the length of satin through the curls Annie had artfully arranged. She found a lap robe that matched Annie's periwinkle blue dress and draped it over her knees.

Annie looked at the Persian blanket with disappointment. "It hides half of my dress."

"It keeps you warm as well as covers the outline of your limbs. Don't be obtuse, Annie."

"It's May, Mama."

"May evenings are cool."

"Then let's take it along and save it for evening." Annie folded the robe and handed it to her mother, then readjusted her skirts.

With a sound of exasperation, her mother tucked the blanket under her arm and pushed Annie's chair from the room.

"You look lovely, my dear," Eldon Sweetwater said to his wife as she pushed Annie's chair down the ramp beside the front steps. Dressed in a dark-brown serge suit and a starched white shirt, he came forward to assist. "And Annie, you're the prettiest little girl a father could ever have."

"Thank you, Daddy."

He lifted her from her chair to the rear seat of their carriage, where she caught her weight with her hands and arms and swung herself onto the upholstery. It was a well-rehearsed routine, one with which they were all accustomed. Her chair took up space beside her, and her mother sat on the front seat with her father.

Side curtains enclosed the vehicle and blocked much of the view, but if she complained, she would be told that they prevented the wind and weather from making her ill, so she peered out the flaps at the scenery and appreciated the much-awaited outing.

The church had been decorated with pink azaleas and delicate baby's breath. Wide bows of gauzy white tulle draped the altar and the end of each wooden pew, and Annie smiled with satisfaction over the hours of preparation in which she'd taken part.

Charmaine located her and bent to give her a hug. "Isn't everything beautiful?" Her pretty face flushed with excitement and yearning. "Come this way, Uncle Eldon, Mama and Papa are already seated and we saved room for you. Annie, your chair can go on the end by the wall."

Which would place her out of view of the proceedings, but she could hardly sit in the middle aisle as the bride came past, so Annie nodded and accepted her cousin's placement.

Sometime later, after the wedding march, after the prayers, while the couple was exchanging vows, Annie's curiosity got the best of her and she glanced across the room. Luke Carpenter, dressed in a smart black suit, his ebony hair combed and glistening, nodded her way.

She smiled a shy greeting and turned back to the ceremony. But her gaze was drawn to him again. He was watching the proceedings, but glanced her way and their eyes met. He smiled this time, a slow, heart-touching expression of recognition and favor that made her stomach flutter.

Seated between Annie and Luke, amidst a sea of onlookers and a row or two back, Burdell caught the direction of Luke's focus and speared Annie with a glare. Annie took her attention from Luke and offered her brother a benign smile. His gaze shot back to Luke, who had looked away and was seemingly engaged with the service. Burdy frowned at Annie.

Beside Burdell, his dark-haired wife, Diana, touched her husband's hand and drew his concentration back to the proceedings. Annie believed that Diana was the best thing that could have happened to Burdy. She was a kind and loving young woman, but she held a will and a mind of her own. She possessed more energy than any three women Annie knew, and was always involved in either a benevolence project or a political campaign. If she believed in a local candidate, she hopped on his bandwagon, distributing flyers and hosting fund-raising teas.

Burdy quite obviously adored Diana, along with everyone who knew her. Her very zest for life and liberty drew people and made her a prominent community figure. She and Burdy had a child now, and with Will's birth, Burdy had pampered and catered to his wife even more.

Annie loved Diana, too.

The ceremony ended and, to the strains of the organ music, the newlyweds linked arms and strolled from the church.

All around, guests stood and spoke in excited voices, milling toward the door, ready for the rest of the festivities to begin.

Annie sat, waiting for one of her family members to come for her. Occasionally wedding guests greeted her on their way past. Times like these, she wished she could fade into the background, where she and her cumbersome chair weren't an eyesore.

Growing impatient, she rolled herself to the back of the building, and as the crowd thinned, toward the door to the small foyer and the three stairs. She knew there were three because her father always found someone to assist him in lifting her and her chair up and down those stairs.

Today it was Ike McPhillips, but his help came too late for her to see the newlyweds depart.

Father pushed her to the social hall building which sat beside the church. The doorways and tables were festooned with swags of white tulle and pink paper flowers. The smooth wooden floor provided space for Annie to push herself independently, and she did so, wheeling away from her parents toward the gathering of young ladies near the refreshment tables.

"May I help?"

Mary Chancelor and Doneta Parker glanced at each other and at the tables. "You can sit right here at the end of this table and pour punch," Doneta told her.

"Okay." Annie accepted the assignment gratefully and took her position.

Though the other girls carried glass bowls and silverware and dashed about arranging things just so, Annie was content to sit at her station and wait for the opportunity to serve someone. She had time to watch the musicians set up and to see people arrive and greet each other. Her mother checked on her, found her occupied, and moved on into the growing throng.

Eventually the food and cake were ready, and guests were encouraged to move through the line.

Annie poured punch, while on her left, Charmaine had assumed the coffee duty.

Annie noticed Luke in the line moving toward her, and her heart beat double-time. Handing Mrs. Whitmore a cup, her sudden trembling caused punch to spill over the side.

"I'm so sorry," she said, quickly handing the woman a napkin and wiping her own fingers.

"That's quite all right, dear," she said, in a kind, yet condescending tone. "Accidents happen to all of us, don't they?"

She hadn't meant it unkindly, but she'd meant that even regular people—people who could walk—spilled things, and the meaning sliced Annie's pride. She blinked back the sting of tears, folded the napkin and poured punch for the next person.

When Luke reached her, she had composed her hands and her feelings.

"That's a pretty color on you, Miss Annie," he said in his soul-pleasing voice. "It does something that brings out the fire in your hair."

Annie looked up, wishing she didn't have to, wishing she could look him in the eye without craning her neck. Her mother had taught her that when approached with flattery, a young woman should never encourage painted words with a smile or a blush. Annie didn't encourage the flattery or blush, but she responded immediately with, "I didn't know I had fire in my hair."

"Oh, yes," he said, extending an empty cup.

She reached to take it, but he held on, their knuckles grazing.

"Sometimes I see a little in your eyes, too," he said. "Before you have a chance to look away or hide it."

His words were disturbing, and she started to tear her gaze away, then caught herself, challenged in some way she couldn't have explained. Was this the flattery she was expected to discourage? She held his stare, his fingers touching hers until she thought she felt the same fire he claimed was in her hair.

He smiled, two rakish slashes forming in his cheeks. "I'll take some punch now."

He released the cup into her hand, and she glanced behind him to see if the next person in line had noticed anything unusual, but Guy Halverson's father spoke to the man behind him conversationally.

Annie dipped liquid and handed Luke his drink.

"Thank you." With a grin, he moved on.

After an hour or so, the line ran out; people finished eating and began to dance. Annie remained at her post. Even though folks could get their own refills, the duty made her feel useful and not quite so out of place.

Finally, Mrs. Jamison shooed her away, telling her to go eat and visit with the young people. She fixed a plate and rolled herself to a secluded spot where she watched the dancing. Trying not to look for him was like trying not to worry a sore tooth with a tongue. She scanned the crowd again and again, occasionally spotting his black hair and then looking quickly away.

She picked at the food without much interest, but holding the plate made her look as though she were doing something.

"Hi, Annie," Burdell said sometime later, coming to take a seat on a wooden chair beside her. He had his little boy, Will, in tow, and pulled him onto his knee.

"Hi, Burdy. Hi, Will."

The two-year-old yawned, then grinned at her. "Hi, Nannie."

"You having a good time?" Burdell asked.

"It's a nice party. Want to sit on my lap, Will?"

Burdy took her plate and handed it to one of the ladies passing by. The child scooted from his dad's knee and used Annie's foot as a step in his eagerness to sit with her.

"Whoa there, William, you'll hurt your aunt."

"No, he won't hurt me," she denied, and brushed his concern aside like swatting at an irritating fly. "We're buddies, aren't we?"

Will nodded. Annie inhaled the sweet fragrance of his baby-fine dark hair and kissed the downy soft skin of his cheek. The twill trousers he wore were miniature replicas of his father's, with suspenders crossing his narrow back.

He said a few words she wished she understood, and pointed to the crowd. Annie nodded and listened. He gave her a comical look with his brown eyes open wide and one corner of his mouth turned up. She laughed aloud. "You're just precious, Will, do you know that?"

"Yup," he said seriously.

She kissed his head and hugged him, enjoying the feel of his sturdy little body in her arms. The evening was full upon them, and Will was probably used to being in bed by now. He snuggled and relaxed contentedly.

Burdy visited for a few minutes, but when he was ready to move on, Annie raised a hand to stop him from taking his son. "Can't he stay with me a while longer? He might fall asleep."

"He'll hurt your legs, Annie."

"He doesn't hurt my legs. I love to hold him."

"He'll tire you out." Burdy picked up the boy, and Will waved to Annie with a disappointed frown and a puckered lip.

She managed a smile for his sake and watched her brother carry him into the crowd.

Annie looked at her empty lap, looked at the dancers smiling and laughing. Then she turned her chair and propelled it toward the back room. She had to pass through a kitchen area to get to the door.

One of the young women standing close by asked, "Need any help using the facility?"

Annie gave her a weak smile. "No, thank you, I can make it on my own."

Darlene held the door open and Annie wheeled past her, out the door and into the dark. The ground near the building was hard packed, easy to roll across, but the farther she got from the social hall, the more grass and stubble covered the earth, and the more difficulty she had pushing the wheels of the chair.

Driven, she struggled until she was hot and frustrated, and made a few more yards. Glancing behind her, she realized she'd come quite a way, almost to the area where the horses were penned and the wagons parked. She had halted between two ancient gnarled trees, and saw now that their roots had finally arrested her progress.

She leaned back, let her aching arms droop, and stared through the branches to the twinkling stars overhead.

"Hell and damnation," she said aloud to the night, the worst words she could think of to express her fury at herself for her self-pity. What was worse, being treated like an invalid, or hating herself for her woeful feelings?

She released a shaky breath, refusing to give way to tears.

"Somethin' bothering you, Annie?"

His voice, coming from the quiet darkness, startled her. She turned to see the blue-black sheen of Luke Carpenter's hair in the moonlight.

Chapter Three

Annie gathered her composure. "No, no, I'm fine. I just came out for a little air."

"Seems to me there was air back by the social hall. I think what you wanted was distance so you could curse a blue streak."

Oh, Lord, he'd heard her! Her cheeks scorched with embarrassment.

He chuckled. "I'm impressed, actually. And glad to know I wasn't wrong about that fire."

"I—I didn't know anyone was out here. I—I'm sorry."

"Don't be sorry on my account. Sometimes a body's gotta let off a little steam. Can't be healthy holding all that in."

Assured that she hadn't alienated or offended him with her outburst, Annie relaxed. That was exactly how she felt much of the time: ready to explode. Sometimes screaming out her frustration was all that kept her sane.

"Feel better now?" he asked.

She thought about it and slanted her head. "Some."

"Not all better?"

No, she would never feel all better. She would always be trapped and stifled and . . . She shook her head.

"What's wrong, Annie?"

His use of her name was disturbing in more ways than one. The familiarity was improper—even her mother called her father Mr. Sweetwater in public—but Annie loved the sound of her name from his lips. She could form no reply and shook her head again.

"Bet I can guess."

She looked up at his silhouette against the dark sky.

"They treat you like a child," he said.

The candid statement hung in the night air. They treated her like a child. Somewhere over the years she'd grown into a woman, but they hadn't acknowledged it. Her mother chided and protected, her father pampered and decided, and Burdy . . . well Burdy was Burdy.

"They don't see me as a person, not a real person," she said, the disclosure tumbling out. "To my parents, to my friends, to the whole world, I'm poor little Annie."

"But not to you," he said.

"Even the things that I can do, they don't allow me to do. I'm able to care for my nephew, I can hold him and play with him. I can help with dinner and chores and all kinds of things." Tears had gathered behind her eyes and she swallowed hard to keep them from her voice. "I'm not just a burden." Annie looked up at him. "I can stand. I can walk . . . a little."

She'd never shared these feelings with anyone. Sharing her secret shame made her feel vulnerable, but also free and, somehow, unburdened.

"Well then, stand up, Annie."

She just stared at him.

"You want to, don't you?"

"Yes. But—it's embarrassing."

"To who? There's just me and you out here."

Annie glanced back at the light pouring from the windowpanes of the social hall. The strains of the music reached them, sounding faraway and off-key. No one would see.

She stepped across the wooden footrest to reach the ground, and pushed against the arms of her chair for leverage. Slowly, she lifted her weight until she was upright. The chair remained safely behind her.

"Have you ever stood outside at night before?"

"Not for years."

He rolled the chair completely away, surprising her. She stood in the open, nothing to fall onto except the hard earth. Her heart hammered and she felt quite vulnerable.

Luke reached for her hand.

She grasped it like a lifeline.

"Let's walk away from the tree and stand under the stars," he coaxed.

"But there are roots."

"If you fall, I'll pick you up."

She pictured herself falling, pictured him

picking her up, dusting her off, as she'd seen Diana do to little Will so many times. She laughed out loud.

Yes, he could pick her up. What was so awful about falling? What was the worst thing that could happen to her? A skinned knee? A dirty dress? A bruised ego?

Holding his strong, callused hand, she moved forward across the grass with her ungainly limp. Since her childhood, she'd stolen only secret steps in her room, never outside on the ground. She'd forgotten how the grass felt beneath her shoes.

"Wrangler's over here," he said, leading her toward the penned horses.

"Is he? You rode him?"

Luke clucked and his horse stepped away from a cluster of animals and walked over to the pine pole fence.

Annie placed her left hand on the fence for support. Luke released her other hand and turned it over, placing her palm on Wrangler's soft nose.

Annie smiled and stroked the horse's bony forehead. He nuzzled the front of Luke's shirt. Luke took something from his pocket and opened his palm. The horse bit it delicately and crunched.

"What was that?"

"A sugar cube. They were on the table with the coffee."

"I think those were intended for the coffee," she said with a grin.

"I had punch, which was delicious, even without whiskey, because you poured it."

She turned toward him. Moonlight bathed his black hair and his broad shoulders, now only an arm's length from her touch.

"I wanted to taste the sweetness on your fingers," he said softly.

Annie's heart kicked against her ribs at his words, at the thought of his lips, his tongue on her fingers. This wasn't just flattery, it was a wicked thing to say, she was sure. "Did you gentlemen drink whiskey and smoke cigars at your gathering?" she asked, to change the subject.

"We did."

It sounded sinful, but not as sinful as him tasting her fingers. Her fingertips tingled at the sugges-tive thought.

And then Annie did the craziest, boldest, most spontaneous thing she'd ever done in her life. She reached across the distance between them and touched his mouth. He had a small scar on his top lip that she remembered seeing in the sunlight, and she traced his lip, searching by feel. "You have a scar on your lip . . . here."

"Mm-hmm."

Beneath her fingers, his lips were warm and smooth, pliant, and ever so sensual. "Where did you get it?"

His mouth formed the word she felt from her fingers to her heart. "Burdell."

The image of that day burst into her mind with cruel vengeance. Luke hadn't stood a chance against her much larger and stronger brother, not to mention his crowd of friends. She vividly remembered the trickle of crimson at the corner of his mouth. She'd cried her heart out night after night, wondering if he was all right. If he hated her.

"Did you hate me, Luke?"

He raised a hand and circled her wrist, his long hard fingers gently enveloping. "Of course not."

"I'm sorry." The words were so inadequate, she was ashamed to have said them.

"The only thing I was ever sorry about was that your family hated *me* after that. I never got close enough to talk to you again."

"They just meant to protect me," she said, knowing that she was defending them, and not meaning to excuse what had happened to Luke.

"They mean well," he agreed against the sensitive pads of her fingers. A moment later, he opened his mouth and touched his warm damp tongue to her skin.

Annie's arm jerked, but she didn't draw away. His breath, hot and moist, sent a shiver up her arm to her breasts and tightened them. Her whole body tingled with unfamiliar anticipation.

"I probably taste like horse," she said in a shaky whisper.

"I eat and sleep horses, so I wouldn't notice," he said. "I think you taste like peppermint ice cream."

She laughed then, an expression of nervous release and tactile enjoyment.

Luke cupped her hand and pulled it away from his mouth at the same time he stepped in and drew her close with his other arm. "I want to kiss you."

Annie'd seen her father give her mother pecks on the cheek. She'd seen Diana kiss Will. But she'd seen Guy Halverson kiss his new bride after they were pronounced man and wife that afternoon, and she knew the kiss Luke intended to give her was more like that one. And she wanted him to.

She moved her hand from the pine rail to his shoulder for support. Beneath her palm he was strong and solid, the arm around her waist muscled, yet unrestricting.

She raised her face expectantly. Luke lowered his head and covered her lips with his, a sweet press of flesh and a gentle bonding of souls. She felt beautiful and desirable and feminine in his arms, heady emotions she'd never felt before.

There was no pity in this kiss, no embarrassment, no condescension. The moment was filled with honeyed yearning, joint appreciation and desire. All the loneliness of a lifetime welled up to be purged by this one kiss.

He raised his head, separating their lips, and

Annie almost cried with disappointment that it was over. But he made no move to pull away, placing a palm along her cheek, grazing the curls at her temple with his fingertips. "You're delicate, Annie," he said, his breath against her cheek. "But you're stronger than anyone thinks."

"I'm not so delicate," she said, denying the frailty she so detested. "I'm not delicate at all." She threaded her fingers into the satiny cool hair at the back of his neck and tightened them as though to hold him captive with that gentle grip.

Luke bracketed her jaw with both hands and kissed her deeply, stealing her breath and her hesitation, and giving her confidence and a newfound sense of delight. She pressed a palm against his shirtfront to steady herself and his warmth seeped into her skin.

The smell and feel and taste of him saturated her senses. Luke was the only person in her entire world at that moment.

Her heart raced, rushing blood to tingle across her skin and pound in her ears. Her body caught fire and thrummed to the beat of Luke's heart beneath her palm.

Luke raised his head, and she had to untangle his hair from her fist. He took her hands and held them firmly, stepping back and placing distance between their bodies. "Annie," he said on a gust of released air. "Sweet, sweet Annie."

Annie's heart soared with a sense of freedom. "I never imagined," she said shakily.

"I did," came his hoarse confession. "But this was better than my dreams."

"You imagined kissing me?"

"Yes."

Why? Why would he even look twice at her when there were so many pretty, healthy girls in Copper Creek? The knowledge astounded her. Pleased her beyond measure.

"You'd better get back," he said, "before they come looking for you."

"I'll see you again?" she asked, then bit her lip at her forwardness.

"I'll find a way," he promised. He placed her hand on the rail and went for her chair. Annie seated herself and Luke pushed her close to the building. "I promise, Annie," he said before he disappeared into the night.

She sat alone for a few minutes, savoring the precious minutes they'd spent together. Finally, she pushed herself toward the rear entrance, but her arms had grown tired, and she paused.

"Annie! There you are!" Burdell rounded the corner of the building. "We've been looking for you."

"I just came out for some air."

"Mama said you didn't have your lap robe."

"I was warm enough."

He pushed her chair toward the social hall, and

Annie didn't even dread spending the rest of the evening sitting in her chair along the wall. She had the priceless memory of Luke's kiss to savor until he found a way to see her again.

"I want to help with the cleaning today, Mama," Annie told her mother the following Monday morning.

"Nonsense, Annie," Mother said, looking up from the tasks she'd been listing on a piece of paper for the young woman who worked for them part-time. "Mrs. Harper can handle the heavy chores as she always does. I am prepared to do the dusting myself."

"I can do the dusting," Annie said, pushing her chair forward.

"It's not an appropriate task for you," her mother disagreed. "You have your books to read and your sewing to keep you busy."

"Well then, just what am I good for?" Annie asked in exasperation.

"We love you, darling," her mother said in her most patronizing voice. "You're our precious girl. We don't expect you to tax yourself with household chores."

"Tax myself? Mother, I'm bored out of my mind most of the time. I feel useless sitting here. Worthless!"

"Get that out of your head right now," her mother said sternly. "You most certainly are not worthless."

"Then let me help," Annie begged. "I have trouble walking, Mama. I don't have a weak heart or a feeble constitution. I need to do something!"

As though Annie's declaration had disoriented her, Mildred laid down the ink pen and stood, glancing about the drawing room, her expression one of bewilderment. "What's come over you, child?"

"She could dust the tables and the lamps, Mrs. Sweetwater," Glenda Harper suggested kindly.

Annie turned and gave the young woman a grateful smile.

Her mother clasped and unclasped her hands. "Well . . . I suppose so."

Glenda brought Annie rags and a tin of lemon polish. "I'll get you an apron, Miss Annie, so you don't soil your pretty dress."

"Your dress is unsuitable," her mother commented.

"I don't have any normal dresses, Mother," Annie told her. Her entire wardrobe consisted of fancy frilly feminine clothing in an array of delicate fabrics and colors. "Everything looks like it belongs on one of those Dresden dolls in my room."

"Don't be ungrateful, young lady," her mother said. "Most girls would be pleased to have the advantages you've had."

"Most girls would, but I'm no longer a girl."

"Annie, this talk is most unbecoming. I've agreed

to allow you to dust, even though it's against my better judgment. Don't be impertinent."

Feeling as though she'd waged a battle and won only a small victory, Annie set herself to the task of waxing the tables and dusting the lamps and the bric-a-brac.

The work was rewarding, though frustrating, because there were so many occasions she had to reach a little higher or a little lower, and had to ask Glenda to hand her something or reach for her. The good-natured young mother took Annie's requests for help in stride, however, encouraging her with warm smiles, and never seeming put out.

"We're dining with the Millers this evening," her mother reminded her. She had finished her chores in time to bathe and dress. "Be ready by seven."

"I'm going to stay home," Annie told her. "I'll find myself something to eat."

"But you can't stay home by yourself."

"Mother. We've been through this before. The Millers are in their seventies, and their house smells like moth cakes. I can stay home by myself, and I can manage just fine. I stayed home last time you went."

"We don't want them to think you're rude."

"Let them think I'm bored, then. I can't take another discussion of Mr. Miller's joint aches."

"He's a business partner of your father's."

"I know that. Sometimes business and dinner

don't mix, especially when one has to dine in that mausoleum of a house."

"The Miller house is a landmark, as you very well know. For someone as fortunate as you, Miss Annie Sweetwater, you have certainly become a complainer."

Chastised, Annie regretted her unkind words. Her parents' friends had been nothing but kind to her. And her mother and father had provided for her in every way they knew how, and to the best of their ability. "I didn't mean to be ungrateful, Mother. I know I'm far more fortunate than many people."

"I know your situation can be frustrating at times, dearling," her mother said, kissing her cheek. "We can go without you tonight."

"Oh, thank you," Annie said, giving her mother a quick hug.

Going about her business, Mildred quickly left the room. Glenda gathered the cleaning supplies.

"Glenda?"

The young woman cast Annie a smile. "Yes?"

"I wonder . . ." Annie rolled her chair to the cherry wood desk. "If I gave you a note, would you mind delivering it on your way home?"

"Not at all."

"It would be our secret," Annie added quickly.

Glenda nodded her agreement. "All right."

Annie took a sheet of parchment and dipped her father's pen in a bottle of ink before writing a brief note, waving the paper to dry the ink, then folding it. She melted a drop of wax and sealed the fold with a brass stamp that smashed the wax into the shape of a horse's head. Annie handed the note to Glenda. "Give it to Mr. Carpenter at the livery, please."

Surprise lit Glenda's honey-colored eyes. "You know who he is?"

Quickly, she looked down at the note in her hands. "I know."

"Thank you, Glenda."

"You're welcome." She slipped the paper into her apron pocket and carried a rolled pile of rags from the room.

Annie's heart reacted belatedly at what she'd done, thumping against her breast like a trapped wild bird. She could trust Glenda. She would give Luke the note without letting Annie's mother know.

Would he think her forward? Scandalous? More importantly—*would he come?*

Annie removed the apron, rolled her chair to her room, and washed the dust and polish from her hands and face.

An hour later, she was in the kitchen when her father called, "Annie!"

"In here, Daddy."

"Your mother tells me you're not going with us this evening."

"No. You have a good time."

64

"What are you doing?"

"I'm fixing myself something to eat."

"You can't cook."

"I'm doing a pretty fair job of pretending that I can, then." Following the directions in a cookbook she'd discovered, she had rolled a pie crust, and was fluting the edges around the dried apple filling she'd stirred together. "Glenda lit the oven for me before she left."

"Well, baking will have to wait until tomorrow. I would worry all evening that you'd burned the house down."

She frowned. "Daddy."

"You don't need to cook for yourself," he said in a discouraging tone.

"Maybe I just want to."

"You always did want to do more than you were capable of. Bank the fire now. I'm sure Mrs. Harper left something you can eat without a fire."

She refused to let his words steal the air from her sails. She'd been flying high all afternoon, but of course she had to be reminded of her limitations on a regular basis. "Perhaps I'm capable of more than you allow," she said softly.

He stepped closer, and she turned to look up at his face. "It's not only injury I protect you from, daughter," he said softly. "It's disappointment and cruelty."

"I know. I'm sure that having a daughter such as I, you understand disappointment."

"Annie," he admonished, coming close and bending to press his freshly shaven cheek against hers. "You're my darling girl, you've never been a disappointment."

Annie returned his hug, then brushed a spot of flour from the collar of his suit. "Enjoy your evening."

"We shall. Good night. Bank the fire now. And you're not to go outside. Keep the door locked."

"I will."

As soon as she heard the Millers' carriage come for them, she opened the oven door and gently placed her pie inside.

By the time she had cleaned up her baking area and washed the utensils, she was so hungry, she sliced herself bread and cheese and nibbled a few olives.

When her pie was finished, she removed it from the oven and admired the golden crust with cinnamon-scented juice bubbling in the slits. Placing it on a counter to cool, she banked the fire, then rolled to her room, washed and changed into a clean dress.

The evening feeling cool now that the sun had gone down, Annie placed a shawl around her shoulders and maneuvered her chair out the front door. The sill of the door frame had been specially constructed for ease in wheeling her chair onto the wide porch where she often sat.

In the day, she read in the west corner, where

the sun warmed her of an afternoon. In the evening, she sat where she could watch the stars and see the moon over the mountains. Tonight the moon was only half-full, but the sky was bright and clear.

The far-off jangle of a piano drifted to her from time to time, probably from one of the entertainment establishments that her friends whispered about. The lonely sound of a train whistle echoed through the night, and Annie imagined travelers bound for exciting destinations. The most exciting far-off places she'd ever been to were to the hospitals and doctors' offices in the East.

The hotel stays had been nightmares because of the flights of stairs and the people who stared at her with pity.

Annie hated pity more than anything.

The night sounds took on an unnatural stillness, and the hair on the back of her neck prickled. Awareness roused her from her musings and she glanced into the darkness.

"Annie?" His voice, hushed, uncertain.

She leaned forward and strained to see. "Luke?" she called softly.

Chapter Four

He emerged from the darkness of the side yard. "You're alone?"

"Yes. They went to dinner at the Millers'. They never come home until after eleven. Where's your horse?"

He climbed the porch stairs. "I walked."

Annie had closed the door and the front drapes, shrouding the porch in darkness. If anyone passed by, they wouldn't be able to make out their shapes. "All that way?"

"It's not so far. It's a nice night."

"You got my note."

"Yes." He sat on a wicker chair across from her. "You took a chance, Annie."

"But you came."

Silence hung between them for a long moment. Finally he said softly, "Yes, I came."

Luke had looked up from the horse he'd been shoeing when the young woman appeared in the doorway of the livery. She'd called out to him, and he'd wiped his hands and greeted her, thinking she needed to rent a rig.

But she'd simply handed him the piece of paper. "This is for you."

She'd been gone by the time he looked up from the unfamiliar handwriting on the outside.

Luke had opened the fancy seal and stood in the doorway so that the sun caught the page, and read the simple words that had leaped from the parchment and into his heart: *Dear Luke, I will be alone this evening. Annie.*

She wanted to see him.

He hadn't set foot on this property in at least ten years. Looking out across the expansive grounds surrounded by a white fence, he could picture the spot where he had returned Annie after their ride and had promptly been set upon by her brother and his friends.

He didn't fear Burdell Sweetwater. He never had. Skin grew back. Noses and ribs healed. He didn't fear the physical harm that could come to him because of his association with Annie. What he feared, and always had, was that her parents would send her away. So he'd kept his distance, knowing that one day she'd be old enough to make her own choices.

And praying that she would.

The fact that she'd wanted him to come to her was almost too good to believe. Why he felt this attachment to Annie, he couldn't explain, but he'd been drawn to her since they'd both been young.

"Luke, I—" she began.

"I've wondered—" he said at the same time.

Both stopped and chuckled nervously.

"Go ahead," Luke said.

Annie smoothed the ruffles on her skirt. "I have

wanted so many times to tell you how sorry I was for that day."

"You don't have to apologize."

"Please let me say this. The words have been in my heart forever."

His chest contracted, and uncomfortably he kept his silence.

"That was the best day I can ever remember. When I think back on how brief it was—how wonderful . . . well, I have no words to say what it meant to me.

"When we got back and my father was so angry, I was shocked. And then when Burdy hit you, Luke . . ." Her voice quavered and her breath escaped tremulously. "I just wanted to die. I felt so helpless. I was angry. I cried and cried, because you took that punishment so unjustly."

"Annie, it's okay."

"It's not okay," she argued. "I wanted to go to you."

"I was all right. It was you I was worried about." He leaned forward, and the chair creaked beneath his weight. "I tried to get back to see you. I wanted to see if you were all right."

"Me? I wasn't the one pounded to a bloody pulp!"

"I wasn't a bloody pulp." He laughed at her dramatic description, but then sobered. "I thought you probably hated me for embarrassin' you at your party."

"Oh, pooh on my party. My parties were all dull, and they still are. How could you think such a thing? You were the only person who ever let me be myself. I never forgot that."

"I don't know why anybody'd want to change you." She was the most delightful person he'd ever met.

"It's like everybody wants to put a rock on my head and keep me in this chair. Why do they do that?"

He shook his head, because he'd wondered the same thing. What did it hurt for her to get up and walk if she wanted? "Have the doctors said it's bad for you to walk?"

"No."

"Well, I'm no doctor, but I know if you don't let a horse exercise, he can't build strong muscles and he tires easily. But if you run him regularly, his strength builds. Seems like your legs are the same. I'll bet if you exercised them, they'd get stronger."

"I think so, too. I've read about some forward-thinking individuals who believe exercise is the key to vitality." She sounded excited about the possibility. "But my parents don't allow me to move about, let alone do calisthenics."

"Annie, is there any way you can contact one of the doctors you've seen and ask if he thinks walking or exercising is harmful for you?"

She seemed to think his question over. "I do

remember one of the kinder doctors. He has even written me on a few occasions."

"Could we telegraph him?"

"I don't know why not. But how would I get to the telegraph office without my parents knowing?"

"I could take your message and send the telegraph."

"Splendid idea! Tomorrow? I can write it tonight."

The excitement in her voice pleased him. "Why not?"

"I baked you an apple pie," she said abruptly. "Wait here and I'll bring you a big slice."

Surprised, he agreed and held the screen door while she rolled her chair into the house. Several minutes later, she returned with a small tray in her lap. "I couldn't fill the glass, because I spill when I cross the doorway," she apologized, handing him a partially full glass of milk.

"I don't mind," he said, taking the cold tumbler from her.

"The pie tastes pretty good. I tried a bite earlier."

He accepted the plate and seated himself on the wicker chair, placing the glass on a small table. He tasted her offering, the apples still warm from the oven. Cinnamon sweetness melted on his tongue. "No one has ever baked me a pie before."

"No?"

He shook his head and enjoyed another mouth-watering bite.

"It's my first one. I just followed a recipe."

"It's better than the pies at Dora Edgewood's café. You could give her a tip or two."

Annie laughed, a delicate ear-pleasing sound of delight. "Are you flattering me?"

"Yes, but it's true." He finished the slice of pie and drank the milk.

"Mother says it's improper to welcome flattery." She set the empty tray on the floor, and Luke placed his dishes on it.

"I guess your mother'd know about things like that."

"A lady may accept a delicate compliment, but she should not appear to expect or encourage them."

"I hardly think you expect compliments, Annie."

She folded her hands in her lap. "I want to go write the telegram, but I don't want to miss another minute with you."

Her honesty warmed him. "Why don't you just tell me what it should say then, and I'll remember."

"But I'll have to find the doctor's address."

"Will it take long?"

"No."

He placed the tray on her lap and opened the screen door for her. "Hurry."

Precious minutes ticked by before she returned with an envelope and handed it to him. He folded it and tucked it into his shirt pocket. "How will I get the reply to you when it arrives?"

73

"Glenda comes every afternoon. You could catch her on her way here and give it to her. She promised to keep my secret when I sent you the note this afternoon. I trust her."

A comfortable silence settled between them. Distant piano music drifted on the night air.

"Luke?"

"Yes."

"It's probably highly improper, but would you mind holding my hand, so I can move over there and sit beside you on the glider?"

"That would be my pleasure," he replied.

She took his hand for support, and using it and the arm of her chair, pushed herself up. Then, with only a few awkward steps, she made it to the padded glider and sat.

Luke lowered his weight to the seat next to her, unwilling to release her hand. She smelled wonderful, an enticing combination of vanilla and lilacs and starched cotton. Her voluminous skirts draped across his knee. He closed his eyes and joyfully inhaled her presence.

"I've thought a lot about the night of the wedding," she said softly.

Thoughts of her kisses had driven him crazy every night since. Even today, he'd found himself staring off into the forge, letting a piece of iron cool, and having to heat it over again. "Me, too."

"Good thoughts?" she asked.

He smiled at her delightful frankness. "Very good thoughts. Was that a delicate enough compliment?"

She smiled and nodded. "Would you mind—kissing me again?"

The question was laughable. "Let me think about it. Hmm. No." He pulled her hand, which brought her face to his, and leaned toward her. She met his lips with hers, a sweet, eager union that immediately had his blood pounding.

He released her hand, and she placed it tentatively on his shoulder. He'd never known she returned his feelings; he'd only hoped, maybe just dreamed. Finding out like this that she was drawn to him, too, gave him so much pleasure, his heart swelled to bursting.

Their lips parted and Luke remembered to draw a breath.

"You taste like cinnamon," she said.

"You smell like lilacs," he replied.

She leaned closer, placing her nose against his neck. A wispy curl grazed his cheek. A shudder passed through his body. "You smell like . . ." she said, her breath against his neck exquisite torture, ". . . I don't know . . . heaven. You smell like heaven."

He turned his face, so that his lips and nose were a scant breath from her ear. "You think there are horses in heaven?"

She moved as though to see his eyes, though it

75

was dark and she couldn't possibly read his expression. "You don't smell like a horse."

"I must. I even sleep in the livery."

"Well, you don't. You smell like . . . like you shaved."

"Mm-hmm," he agreed. He had shaved before he'd come to see her. "And how would you know what that smells like?"

"My father shaves. But he doesn't smell nearly as good as you do."

"Your mother probably thinks so."

Annie sat up straight and her eyes widened in the moonlight. "What a thought! Don't you ever place another thought like that in my mind! Goodness, if I imagine my mother sniffing my father, I'll die of laughter and you'll never get to kiss me again."

"Well, we can't have that, so forget all thoughts of your parents. They probably don't even sleep in the same room."

"Luke Carpenter, you're incorrigible!" She laughed out loud that time, however. Lord, she was having fun.

He wrapped his arm around her shoulders, felt her delicate bones beneath the fabric of her dress, and pulled her toward him. She came willingly, eagerly, all softness and sighs.

Luke nuzzled the springy curls at her temple, the delicate skin behind her ear, and placed a kiss there. She leaned more fully into him, pressing her breasts against his chest, and he tried to feel and taste and smell every vivid sensation and press it into his mind for later.

Their lips met again, this time more forcefully, and when he touched her lip with his tongue, she intuitively allowed him access. Her whole body stilled and her breathing grew shallow, as though she were concentrating fully on this exploratory kiss.

Luke had to bracket her face with his palms and end the torture before he allowed himself more liberties. Because she was willing. And he was weak.

"I'm going to leave, Annie," he whispered hoarsely.

"But we still have time."

"That's what I'm afraid of."

"What are you afraid of?"

"If I don't go, I might do somethin' very ungentlemanly. And I think too much of you to let that happen. So I'm leaving."

He stood, swept her up into his arms, and deposited her in her chair. He leaned over her, his palms on the armrests.

She placed her soft hands on the backs of his, and slowly, he backed away until only their fingers were touching, even that tentative contact a tactile pleasure.

"There will be a next time," he promised.

"It'll seem like forever."

"I'll be thinkin' of you."

"And I of you."

"Good night, sweet Annie."

"Night, Luke."

He released her fingers, moved to the stairs and disappeared into the night. Annie placed her empty palms over her racing heart. Adrift in heavenly sensations and riotous feelings, she slowly came back down to earth, the chair beneath her a cold reality.

But Luke didn't care. He didn't see her and this chair as one. He saw her as she saw herself, as she dreamed to be. A whole, unfettered person.

How would she ever sleep again?

For a week, Annie anticipated Glenda's daily arrival. The weekend seemed endless and unbearable, because the housekeeper didn't come on Saturday, and it wasn't her Sunday to help with dinner. But on the following Monday, as Annie sat waiting on the shady porch, Glenda climbed the stairs with a sly smile.

Annie's heart fluttered. "Do you have something for me?"

Glenda glanced through the open doorway. "Where's your mother?"

"She's upstairs packing. I'm to be shipped off to my aunt and uncle's again while Mother and Daddy travel to Denver."

Glenda slipped folded papers from her pocket and handed them to Annie.

Opening them quickly, Annie discovered there were two pages to the missive, the first a Western Union telegram from Dr. Mulvaney: "I wager that the benefits of exercise would greatly strengthen muscles. Stop. To my knowledge there is no damage that can be done by walking. Stop. I should be interested to know results after an adequate period. Stop. Regards to your family. Stop."

Giddy at the encouragement, Annie pressed the papers to her chest and grinned. She hadn't been wrong. She could walk and not harm herself as long as she was careful.

Remembering the piece of brown paper, Annie opened it and read the words scrawled in black ink: "Sweet Annie, I should be interested to know the results, too. I believe you can do anything you put your mind to. The scent of lilacs fills my dreams. Luke."

She must have been grinning foolishly, because Glenda chuckled. "Your cheeks are pinker than the snapdragons beside the porch, Miss Annie. Your mother will suspect something for sure."

"She'll just think I'm still put out over our argument about letting Charmaine come here and stay with me for the week, instead of me going to their house. I lost—again." Annie quickly tucked the papers beneath the folds of her dress. "You won't tell?"

"What's to tell?" Glenda removed her bonnet.

"You and Luke Carpenter exchanged letters. Nothing scandalous about that. Besides, your folks are far too protective. Pretty thing like you should have been courted by now."

"Did your husband court you?" Annie asked.

"Lands, yes. He brought me flowers and trinkets of all sorts. My mama liked him right off, but my father took a while to come around."

"What convinced him?"

"I think it was the fact that Tim plucked him from the midst of a saloon fight and brought him home without my mama being any the wiser."

"I doubt my father will be in a saloon fight any time soon," Annie said dejectedly.

"I 'spect not. Well, I have chores to do."

"Thank you, Glenda."

Glenda patted her arm. "You're welcome. Now you'd better get in there and pack your things before your mother starts doin' it for you."

Glenda held the door and Annie wheeled herself into the house. She hid her note and the telegram in between the pages of the Bible on her night table.

She would be staying at the Renlows' until Friday. Surely she could find an occasion in those three days and nights to see Luke. Perhaps Charmaine would want to go into town again, like they'd done the last time. Charmaine loved to shop, or Annie could suggest a visit to the public library. It was open every weekday. Packing took on more excitement at the hope of seeing Luke soon.

That evening she sat at her aunt and uncle's table, a more relaxed affair than dinner at her home, and joined her uncle in a conversation about the man who was running for governor.

"How do you know about such things, Annie?" Charmaine asked.

"News of the upcoming election has been in the newspaper every day," she replied. "I can't talk about it at home, though. Mother has a fit."

"Does she have something against one of the candidates?"

"No, you know Mother. She thinks ladies are supposed to avoid pretentions of learning."

"My friends had instructions on that, too," Charmaine offered. "Young women aren't supposed to let on that they know as much as gentlemen. It's pedantic, they say."

"So you're supposed to pretend to be dumb?" Uncle Mort asked the girls. "What kind of man wants a dumb wife? Or daughter for that matter?"

"A gentleman, I guess," Charmaine said with a sigh.

"What about Diana? She's not one to hold her opinions to herself," Mort said. "My nephew obviously didn't take to that thinkin'."

"Diana drives Mother crazy," Annie said with a grin. "Although she does know a lot of influential people, and Mother is impressed by that. There's bitter mixed with the sweet, I guess."

"Mama, may I stay home from school while Annie's here?"

Annie's Aunt Vera cast her daughter a knowing look. "The answer is the same as last time and the time before. Annie and I get along just fine while you're in school."

Charmaine pouted prettily for all of thirty seconds, then turned to Annie. "What shall we do after school tomorrow?"

Annie's heart gave a little leap. "Would you like to shop?"

Charmaine appeared to be thinking. "I'll bet there are more interesting places to shop in Denver. Wouldn't you like to go with your parents one of these days?"

Annie pushed some turnips around on her plate. "I don't know. I don't much like going into cities—there are too many people. I feel awkward."

"Well if you should ever want to, you know I'd be happy to accompany you."

Annie gave her cousin an amused smile. "Thank you for the offer. We could go to the library."

"All right. Let's help Mama with the dishes, and then she'll have more time to work on the dress she's making for me."

Annie was always more than glad to help with the dinner chores. The Renlows didn't treat her as though she were an invalid; they allowed her to help with meals and dishes and any household task she put her hand to. Here it was as if her help was expected, and that tiny measure of normalcy gave Annie a deep-down sense of value.

Mort went off to the barn, and the ladies completed the dishes, then Vera had Charmaine try on the bodice of the new dress. The creation was a lovely moss-green print, with a high collar and a cinched waist.

Annie fingered the fabric of the basted skirt lying on the dining room table. "Oh, this is just lovely."

Charmaine and her mother turned their heads toward Annie at the same time.

"It's a simple pattern," Charmaine said. "And not an expensive fabric."

Annie glanced at her own dress: silk taffeta with outsize cap sleeves and three layers of ruffles around her neck and at the hem. People had seen her dressed like this her entire life; why it should matter now, she didn't know. But it did. She wondered how others saw her—how Luke saw her. "My clothes are childish," she said honestly.

"They're elegant, Annie," her aunt said.

"And expensive," Charmaine added.

Vera nudged her daughter.

"Well, they are."

"I stand out enough in this chair." Annie tapped the arm. "But combined with the dresses, I'm a carnival act. I should learn to juggle."

"Stop it, Annie, you are not a freak." Charmaine came and knelt beside her. Charmaine picked up Annie's hand and brought the backs of her fingers to her cheek. "You are the most special person I know, and I love you. Please don't belittle yourself."

Annie caressed Charmaine's soft cheek. "You're my best friend, you know that."

"Mama could make you a dress like this if you'd like one."

Annie looked to her aunt hopefully. "Would you, Aunt Vera?"

Vera dropped her gaze to the basted fabric on the table. "I'm not a seamstress, girls. Annie, your clothes are exquisitely made by professionals. My sewing doesn't hold a candle."

Annie's initial hope ebbed back into complacency. "And you're busy, I know. You have many important things to do, as well as things to make for Charmaine. It's all right, really." She drew her hand from her cousin. "What can I do to help? I can sew a straight seam, or I could iron the hem for you."

Vera and Charmaine exchanged a glance. "Annie, would you really like a dress like this?" Vera asked.

Tears smarted behind Annie's eyes at the fierce longing for something so normal and grown-up looking. Somehow it symbolized a passage to adulthood that she longed for. Keeping her eyes averted, she nodded.

"Well then, we'd better have you stand up here and let us measure you."

Annie met her aunt's eyes. Understanding passed between them. A lump formed in her throat and she swallowed past it.

"Better yet, let's go into your room and measure you without your dress. I'm sure those ruffles add inches."

Annie laughed and wheeled herself toward the modestly furnished room she used when she stayed at the Renlows'. Vera measured and jotted numbers, while the girls discussed colors and fabrics. Annie planned to buy fabric during their visit to Copper Creek.

The following day after Charmaine returned from school, she and Annie set off for town in the wagon. "Missy Sharpe is such a flirt," Charmaine called over her shoulder. "She had all the boys gathered around her today because she brought lemon tarts to share."

"Maybe we could bake something for you to take," Annie suggested.

"Oh, they're just silly boys," her cousin replied. "I'd much rather bake something for someone more mature. Say, Luke Carpenter, for example."

Annie blinked her surprise, but said nothing.

"He's ever so handsome, don't you think?"

"I guess so." He was so handsome, she could hardly breathe when she looked at him.

"And ambitious, with his own business, even if it's a livery."

"Yes, he's ambitious." Not enough for her parents' standards however.

"He's become the best part of coming into town, don't you think?"

She'd thought of little else and knew without a doubt that Luke was the best part of coming to town. He was the best part of any week in which she saw him, and thinking about him was the best part of the numerous days she didn't see him. She looked toward town in anticipation and said, "I haven't really thought about it."

Chapter Five

They entered Copper Creek and Charmaine guided the horse to the livery. To Annie's disappointment, a fatherly looking man with a dark beard greeted them and assisted Annie and the chair from the back of the wagon.

Charmaine stood beside Annie's chair. "We were expecting to see Mr. Carpenter."

"Guess he had business this afternoon."

"Do you work for him?"

"I help him out once in a while."

"We'll be back for the wagon when the library closes."

"I'll be here."

The library was only a short distance from the livery, but the building itself had several stairs. Annie stood by while Charmaine wrangled her chair up the stairs and inside the library, then came back for her.

She clung to Charmaine's arm, managed the steps, and went inside. It didn't matter that her cousin couldn't lift and carry her, because Charmaine didn't mind her awkward stumblings, and was always ready to offer her strength as support.

"Good afternoon," Mrs. Krenshaw said in the

loud whisper she used even when not in her natural habitat. She stood behind the loan desk, a pencil tucked into the lopsided graying bun on the top of her head.

The cousins greeted her quietly.

Annie seated herself in her chair and Charmaine handed the librarian a few books they were returning.

Annie rolled herself across the spacious open floor toward one of the sections of wooden shelving.

She had been spending an hour a day, in twenty-minute intervals, standing and walking in the privacy of her room. So far, the practice had had no ill effects aside from a few sore muscles.

Today it gave her a feeling of accomplishment and independence to leave her chair at the end of a row of shelves and inch along the books, examining spines, reaching tomes on the top shelves.

"Goodness, Annie, look at you!" Charmaine said. The building was large and open, with wooden walls and ceiling, and sound carried clear to the desk.

Annie placed her finger to her lips to silence her. "I've been practicing," she confessed.

"Standing?"

"Walking."

"What does your mother think?"

"She doesn't know. Don't tell her, please."

"You know I won't. I think it's positively wonderful." After voicing her approval, she moved away, browsing though the books.

Annie found a few she wanted to borrow, placed them on her chair and began another search. Many she'd read before, but she didn't mind reading them again. Some were beloved old friends she visited often. Locating a favorite she'd borrowed half a dozen times, she opened it and scanned the familiar worn pages.

She'd become engrossed in the scene in which a young boy who has raised a colt is forced to sell him when a step behind her caught her attention. The back of her neck prickled.

"Hello, Annie." The greeting was whispered so near her ear that warm breath touched her neck and scattered shivers across her shoulders. The masculine voice was unmistakable.

She turned and found Luke standing so close, her skirts brushed his pant legs. He smiled, deep crevices slashing his cheeks and making him appear rakishly handsome.

Annie pressed the book to her pounding chest. "Luke," she whispered.

A faded blue shirt encased his broad chest, open at the throat, and he wore a pair of dark trousers. "Afternoon," he said softly.

A tremor of excitement passed through her. She glanced behind him, seeing no one. "What are you doing here?"

"I saw the Renlows' horse and Burt told me you and your cousin came over here."

And he'd come away from his business to see her? His interest flattered her like nothing else could. Her neck and cheeks warmed.

"Shouldn't I have come?" he asked, doubt etching his brow.

"I—I'm just surprised," she managed. "I'm glad you came."

"And I'm surprised to see you standing."

"I've been practicing," she told him.

"Any problems?"

She shook her head. "A few aches in the unused muscles, but it's getting better—and easier. I can stand for longer periods of time now."

"I'm proud of you."

Everything inside her warmed at those words, but the sentiment embarrassed her, too. "Nothing most people don't take for granted."

"Most people don't have the same challenge."

She smiled, his appreciation for her small achievement a joy she felt all the way to her toes. "I guess not."

"Maybe you could stay in town for supper?"

"Aunt Vera is expecting us back. She would worry."

His expression fell. "Oh."

"But tomorrow. We could plan it for tomorrow and tell her ahead of time."

He raised a brow as though having second

thoughts. "What if someone sees us and tells Burdell or your parents?"

"Someone will see us, that's for sure." She thought a moment. "What comes after that, I don't know."

"Maybe we shouldn't then. If you're afraid of what will happen."

Annie studied the concern in his sky-blue eyes, the scar on his lip, weighing her parents' anger against the pleasure of spending time with him. "I'm only afraid for you."

"I'm not afraid," he replied. "I was never afraid except that I thought they might send you away."

"I'm a big girl now," she said, a soft declaration, a pronouncement of the maturity and independence she craved. "Even if they don't acknowledge the fact."

"Then you want to? Meet me for dinner?"

There had never been a doubt. "I want to."

"And if they find out?"

"Then we deal with that."

"Okay, Annie." He took a step closer. Her heart skipped a frantic beat. She looked up into his eyes, glad she was standing on his level and not staring up from her chair. His slow smile turned her insides to liquid.

A footstep sounded in the next row of books. Mrs. Krenshaw's loud whisper echoed from the desk, instructing someone where to find a volume.

The sound of swishing fabric and footsteps came up behind her, and Annie stepped away from Luke.

Charmaine rushed to her side. "Mr. Carpenter! What a pleasure to see you."

"You too, Miss Renlow."

"I didn't know you came here."

He glanced from Annie to her cousin. "It's a library. A lot of people come here."

Charmaine giggled. "Of course. How silly of me."

"I was wondering if you and Annie would meet me for dinner at Mrs. Edgewood's café tomorrow night? Not very fancy, but the food is good. I would sure like your company."

Charmaine blushed to the roots of her hair. "Why, that would be delightful! Wouldn't that be delightful, Annie?"

"Shhh!" came an admonition from the front of the library.

"Yes, it would," Annie whispered. "What time, Mr. Carpenter?"

They settled the details and he wished them a good day, turning away and walking toward the door, his boot heels loud in the echoing silence.

"Oh, my gracious, Annie!" Charmaine said, leaning on her cousin's arm and nearly toppling her over. Annie grabbed a shelf for support. "Oh, oh, I'm sorry. You must be getting tired. Here." She retrieved Annie's chair from the end of the aisle and Annie picked up her books and settled into it. "He invited us to dinner! This is the most thrilling event! Can you even imagine?"

"Shhh!" came the expected admonition from the front of the building.

"Keep your voice down," Annie shushed her.

"I've never been invited to dinner before." She glanced at Annie. "Well, of course, neither have you, but it's ever so flattering. He's not even a boy, he's a grown man!"

Annie had been flattered, too; naturally Charmaine would be ecstatic. She thought Luke was a prince. And she had no idea that Luke had invited them so that he could see Annie. Hadn't he? Or was Annie attributing too much meaning to the kisses that had passed between them? It was almost too good to be true that he thought of Annie as fondly as she thought of him.

Perhaps he shared kisses and dinners with other young ladies all the time. Or perhaps it was actually Charmaine who'd captured his interest and Annie was a harmless distraction.

No, no, he had voiced his interest on more than one occasion. He genuinely wanted to see her in spite of her family's disapproval. She almost wrapped her arms around herself and laughed. *Her!* Luke Carpenter was interested in *her!*

"We'll have to decide what to wear," Charmaine said from behind, pushing her toward the loan desk. "We'd better go home and plan."

Guiltily, she hoped Charmaine's feelings wouldn't be hurt when she realized that it was Annie whom Luke wanted to see. Perhaps she should tell her. But that would seem as though she were full of herself—and she wasn't. She could hardly believe it herself.

What would her cousin think if she knew about the kisses she had shared with Luke? She'd better wait and see what happened next. She could be wrong about his intentions.

And if she was, she would die of disappointment.

Her emotions were in turmoil for an entire day. Charmaine told her mother about their dinner plans and proceeded to try on every dress she possessed, as well as arranging her hair and holding earbobs to her ears and turning this way and that before the mirror. Annie felt like a traitor. She didn't want Charmaine to get her hopes up. She didn't want to get her own hopes up. She didn't want Charmaine to be embarrassed. She didn't want to be embarrassed herself.

What a predicament she'd landed in.

By the time they were dressed and ready to take the wagon into town the next night, Charmaine's whirlwind chattering and primping had Annie's nerves frayed. She surveyed the scenery between the ranch and town and took slow calm breaths, tuning out her cousin's continual stream of girlish talk.

They entered Copper Creek and Annie's heart kicked into a frenetic beating. Luke, dressed in dark trousers and a white shirt and black string tie, met them at the livery. "Evenin', ladies. Aren't you the prettiest creatures in these parts?"

Annie had borrowed a blue shirtwaist dress from Charmaine. Charmaine thought the dress was too plain, but that was exactly why Annie loved it. She didn't feel like a child in the garment.

"Stay where you are," he said and climbed up to sit beside Charmaine. "I'll leave the wagon in the alley while we eat."

He drove the horse and wagon to the café and assisted the ladies to the door, then left to move the wagon.

"Isn't he charming?" Charmaine asked breathlessly.

Annie nodded.

"I wish Mary Lou could see me," she said. "She's always bragging about that Nelson boy calling on her."

"This isn't exactly calling," Annie dared to mention.

"Of course it is," her cousin argued. "He's courting minded."

"But there are two of us," Annie reminded her.

"That keeps it proper. Watch how outrageously he flirts."

"He's simply being nice."

"No. He's of an age to be married. Don't be so dull, Annie. When a young man shows interest in a young lady, it's courting."

Luke came toward them and the conversation ended. He led them into the café, held Charmaine's chair while she sat, and moved a chair aside to wheel Annie up close.

Noting the high color in Annie's cheeks, Luke sat between the cousins and glanced from one to the other.

Annie was lovely in a dark-blue dress with a ruffled collar standing up around her ivory throat. The color set off the red-gold highlights in her curly hair and brought a sparkle to her eyes. "You look—you *both* look so pretty."

Annie smiled and blushed, and Charmaine thanked him.

Dora took their orders and brought the ladies cups of tea and Luke coffee. He stirred in a spoonful of sugar.

"Rachel Maye said she ate at an elegant restaurant when she went to Denver with her family," Charmaine said. "Have you been to any of those types of places?"

"Restaurants, you mean?" he asked.

She nodded.

"I've eaten in some nice places. Dora's cookin' is right up there with the best, though. 'Course it was always just Gil and me cooking for each other, so I'd probably think anything was good if we didn't fix it."

"Your uncle doesn't have a wife?" Annie asked.

"Guess he had one once, but she ran off. He never talked about her. I never knew her—that was before I came here."

Annie's gray-green eyes studied him as he spoke, her sincere interest obvious. "You weren't born here, were you? In Colorado?"

"No. I was born in Illinois. My father worked in a newspaper office. My mother died when I was about six or seven, and my father was killed when I was fourteen. That's when I came to live with my Uncle Gil."

"It must have been awful for you, losing your parents like that," Charmaine said.

"My mother and my younger sister died of whooping cough. After that I sort of took care of myself when I wasn't in school. I was fortunate that Gil asked me to come out here. I'd been workin' at the paper, just doing the clean-up jobs, but when I got to Colorado I discovered how much I loved horses."

"You didn't get Wrangler until you moved here then?" Annie asked.

"Actually we found him on the way from Illinois," he replied. "We stopped over at a stage station near Wichita and Gil bought him from a trader for me."

"A Swedish Warmblood," she said.

Luke raised his brows. "You remembered that?"

She nodded and changed the subject. "Your Uncle Gil sounds nice."

"He is. You'll have to meet him."

"I'd like that."

Charmaine glanced from Luke to Annie curiously.

Annie's face turned pink and she looked down at her hands. What had been said that had embarrassed her?

She glanced up again, and the cousins exchanged a look.

Annie's gaze turned to other patrons in the room, and Luke followed her glance. Five or six other tables were filled, mostly town people he knew because he did business with them.

She was obviously wondering who would notice them together and take the news back to her family.

The door opened and closed.

"Annie," Charmaine whispered, "it's Mary Lou with her parents and that awful brother of hers." Charmaine almost squirmed in delight. She sat up straighter, and Luke wondered what was so exciting about the arrival of the people she'd mentioned.

A glance told him it was Daniel Holister with his wife and children. The girl, Charmaine's age, stared wide-eyed at their trio. Luke smiled politely and her cheeks turned crimson.

Dora brought their meals, and the attention moved to the savory roast beef and new potatoes.

"Annie's mother has someone to help with the cooking, but my mother only has me," Charmaine said. "You don't know how nice it is to eat away from home."

"Sure I do," Luke replied. "I get tired of food out of tins, so I eat over here a lot."

"What's your favorite dessert?" Charmaine asked, glancing at the chalkboard on a wall.

"Apple pie." It had become his favorite when Annie had baked one just for him. And since she'd said his kisses tasted like cinnamon. He couldn't repress a smile at the memory.

Annie wouldn't meet his eyes. She dabbed her mouth with her napkin and folded it into a neat square.

"Annie, you're positively scarlet!" Charmaine said, and touched her cousin's cheek with the back of her fingers. "Are you feeling well?"

Annie caught Charmaine's wrist and lowered their hands to the tabletop. "I'm fine. Can we change the subject?"

"From *apple pie?*" Her voice held puzzlement.

A laugh worked its way up from Luke's chest and he tried to hold it back by taking a sip of coffee. But Annie's red face and Charmaine's quizzical look struck him so funny that the laugh rumbled out, and he choked.

He coughed to cover his amusement, making the situation worse, and covered his mouth with his napkin.

Annie leaned sideways in her chair and slapped her palm against the center of his back a few times. "Are you all right?"

He glanced down at the warm touch of her other hand on his forearm, able to think of nothing but her hand on him.

She caught herself and snatched it back.

"Yes, thanks," he managed to reply finally.

She met his eyes then, and leaning close this way, he could see the tiny green flecks that circled her gray irises like sunbursts. Her brows were delicately shaped and tinged with red like her hair, her lashes a spiky fringe.

His focus lowered to her mouth, a lovely smooth pink bow with a full lower lip. He'd kissed those lips.

The corners twitched. She was fighting laughter now, too.

She chuckled and straightened, pulling away from him. One glance at her cousin and laughter spilled out.

Luke joined her, and they laughed until his side hurt.

Charmaine glanced around the room with a halfhearted smile.

Finally, the mirth subsided and Dora came to remove their dinner plates. "Will you be having dessert?"

"I guess apple pie is out of the question," Charmaine said owlishly.

Luke didn't look up. "I'll have the bread pudding, please."

His dinner companions agreed with his decision, and Dora cleared the table. She returned with their desserts, filled Luke's coffee cup and set a fresh pot of tea on the table.

"This is delicious," Charmaine said. "I wonder how you make it."

"Eggs and bread and . . . cinnamon," Annie replied. "I—I saw a recipe in a cookbook."

"Well, it's delicious."

She glanced over and he knew her thoughts. *Cinnamon.* Lord, he had it bad for this woman when he thought of nothing but kissing her, even when they were sitting in a restaurant surrounded by other people.

Too soon, the meal was over. Luke paid the bill and escorted the ladies from the building and brought the wagon around. Annie stood and he took her hand, walking beside her in the twilight as she made her way to the back of the wagon.

"Why don't I get a horse and see you home?" he said, not wanting to end their time together, even if they had no privacy.

Charmaine expressed her agreement and he helped Annie into the back and Charmaine up to the seat, then rode beside her as far as the livery.

He entered the stable and saddled Wrangler. "We're goin' for a ride this evenin'," he told the animal, then led him out and tied his reins to the back of the wagon. He wanted only to climb into the back with Annie, but he did the gentlemanly thing and took the leads from her cousin.

Charmaine seemed a little subdued, and he appreciated a few welcome stretches of silence. Before long the Renlow ranch came into view beneath the darkening sky, a modest spread with good water and healthy stock. He pulled the wagon up before the house, and Mort came out the door.

Luke helped Charmaine down. "Luke came home with us, Daddy."

"Son." Mort shook his hand.

"Mr. Renlow."

Annie's uncle lowered her to the ground while Luke got her chair. She thanked her uncle and seated herself.

"The missus just made some fresh coffee," Mort said.

"No, thanks," Luke replied.

"She made raisin cookies."

"Now I could probably tuck away a cookie."

They headed for the house. Once again, Mort

picked up Annie and carried her while Luke got her chair.

The Renlow place was spacious and adequately furnished. They weren't well-to-do, but they were comfortable and their house was a real home. They were genuinely nice warm people. Vera Renlow brought a tray of cookies to the kitchen table and they nibbled and talked.

She offered a pitcher of cold milk and Luke accepted a glass.

He felt as though he'd broken through a wall that had been standing in front of him most of his life. A wall separating him and Annie. These people treated him as though he were any other person. They accepted him.

But then they weren't Annie's parents.

Charmaine behaved less silly in her home and in the company of her parents, and he actually saw a side of her he liked. She offered Mort more coffee and Luke more milk. She filled her father's cup with her hand on his shoulder. Mort gave his daughter an affectionate smile.

Annie seemed comfortable and at ease with the Renlows, too, exchanging banter and waving her hand at her uncle when he told a story about her thinking a baby rabbit was a baby pig when she was twelve years old.

"Well, they look the same," she said, laughing. "Those baby bunnies didn't have one lick of fur and their ears were short. Now, what would you think if you'd never seen one before?"

The question was directed at Luke, and he shook his head and grinned, saying, "I think pigs are a little bigger, but then it's probably an easy mistake."

"Well, Charmaine came carrying it to show me, and I didn't see its mother. It looked like a pig to me!"

Mort laughed again, and Annie cast him a mock scowl. "You wouldn't want anyone to mention the time you climbed down the ladder and stepped into the paint bucket, would you?"

Vera got a laugh over that one and joined Annie in regaling Luke with the tale.

Their family and their easy camaraderie charmed Luke. As a boy, there'd been only him and his father, and as a youth it had been him and Gil, with no women in their lives. Women sure brightened a house . . . and a heart.

"How are you related to the Sweetwaters?" Luke asked conversationally. He couldn't imagine the Sweetwater family being this unpretentious.

"Mort and Annie's mother are brother and sister," Vera said.

"Oh. They don't—*look* alike."

Mort and the girls said nothing. Luke glanced at them, hoping his question hadn't put a damper on the enjoyable evening.

Annie offered him her sweet smile.

"Both nice looking, though," Luke said, and the others chuckled.

Mort smiled at Vera. "My wife was the prettiest girl in Fairfax County. Now she has a little competition, what with Charmaine and Annie here, don't you think?"

"It would be a three-way tie if I had to vote."

Annie's uncle finished his coffee. "You're a smart man, Mr. Carpenter."

"I just know when not to hang myself."

Mort chortled and pushed his chair back to stand. "I'm turnin' in." He offered his hand. "Come back any time."

"Thank you, sir."

The older man started for the doorway, then turned back with his forehead creased in curiosity. "Say, which of these young ladies is it you're callin' on, anyway?"

Chapter Six

He'd been too quick to say he knew how not to hang himself. Mort Renlow's words had created the first tension he'd felt in this house since he'd arrived. What should he say? Did the man think that he might be coming around to see his daughter? The truth of how it must look hit Luke square between the eyes.

Of course he could think that. Luke had invited both girls for ice cream and then for dinner. While he'd been thinking that Charmaine's presence kept his and Annie's relationship respectable in public, others might have been thinking he was using Annie as a chaperon. The thought angered him momentarily. But Mort wasn't thinking any less of Annie; he just truly wasn't sure of Luke's intent and his question was honest.

For the first time, Luke considered Charmaine's feelings and felt like a heel. If Annie hadn't confided in her, then she might be thinking he was interested in her. All along, he'd assumed she'd known his attraction was for Annie.

Mort stood in the doorway, one hand on the frame, waiting.

Luke met Annie's eyes and read the panic behind them. He glanced at Charmaine, seeing a touch of color in her cheeks and an expectant lift to her eyebrows. No. Annie hadn't shared what had gone on between them. Why not?

He didn't know any other way than honesty, so he said, "Charmaine is pretty and charming, and I'm sure the fellows will be flockin' around soon, but your daughter is a trifle too young for me, Mr. Renlow."

Mort nodded as though that simple declaration was all that need be said. "It's Annie, then."

Luke nodded affirmatively. It most certainly was Annie.

Annie saw his nod and felt the rush of pleasure and relief sluice through her insides. She had waited with dread, not knowing if she wanted Luke to make a declaration or not. His admission brought a lump to her throat. She wanted to jump up and hug him, but she turned instead to her cousin.

Charmaine had cast her gaze to the tabletop and it was a full minute before her lashes swept up and she looked Annie in the eye. Annie wanted to spare her embarrassment, but she didn't know what to say. She'd never known what to say, and that's why this moment had come. She hadn't possessed the courage or the confidence to really believe that Luke was interested in her.

Now she knew. And so did Charmaine.

"You're gonna have a tough time with Annie's folks," Mort said. "I hope you know what you're doin'."

107

"I think I do," Luke replied. "I know I don't have a good history with the Sweetwaters. But Annie's grown-up now. She should be able to make decisions for herself."

Vera stood behind Charmaine's chair. "Nothing I've ever said to my brother-in-law has made a difference, but you have our support. Annie deserves to be happy, and whatever makes her happy will be what we want, too."

Annie blinked at her aunt's approving words, not surprised because she knew her character, but moved by her understanding.

Her uncle took his leave and Luke stood. "Thank you, Mrs. Renlow. Thanks for everything."

"You're welcome here any time."

"Good night, Charmaine," he said tentatively.

Charmaine mumbled something.

"Annie," Luke said to her.

She wished they had a few minutes to talk privately, but right now she didn't know what she'd have said. "Good night."

He looked as though he wanted to say more, but he exited through the kitchen door.

Vera left the room and her footsteps sounded on the stairs.

Annie would have liked to hug this new information to her heart and enjoy the amazing fact that Luke was interested in her, but, concerned for her cousin's feelings, she reached for Charmaine's arm.

"Oh, Annie, you're positively the luckiest girl in all of Colorado!" her cousin said breathlessly.

Annie blinked back tears in agreement.

"Of course, it was you all along," she said, her tone self-deprecating. "Why, you're bright and beautiful and poised, far more sophisticated than me."

"All those things have nothing to do with it," Annie disagreed. "You are all those and more. It's just that Luke and I have this . . . this *history*."

"Yes. And it's so romantic. Oh, Annie, he's loved you since you were a girl!"

She didn't know if he loved her, exactly, but he had always been kind and shown respect. He treated her as an equal, as very few people in her life ever had. As Charmaine always had. "I only hoped," she told her. "I didn't know. I thought maybe it was you. You deserve someone wonderful, too."

"Well, I'm disappointed," Charmaine said. "No use denying it. But I'm thrilled for you! Good Lord, what will your mother say?" She blinked. "What will Burdell do?"

Annie could only imagine the answers to those questions. She shook her head. She was so grateful for Charmaine's loving acceptance, she threw her arms around her, rather awkwardly because she was in her chair and Charmaine was seated, too, and hugged her soundly. All the emotions of the past days and weeks built up and exploded in a burst of tears.

"Annie! There's an honorable sheriff now, he won't let Burdell do anything bad to Luke."

That was true. People couldn't just go around beating up one another without the law stepping in. But what if Burdy hurt Luke and went to jail? He had a family. Her worry for Luke hadn't been the only cause of this emotional torrent. The reality of Luke's intent, her aunt and uncle's acceptance, Charmaine's selfless joy for her, years and years of inadequacy and wishful thinking . . . all those poignant feelings, plus more, confused her heart and her head. "I—I know. It's more than th-that. It's everything."

Charmaine slid from her chair to kneel before Annie and hug her, rubbing her back comfortingly. "I haven't heard you cry like this since Uncle Eldon made you give that puppy back to the Deets boy. You'd think you'd lost something, rather than gained a handsome, attentive admirer."

Annie pulled away and swiped at her cheeks. "I know, I'm ungrateful, aren't I?"

"No, you're just sensitive."

"You're so good to me." Annie squeezed Charmaine's hand.

"Well, remember that," Charmaine said, sitting back on her heels. "Because the next too-good-to-be-true man is mine."

Annie laughed. "Of course he is."

Charmaine stood. "I'd better get up to bed, so I can be fresh for school in the morning. You can sleep in, you lucky duck."

"Be glad you get to go to school and that you don't have to be bored out of your wits by tutors. I used to sit and daydream about going to class like the others." Annie stood and blew out the lantern hanging over the table and pointed to the one on the kitchen wall.

Charmaine lifted the chimney and extinguished the wick. "All right, all right, I'm grateful. Night, Annie," she said into the darkness.

"Night."

Annie wheeled herself into her room where her aunt had lit a lamp. Leaving her chair in a corner, she walked to the dresser for her night-rail, picked up her silver-backed hairbrush and sat on the edge of the bed to brush her hair.

She paused with the bristles in the ends and stared at her reflection in the window glass. Looking back at her couldn't be the same girl who'd only wistfully dreamed of a normal life while spending hers in a wheelchair and watching everyone else have fun and do the things she yearned to do. The girl looking back at her looked like every other young woman in Copper Creek, a normal girl doing normal things.

Annie hugged the thoughts close, her mind reeling with images of the future.

She didn't watch her reflection as she got to her

feet; that wasn't as graceful as she wished. Walking to the window, she drew the curtains closed. It was as if her life had only just begun, that all that had come before was only a foreshadow to the real thing.

Everything would be perfect if only her parents could see Luke the same way the Renlows did. But they didn't see her the same way the Renlows did, so that was undoubtedly too much to dream for. She changed into her nightclothes.

A black cloud hung over her happiness. She was too cowardly to even say his name to her parents yet. Things could stay like this for the time being. The situation wasn't perfect, but it was exciting and new and she wanted to enjoy it a while longer. Right now she wasn't up to facing the possibilities that the future held.

Right now she wanted to let the fact that Luke had declared himself soak in. The memories of his words, of all their moments together buoyed her flagging spirit, and she turned down the lamp wick and crawled into bed.

She would take this day by day.

"Your brother will be here in a few minutes," Mildred Sweetwater called to Annie.

Annie jumped and stuffed her new dress back into the corner of her wardrobe where her mother wouldn't find it, running her fingers over the spring-green brocade one last time. "I'll be there in a minute!"

She closed the cabinet door with satisfaction. Aunt Vera had been impressed with Annie's skill with a needle and thread. After years of needlepoint practice, she'd been a natural at precise, even stitches, and had turned out the collar and facings so that they lay smooth and flat. They'd finished it a week ago, and she'd brought it home in her trunk.

The dress fit her perfectly and was like nothing she'd ever owned before. She couldn't wait to wear it. But she could wait to see her mother's reaction.

She wheeled herself into the kitchen, where Glenda was stirring gravy on the stove. "Can I help?"

Glenda cast her a sideways glance. "You can if you want to hear your mother's sermon on why you shouldn't be in the kitchen."

"I've heard that one. I'm pretty good at turning a deaf ear. I don't want her angry at you, though."

"Now could I stop you from going over there and slicing up that ham?"

Annie left her chair at the end of a counter and stood to slice the aromatic glazed ham. "How thick?"

Glenda glanced over at the slice Annie'd made. "About like that."

"Annie!" her mother shrieked, and the knife clattered to the floor.

Glenda picked it up and rinsed it.

Mildred stood with her hand on her hip. "You know you shouldn't be in here. It's far too hazardous."

"It is when you scare the pea-wadden out of me while I have a knife in my hand."

"Don't be insolent, child. And what are you doing out of your chair?"

"I was helping Glenda."

"Glenda has performed these tasks many times without your help, she doesn't need it now. Go out on the lawn and direct your father in setting up the croquet game."

Deciding she'd rather save her battles for the important things to come, Annie sat and rolled out the back door that her mother held open for her.

She wheeled down the ramp and several feet into the yard. Her father came and pushed her closer to where he'd been poking U-shaped wires into the ground.

"Daddy?" she asked.

He adjusted a wire and straightened, glancing her way.

"What did you and mother always think would become of me? I mean, did you think I would always live here with you?"

"You're our daughter, we'll always take care of you."

"You'll be old someday. What did you think would become of me then?"

A pained expression crossed his features, and she knew it was something he'd given considerable thought. "There's Burdell and Diana. Or Charmaine."

"Burdy has his own family, and soon enough Charmaine will, too."

"There will always be someone who loves you and wants to take care of you."

"You know," she risked saying, "I can take care of myself."

"Money won't be a problem after we're gone," he added. "You could hire a nurse or a companion."

"A nurse?" Like she was sick? "Didn't you ever imagine I'd meet someone . . . a man, I mean . . . and have a husband?"

Her father stared at her as though her hair had turned to snakes. "You're not like other girls," he said, as gently as he could. "You have to look at your life in other perspectives."

What other perspectives? They hadn't allowed her any outside interests or friends. She wasn't allowed to be productive in any way. Just what in heaven's name did they think would become of her? They treated her as though she were a porcelain doll they could just dress and pose, a doll that simply sat on a shelf looking pretty, with no feelings or desires or life.

Annie closed her eyes. It had been over a week

since she'd seen Luke. Glenda had brought her one note in that time. It had been seven whole days since she'd returned from the Renlows, where she at least felt like a whole person.

"Hi, Nannie!" a tiny voice called.

She opened her eyes and shaded them to see Burdell and Diana walking toward the gate. Burdell carried Will on one shoulder. She waved and smiled.

Inside the yard, Burdell stood Will on his feet and the little boy ran toward Annie, an adorable cherub with huge round dark eyes and perfect tiny teeth visible through that wide smile.

She leaned to scoop him up and he wrapped his arms around her neck and hugged her fiercely. "How's my boy?"

"Meow!" he said and jabbered something she assumed was about a cat they'd seen on their walk over.

"Ooh, a kitty, huh?"

He nodded and then pointed to his brown leather shoes. "Shoes."

"Those are nice shoes. Are they new?"

He nodded.

"Will, come now, don't wear out your aunt," Burdell said, coming close enough to reach for the boy.

Annie settled him more firmly in her lap, clamped her arms around his waist and glared at her brother.

He would have had to wrestle Will from her, which might have hurt the child, so he appeared to change his mind and backed away.

"Hi, Annie," Diana said. The open, friendly smile on her round face allowed Annie to lower her defenses. Burdell strolled toward their father.

Annie kissed Will's cheek and loosened her grip.

"You're just in time," Mildred called from the edge of the porch. "Dinner is ready."

Diana pushed Annie and Will across the lawn, up the ramp and into the house. There was never a chair on Annie's side of the table. Her wheelchair fit neatly in its spot.

The food was all on platters and in bowls and in minutes it was served and the family ate. Sounds of cleanup came from the kitchen where Glenda was no doubt eager to get home to her own family. She agreed to come in and cook for the Sweetwaters two Sundays a month, and Annie knew it was because Mildred paid her so well and she needed the money for her two children.

"Would you like some potatoes, Will?" Diana asked her son.

He nodded and she served him. He sat on a stack of books across from Annie, a dish towel tied around his neck to protect his clothing.

Annie loved watching his animated expressions as he sampled the food on his plate. Everything he did was an adventure. The sliced potatoes kept slipping off his fork, so using Will's fork, Burdy patiently stabbed a slice at a time for the boy to get them to his mouth himself.

"You're a good daddy," she told her brother softly.

He shrugged modestly and took a bite of his own meal. He'd been a good brother, too, if a bit overzealous in protecting her.

"He's a very good daddy," Diana agreed. "He even reads Will a bedtime story every night."

The scenario sounded so normal. Annie couldn't have been happier for her nephew, having a kind mother and an attentive father . . . enjoying his health and a typical childhood.

All the things she'd longed for. All the things that had never been hers. Her thoughts kept straying to Luke's intent, as they had every day since the night he'd expressed his interest in her. Charmaine had been right—about the courting part.

Could something so ordinary and so wonderful truly be happening to her? Should she allow her dreams to include a family of her own—a husband—children like Will?

For the first time she'd begun to think that those things were possible for her. Happiness bubbled up inside without a means of expression.

After coffee and dessert, which Mildred served herself, the family headed back outside. Annie remained in the kitchen to help Glenda finish.

"Will you take this note for me?" she asked. She'd prepared it that morning.

"Glad to help a budding romance," Glenda said with a sly grin and took the paper, tucking it into her pocket.

"Go on now, I'll dry that pan," Annie told her.

Glenda thanked her, hung her apron on a peg in the pantry and wished her a good afternoon.

"You, too." Annie dried the pan, put it away and took herself out back.

The three adults were engaged in a game of croquet, and Will was getting in trouble trying to play with the wooden balls.

"Here, Will!" she called. "There's a rubber ball on the porch right there." She got the message across to him and he ran up the ramp, got the ball and carried it back to her.

"Let's move over here and throw it."

Of course Will's pitches landed on all sides of her, rarely reaching her unless they caught her in the head or the chest. It would have been so easy for her to get out of her chair and simply walk to the ball each time. Her arms grew tired of pushing the wheels over the grass, and her frustration became a coppery taste in her mouth.

The ball sailed six feet to her right and the temptation to stand grew so strong, she drew a deep breath.

Standing, she limped to retrieve it and tossed it back.

Wide-eyed, Will grinned and picked it up, only to toss it in the other direction. Annie went after it. This was so much easier—and so much fun! Will was delighted, too, crying, "Nannie! Nannie!"

"Annie!" Her mother's shriek broke into their joyful game. Burdell was at her side in an instant, pushing her chair up behind her.

"What are you doing, child?" her mother cried in horror. "Thank goodness there was no one here to see this!"

Annie sat and stared up at her, a sick feeling sinking in her chest. "What do you mean?"

"I mean—you could have hurt yourself! You could have fallen! You may already have been hurt." She turned to Eldon. "Do you think we should send for the doctor?"

"I'm fine, Mother," Annie said with disgust.

"Are you certain?" her father asked. "Does anything hurt?"

They had no idea, no idea whatsoever. "Yes, my arms, from pushing this damned chair across the grass."

"Annie!" Mildred's hand flattened on her breast in offense. "Such language is inappropriate for a lady!"

"It's my fault," Burdell said. "I wasn't paying attention and Will wore her out."

"Will didn't wear me out," Annie disagreed with a disgusted flick of her hand. "All this invalid stuff is wearing me out."

Her mother's pale face took on a positively stricken expression. She grabbed her husband's arm. "That tea that the Philadelphia hospital suggested. That will relax her. I'll go prepare it immediately."

"I don't need to be 'relaxed', Mother!" Annie called to her back. She studied her father's helpless expression, Burdell's smothering look of concern, and noted that Diana was giving the two men curious looks.

She met Annie's gaze.

"Diana, will you push me to my room?"

Diana stepped behind her. "Of course."

She wheeled Annie past her mother, who was fanning the fire in the stove, and got her to her room.

"You are all right, aren't you?" Diana said, more of a statement than a question.

"I'm perfectly fine except for wanting to tear my hair out and scream."

"Don't do that. Your hair is too pretty to tear out."

Annie couldn't suppress a smile. "I'm just so tired of being treated as though I'm worthless," she said wearily. "I can do things! I can *walk!* They just won't let me." She got out of her chair and demonstrated, walking first to the window and then to the wardrobe. The enormous room allowed her space to walk in a circle and she did so, as she'd done every day for weeks and weeks.

"Is this so awful? Is my limping so hideous that I should be ashamed and hide myself away? Is it? Do I embarrass you?"

"Not in the least! I'm thrilled you can walk so well. I had no idea."

"Because they don't allow it." Her temper had cooled and she stepped to the overstuffed chair near the window seat and sat, cradling this new injury to her pride and confidence.

Her sister-in-law took a seat on the padded window bench. "Maybe they just need some time," she said.

"How much time? Nineteen years, would that be long enough?" She hated the catch in her voice that gave away her hurt feelings.

Diana's glance at the ceiling and bob of her head said she'd gotten the point. Nineteen years hadn't been enough to show them she was capable of anything more than the slim allowances they'd permitted.

"I'll speak to Burdell," she promised. "Maybe that'll make a difference."

Annie didn't hold much hope that it would, but she was grateful that Diana understood and cared. "Thanks."

Mildred tapped on the door and opened it, a tray balanced between her hip and forearm. "Annie?"

Annie rolled her eyes at Diana. "Come in, Mother. You'll notice I'm not foaming at the mouth."

"I've made you tea."

"I'm not going to drink it."

"Of course you will. The doctors warned us you might become agitated from time to time."

"Yes, I get agitated. So would anyone in my situation. But I don't want to be drugged."

"Don't be difficult, dear—"

"Mother, please. I'm not a child. I'm not being difficult. Please stop treating me as if I were six years old."

Her mother sat the tray on a cherry wood table and wrung her hands, her dismay evident. "I don't know where this attitude has come from. Diana, talk some sense into her."

Startled, Diana glanced up. "She makes perfect sense to me. I can't imagine anything I'd have to say. She has some valid points if anyone cared long enough to listen."

Mildred stiffened and clasped her hands together. "I might have expected as much from you."

She turned and quit the room in a huff.

Diana shrugged.

"I have something to show you." Annie got up and walked over to her wardrobe. She withdrew the green dress and held it for her sister-in-law to see.

"That's a pretty dress."

"Isn't it positively *normal?*" She held it against herself and gazed down fondly. "I sewed most of it myself, too. Aunt Vera showed me how and helped when I made a mistake, but I pretty much did it on my own."

"That's impressive. I've never sewn a dress for myself."

"Really? Well then I guess I'm impressed, too." She grinned. "But you can do so many things. You're independent and smart and politically savvy."

"Not exactly sterling qualities in your mother's book, are they?" Diana asked with a wry tone.

"And you have a beautiful little boy, who is bright and happy."

"He is, isn't he?" Pride shone in her dark eyes.

"And you obviously make my brother very happy. He adores you."

"He adores you, too, Annie. But he treats me completely different than he treats you."

"Because he looks at you as an adult," Annie said. "An equal."

"He's overprotective because he loves you."

"I know that. But it's smothering."

"I promised you I would talk to him, and I will."

Annie nodded her understanding. "I know. Thank you."

After a few more minutes, Diana left to join her husband and son. Annie stayed in her room, pacing for a time, then lying on the bed and allowing her thoughts to roam.

She opened her eyes and discovered she'd

fallen asleep. Darkness shrouded her room. She sat, finding her arms and legs achy from excessive use that day. Flexing the muscles, she brushed the wrinkles from her clothing and wheeled herself to the kitchen for water to wash and clean her teeth.

The house sat dark and silent; her parents had been upstairs for quite some time. After washing, she checked the Seth Thomas clock on the mantel, then silently unlocked the back door and wheeled down the ramp and along the hard-packed path to the gate. By the time she reached the end of her street, her arms were trembling, but the pain was forgotten as soon as she saw the dark horse and the tall man beneath the glow of the silvery moon.

Chapter Seven

"You got the note. I'm sorry I'm late," she said. "I fell asleep."

"I didn't mind the wait." The nearest house here at the edge of town was several hundred yards away, and a dozen pine trees plus a blooming hedge of spiraea prevented anyone from seeing where Luke waited.

"It's been so long," she said, hearing the breathlessness in her own voice.

"I'm glad you sent the note." He glanced down the lane. "We probably shouldn't stay here."

"Let's go somewhere, then," she suggested, even though her suggestion was a risky idea. She really didn't worry about her parents waking and checking on her; they never did any more. But someone might see them together.

"All right." He appeared to think for a moment. "Stand up."

Willing to take the risk, she did.

He pushed her chair into the spiraea bushes where it couldn't be seen. "You up to a ride?"

She glanced at the horse. "You brought Wrangler."

"He wanted to see you."

Annie laughed softly. "Yes, I'm up to it."

He moved the animal closer to where an

abandoned cart sat at the corner of the neighbor's property. June flowers bloomed in the back. Luke dipped to sweep her up and carry her to the cart, where he placed her on the top of the wheel and held her hand for balance. "Can you reach his back from there?"

She grabbed the saddle horn and made the transference easily. Using the stirrup, Luke swung up behind her.

He was bigger than the last time they'd done this, harder, more muscled, and she was aware of his chest and thighs against her back and hips, his breath grazing her neck.

"Can Wrangler handle this?" she asked.

"We're not going far." Luke took the reins and with a flex of his hard thighs against hers, the horse stepped forward.

Elated, Annie clung to the saddle horn and leaned back against his solid reassuring form. Her second ride was every bit as exhilarating as her first, in fact even more so. Now she was aware of Luke as a man. She had eagerly anticipated their stolen time together.

He led the horse through the dark silent streets of town, passed businesses with living quarters overhead. Annie glanced up at the dark windows. Luke halted the horse before the livery. The wide door that stood open during the day was closed, and the horse stopped near a door to the side.

Luke dismounted, then reached up. She leaned

toward him and he took her weight easily, carrying her and leading the horse through the doorway and into the dark interior of the stable that smelled of hay and horses.

He paused and told her where to reach to locate a lamp and matches. She lit the wick and carried the lantern, letting the light guide their way as he carried her down a double row of box stalls.

Luke lowered her to her feet. "There's a bench there, if you want to sit."

She did.

He led Wrangler into a stall, removed his saddle, and scooped grain into a bucket. "You deserve extra oats, boy," he said, slapping his hindquarters. "I'll brush you down good later."

The horse nickered as though he'd understood, and Annie smiled to herself.

Luke fastened the stall door behind him. "Want to walk or shall I carry you?"

"I'll walk."

She stood and he took her hand, leading her past the stalls, telling her which horses were his, which he boarded. He tucked her hand into the crook of his arm and against the solid warmth of his body. They turned a corner and entered a large room with a waist-high brick fireplace that took up the outside wall.

"This is the forge." He showed her his tools: hammers, tongs, punches and chisels. He pointed out the double-chambered bellows above the forge. Two sizes of anvils had been mounted to tree trunks of a height he could easily reach to work. Right now the chilly room smelled of coals, and she could only imagine how hot it would be when the fire was blazing enough to shape and beat iron.

"I heard the sound of the hammers building this place, and sometimes on a clear day I can hear the ring of the hammer on the iron. Now when I hear it, I'll picture you here. You'll seem closer."

He gave her a gentle smile and touched one finger to her cheek before continuing on.

Another room was completely filled with tack, and the scent of leather and oil permeated her nostrils.

"Why so many different harnesses and bits?" she asked after he told her what each was.

"All horses are unique and work differently. Some like one kind of bit, some another. You don't want your animal to obey because of pain, so you make sure the bit fits his mouth."

"Oh." She turned back and he was standing so close that she stepped into his arms. She wrapped her arms around his waist more because of her pleasure to be with him than for balance.

He ran his thumb down her spine to her waistband and back up, and Annie experienced a stunning rush of excitement. Being alone with a man and any physical contact was strictly forbidden according to the way she and every other girl she knew had been raised. If she'd been severely warned about flirtation and flattery, how much more taboo was *this?*

But she just couldn't see this beautiful thing they shared as wrong.

He lowered his head and her heart fluttered in response. She raised her lips and met his warm damp mouth with a soft exhale and a tiny sound of pleasure.

The kiss mounted and swelled, and he nipped the corner of her lips, dragged his mouth to her chin, then to her neck.

Annie let her head fall back and enjoyed the pleasurable sensations his mouth created on her sensitive skin. Deep inside, tiny bursts of warmth flooded her heart and chugged through her veins.

"I like you in the daytime, Annie, when the sunlight is bright on your hair, making it look like fire and fool's gold. Your lashes are so light and your skin is as fine as a baby's, so fair and so delicate."

Just those words made her breasts feel hard and achy. Her breath caught in her throat.

"But I like you in the dark, too, when I have to rely on my nose and my hands and the sound of your voice and your sighs. In the dark it seems like we're the only two people in the world."

She let her eyelids close and imagined being alone with no distractions, no parents, no one waiting to correct her or stop her from being herself. "I wish we were."

He hugged her tightly, and she buried her cheek against his chest and the erratic pounding of his heart.

"Where do you live?" she asked. "You haven't shown me yet."

"It's not much to see."

"I want to see anyway."

"Okay." He took one of her hands and the lantern and led her through a narrow corridor, then held open a door for her to pass inside.

Annie limped into the long, narrow room. The space held a small woodstove, a chest of drawers, a normal-size bed, a stack of crates atop which sat folded toweling and a pail for water. Pegs in one wall held coats and overalls and hats she'd never seen him wear.

Another stack of crates held books and a few personal items. A worn braided rug covered the plank floor.

"I told you it wasn't much."

She glanced around the austere space. "It's not bad."

"It's only temporary until I build a house."

"I said it's not bad."

"It's not what you're used to."

She glanced up at him. "I've never had to pay for anything myself."

An uncomfortable silence stretched between

them. Annie's tired legs wobbled, and she made her way to the edge of his bed and sat. "I had an abysmal day."

Luke set the lantern on the chest of drawers. "What happened?"

She told him about the ham and the incident with Will and the ball and the tea. He pulled an upended nail keg from a corner and perched atop it in front of her.

"Sometimes I feel like I'm swimming upstream and all the other fish are going the other direction. I'm the only one fighting the current and it's a losing battle. The other fish all say, 'Why don't you turn around and go the way we're going?' and I wonder that myself sometimes.

"But I'll die. I'll just die if I have to wither away in that chair and be treated like an invalid for the rest of my life." Her mother's words pierced her again. "Do you know what she said? Her first words were 'What if someone had seen you?' As if that were the worst thing that could happen. As if I'm so gauche and ugly that she's ashamed of me."

Luke lifted her hands and pressed his lips to their backs. "I can't believe she's ashamed of you," he denied. "She loves you, and she's protective."

"It's more than that. It's as though I'm a pretty pet when I stay in my chair, but if I look awkward she's embarrassed."

"I think you're beautiful just the way you are."

132

She smiled into his eyes, still disbelieving he saw her the way he claimed. But she even felt pretty when she was with him. "I did discover that I have an ally in Diana, however. I'd suspected all along, but today confirmed it."

"Well then, somethin' good did happen today."

"And tonight," she said softly. "Something real good is happening tonight."

He smiled that devastating smile that carved slashes in his cheeks.

Annie pulled a hand from his easy grasp to reach up and tentatively stroke one long dimple with her fingertips. His skin was surprisingly smooth and warm. She drew the caress across his lips and he kissed her fingers in passing.

Her stomach fluttered crazily.

She touched his eyebrows next, so black, and yet they, too, were remarkably soft.

He circled her wrists and brought her palms to his cheeks to frame his face, and her skin felt cool against the divine heat of his. His ebony lashes swept down and his eyes closed.

He was beautiful, with strong sharply angled lines to his face, a soft sensuous mouth, hair and brows as black as midnight, his chin and jaw molded in clean lines. She could look at him forever. She could touch him forever. Her throat tightened with the sweet ache of emotion she felt toward this forbidden man.

What was it she felt? Gratitude? Of course.

Friendship? Not really, not compared to what she felt toward Charmaine or Diana. These feelings were more intense . . . more consuming . . . more—*physical.*

Was this lust or love or a combination?

All she knew was that she couldn't get close enough, couldn't spend enough time in his company, couldn't draw enough pleasure from their touches and kisses to satisfy this wild greedy hunger she had for him.

"Come closer," she begged softly.

His eyelids rose and he slid from the keg to kneel on the braided rug at her feet. She turned her knees to one side to allow him to lean in close and he released her wrists to circle her waist.

She felt his mouth move over hers as much in her hands as against her lips. His jaw moved as he angled his head and parted his lips against hers.

His tongue dipped out to taste her, hot and satiny textured. Hesitantly she parted her lips and his next sweep brushed his tongue against hers.

The erotic contact reached to her very core. Threading her hands into his silky hair, she held him fast, returned his kiss, relished each thrust and foray and bewildering jolt of sensation.

His hands, bracketing her waist, rubbed up and down her ribs through the fabric of her dress and underthings. The heat melded right through the fabric to her flesh. His thumbs brushed the undersides of her breasts, and her heart hammered double-time.

She must have taken over someone else's body, someone beautiful and healthy and desirable for him to want her like this. Someone else must be occupying her mind for her to have cast caution and upbringing aside to engage in fleshly pleasures. Because she sure wasn't Annie, not the hesitant, self-conscious girl she'd been only a few months ago.

His attentions lent her boldness and confidence, and combined with the reactions of her body, she felt completely new—completely whole. She'd done things the way her parents expected her to for as long as she could bear. No matter how dangerous this was, she wanted it. She wanted Luke.

She pulled her mouth away and rested her forehead against his. "This was the longest week of my life."

"Once when I couldn't sleep for thinking of you, I walked over to your house in the middle of the night and watched the windows."

"You did?"

He nodded and her head bobbed against his. She smiled a foolishly giddy smile. "My room is downstairs on the east corner. Next time you'll know."

"You think there'll be a next time?" he asked,

his lazy stroking through her dress keeping her nerves at a fevered pitch.

"Do you?" she countered.

"I hope not. I can't afford to lose sleep and I definitely can't afford to have your neighbors call the sheriff on me."

Finally, she reached for his hands, placed them firmly over her breasts and leaned into him. She closed her eyes and absorbed the sensations. One summer when a temporary librarian had taken over for Mrs. Krenshaw, she and Charmaine had read the books they weren't allowed to check out. They'd found the anatomy books highly informative, and the fiction fascinating, though the romantic parts regarding physical details between men and women had been sketchy.

They hadn't been able to imagine how two people performed such acts with a straight face. Now she knew. She knew the pleasure and the heat, and she welcomed learning more, experiencing more.

Luke rose and guided her down upon the rough wool blanket that covered his bed. She went willingly, wrapping her arms around his shoulders. This kiss was a wet fusion of lips and breath, and it was new in that he lay with his body molded along the side of hers, chest to breast, belly to hip, thigh to thigh, hard to soft, his head and shoulders above her in the golden lamplight.

She loved the feel of his muscled body pressed against her, the scrape of his chin on her neck, the pressure of his hand, molding and shaping her breast through layers of fabric. He pressed his cheek to hers and she found his velvety earlobe with her lips . . . her tongue.

He lifted a thigh over hers, shifting his weight, urging her down into the mattress with firm gentleness. "Does this hurt you anywhere?"

"Oh, no," came her hoarse encouraging reply.

Their mouths fused, tongues and lips sleek and seeking. Annie rocked up against him, pressing as close as she could. His body stilled, then he ended the kiss with a series of plucks across her jaw.

Luke moved his weight to the side and drew her into the fold of his arm, stroking her shoulder, her hair, her cheek. Annie lay with her head against his chest and listened to the rhythmic beat of his thudding heart as it slowed. She'd never dreamed of anything so good, of anyone so— *alive.* Alive and warm and exciting and real. Those were only a few of the words that described this man she wanted, this man she loved.

A cat meowed somewhere in the darkened depths of the stable.

"Luke, I lo—"

He pressed his fingers against her lips. "It'll only make it worse if we say it."

She pulled his hand away and tipped her head to look at him. "We?" she asked hopefully.

"Even if your family didn't hate me, I couldn't offer to marry you, Annie," he said, regret tingeing his words with roughness she knew he didn't intend. "I couldn't bring you here to live. I have to have a house first."

"It wouldn't matter to me," she said. "I would live anywhere with you."

"It would matter to me. And to your family. And to the people of Copper Creek. I have to do better than this for you."

She shifted and turned to her side, raising her head to see his face. "You talked about building a house."

"In the future. I spent every dime I ever earned and saved to build this livery. It's barely started to make money."

"The waiting is so hard," she said.

He curled a springy tendril of her hair around his forefinger. "You're not tellin' me anything I don't know."

"Well, why do we have to wait for a house? I'd have all I'd ever need right here."

"There isn't even a real stove."

"I can barely cook anyway."

He chuckled, but then sobered. "Annie, babies come when people get married. We couldn't bring a baby to this place."

Warmth seeped through her belly and her limbs at those astonishing words. Tears burned behind her eyes at the miraculous thought of having her own baby. She laid her forehead on his chest. "You're so sensible and so wise and . . . and I can't believe you want me. I've always thought no one would want me—that I couldn't have a life like other people. Now I believe I can."

She raised her head and met his glistening black eyes. "I believe you can, too," he said. "I believe you can do anything you want to."

"Well, I want to marry you," she declared.

He pulled her up for a sweet lingering kiss. "I want that, too. Let's be patient a while longer."

"They're not going to change their minds," she warned him. "I've been fighting their constraints my entire life."

"I know," he said, threading his fingers through hers, palm to palm. "But we have to wait, so let's hope that somethin' changes in the meantime."

Change didn't seem likely to her, but she guessed she could hope if he could.

"I'd better take you home," he said a short time later. "We both need our sleep. If your parents woke up, we'd both be in more trouble than we can deal with. We took a big chance tonight."

"I know. But I wish I didn't have to leave."

He stood and pulled her to her feet with a pained expression. "Let's go."

"We can do this again," she suggested.

"We have to be careful," he replied. "I don't want to give them fuel for their hatred."

"They don't hate you, really."

"They'd rather see me hit by a train than living in the same town," he disagreed. "It's cooled off out there, you'd better wear my coat for the ride home." He lifted a wool jacket down from a peg and held it out. Annie slipped her arms into the engulfing garment that carried his scent.

He saddled a different mount for the short ride home, helped Annie atop the horse's back from a barrel near the door, and led him outside. He climbed up behind her and she leaned back against him.

Luke buried his nose in her hair, inhaled her sweet fragrance, and wished their time together didn't have to be only a stolen hour here and there.

He walked the horse along the shadowy black streets, taking as long as he could to reach the lane where the stately Sweetwater house stood. He never traveled this way that he didn't remember the day they'd met and think of the vivacious girl who had captured his admiration and interest.

Annie still possessed that same zest for life, the same youthful spontaneity and deep appreciation for things most people took for granted.

"It's torture not being together," she told him after he'd lifted her down and helped her into her chair.

"How well I know," he agreed.

"I'm so happy," she whispered, and he knelt in front of her to kiss her one last time. "Nothing has ever made me as happy as being with you. Not in my whole life."

"Then I'm a very lucky man." He took her hand from his cheek and pressed it against his heart. "You're in here," he told her. "I'm taking you with me."

"It's a good place to be," she said, closing her eyes in the moonlight. "Safe. Warm. Loving."

He kissed her lips. "Remember that."

When she opened her eyes, tears glistened. "I will."

"Shall I push you closer to the house?"

"Just a little."

He stepped behind her chair and propelled it toward the Sweetwater home.

"That's far enough," she said and handed him his coat.

"Remember," he said into her ear from behind, then turned and loped back to his horse. From his vantage point, he watched through the trees and she rolled herself up the ramp to the porch. Several minutes later, the light in the window she'd indicated came on, and after a brief moment, was extinguished.

Shrugging into the coat that now smelled faintly of lilacs, Luke hauled himself up onto the gelding's back and with the command of his heels, rode away.

He turned the animal's head away from town and bent low over his neck, urging him to run. He rode with abandon, the instructions to the horse automatic, because his mind was anywhere but on the ride.

Leaving the road, he skirted the edge of a lake, pounded along a trail above a canyon, and continued on. They had taken a foolish risk tonight. What if someone had seen them—what if her parents had missed her and been waiting? What if they sent her away to keep her from him?

That had always been his fear, and now the fear of separation was greater. Would the fact that she was an adult keep them from sending her off? Perhaps they would have missed her as much as he would've, and that's why they'd never done it. He didn't want to take her from them. He just wanted to love her.

Because he did love her. As much as he directed his mind to steer from that thinking, the fact was inevitable. Indisputable. He loved her. He wanted her. He needed her. Annie. His sweet Annie.

He had reined in the horse and now walked him around the edge of the lake to which he'd somehow returned. His blood still pounded hot and thick in his veins. Even after the wind had seared his face and nostrils he could smell her on his hands and his clothes and see her face in the star-studded sky.

Luke stopped walking and stared up into the heavens. He hadn't told her. He hadn't said the words that would make being separated even harder. The words welled in his chest, burned on his tongue, blurred his vision and made the stars overhead streak together. They'd been there for so long, for an eternity, without recognition or expression. They tore from his throat like a volcanic explosion.

"I love her!" he shouted across the water and his tortured voice echoed back to him: *I love her-er-er!* "I love Annie Sweetwater!" *I love Annie Sweetwater-ater-ater.*

A frog or a turtle splashed into the water from the nearby bank.

The night remained as silent as death, the stars bright pinpoints of icy brilliance. She knew. And she felt the same.

Her frustration must be a hundred times as bad as his, because she couldn't ride out her release, couldn't shout to the heavens, couldn't work up a sweat over the forge and purge her mind and body with work.

The toe of his boot came in contact with a good-size rock. He kicked it and winced at the pain that shot through his foot. Picking up the heavy stone, raising both hands over his head, he heaved it as far as he could into the water.

After a satisfying splash, a ring of circles expanded in increasing sizes in the moonlight.

But she loved him. He'd stopped the words from falling from her sweet lips. In her heart she was his.

Now he had to find a way to make her his in all respects. He needed a house. That was the first order of business. And he set his mind to planning just how he could make that happen. He would build Annie a house. And then he would make her his wife. And then he could stop scaring night creatures and maybe even sleep . . . in her arms.

Luke mounted the horse and kicked him into a run.

Chapter Eight

Luke sat in the lobby of the bank, the warmth of the summer morning not enough to cause the heat prickling along his spine and the moisture forming on his upper lip. He withdrew the handkerchief he'd tucked into the inside pocket of his best worsted wool coat and dabbed at his skin, hoping no one noticed.

He'd never done this. He'd never had to ask anyone for money. He'd built his livery the hard way, the honest way, through sweat and labor, a dollar at a time, a horse at a time, a board at a time, until his dream had taken shape.

He'd hoped, planned maybe, in the back of his mind, that it would never come to this—that he'd never be sitting here—never be asking for a loan. But when life boiled down to just the bare facts, Annie meant more than his pride.

The man at the one open teller window cast him another quizzical glance from behind steel bars. The bald-headed man sitting at a desk outside Eldon Sweetwater's office had been eyeballing Luke ever since he'd arrived forty-five minutes ago. Luke'd never been inside this bank before. He didn't trust his money here, and he'd never doubted the wisdom of that choice.

As luck would have it, Burdell arrived through

the front door just then, did a double take when he saw Luke sitting in the straight-backed chair, and with a scowl, marched to his father's office and entered without knocking.

The bald fellow jerked his gaze from Luke to a stack of papers in front of him. Undoubtedly Sweetwater had deliberately kept Luke waiting just to see him sweat.

Finally, several irritated swipes of the handkerchief later, Burdell opened the door. "Come in, Mr. Carpenter."

Luke crossed the floor and stepped into the lion's den. Burdell entered behind him and jabbed a finger at a chair.

Luke glanced around the handsomely furnished office, from the enormous glossy desk topped with brass accessories and a humidor to the leather chairs and the painting of a fox hunt on the wall over a library table.

Eldon Sweetwater sat in the chair behind the desk, calmly puffing on a cigar. They had spoken in the months since Luke had opened the livery. The man who'd owned and operated the old one had been glad to retire and move to Nebraska to live with his son. The Sweetwaters had no choice if they wanted to rent a rig; they were forced to do business with Luke . . . but they didn't have to be civil. They used his rigs and his horses and they paid him and left. They didn't like it one bit.

"You must have a good reason for being here."
Eldon folded his hands over his stomach.

Burdell made himself comfortable in a chair
and crossed one ankle over his knee to watch.

They hadn't lynched him at the door, so Luke
took encouragement from that small fact. "It's
business."

"I don't have any business with you," Eldon
replied.

Maybe he should start over. "Thank you for
seeing me."

The man said nothing.

"I've come to ask for a loan. To build a house."

Sweetwater raised his brows, looked at his son,
then back at Luke. "You didn't need my help
before."

He referred to the livery. Luke hadn't wanted to
ask for help then any more than he did now. But
things had changed. "I managed the livery on my
own. Now I need a loan."

"Takes a lot of money to build a house."

Luke nodded. "I think you can see that I'm
reliable and hardworking. I'm good for the
money."

"Loans require collateral."

"I have the livery. You know that."

"Free and clear?"

"I paid cash for every last nail."

"I'm supposed to be impressed, I imagine."

"Not at all. But you know I'm good for it."

147

"I don't know that. You could default on the loan."

"I won't."

"Things happen."

"Then you'd get the livery." He had to swallow hard to get that one out.

"I have no use for a livery."

"You'd sell it. It's worth a pretty penny and it's making money now."

"Then why don't you pay for your own house?"

"Well, I haven't made that much money. Not yet anyway. But I will. I'm the only farrier in sixty miles."

Eldon leaned back into his leather chair and puffed until a cloud of smoke circled his head. "Dirty work," he said and brushed a speck of lint from his tailored sleeve with a clean uncallused finger.

Burdell made a point of casually examining his fingernails, and Luke held no doubt there wasn't a speck of dirt under a one of them.

The warmth of slow-mounting anger inched its way up Luke's collar. He kept his own work-roughened hands on his thighs and refused to look down at the nails he'd scrubbed for ten minutes that morning. "It's honest work."

The older man's brows lowered in disapproval. He deliberately waited before speaking again. "Do you have anything else to use as collateral? Jewelry? Gold?"

"Horses."

"I don't have much use for horses, either."

Luke's anger mounted. The horses would bring plenty at auction and they all knew it. The man was baiting him. He took several even breaths and relaxed his hands on his thighs. "I'm asking honestly for a loan, Mr. Sweetwater. You can turn me down for any reason you choose. I wouldn't have asked if I didn't have a need."

"Seems for a man in your position, a house would be a luxury."

"You judge every man who comes in for a loan?"

"It's necessary for me to judge a man's ability to pay my investment back. Banks don't stay in business by losing money."

"I can pay it back."

Leaning forward, Eldon placed his cigar on the edge of a brass ashtray and stood. "I'm not convinced. You're not a good risk. This meeting is over."

Luke met Burdell's eyes, but surprisingly they revealed only mild interest in the exchange. He'd expected gloating or in the very least superiority.

Eldon had turned him down flat.

He'd expected as much, so the humiliation didn't consume him. This was Annie's father, and though he didn't think he owed the man undue respect, he felt obliged to keep things civil. He extended his hand. "Well, I thank you for your time."

Eldon acted as though he hadn't seen the gesture or heard the words. "Do you have those ledgers prepared?" he asked Burdell.

Burdell stood and gathered a pile of account books from the top of a wooden cabinet.

Luke dropped his hand to his side. He gathered his composure and exited the office. The hairless man outside the door stared as he passed. The man at the teller window gave him a nod.

Standing on the dirt in the street, Luke loosened his tie, unbuttoned the top button of his good white shirt and glanced at his nails. The Sweetwater bank would have been the most convenient to do business with. But it wasn't the only bank in the county. He could take the deed to his property and ride to Fort Parker.

After making arrangements with Burt, he packed provisions for a night and saddled a horse.

During the ride he had plenty of time to regret going to the Sweetwaters' bank. Father and son were probably laughing their guts out right about now. What had he thought would happen? That the man would have a sudden change of heart? If he knew the house was for Annie, would it make one bit of difference or would it make him fight Luke all the harder? The latter, he feared.

A suitor was supposed to approach a man for his daughter's hand. The way Luke had been going about this made him uncomfortable. But what choice did he have? It was this way or no way. The Sweetwaters would never give him the time of day without a fight.

He wanted Annie. And he was ready to fight.

In the afternoon shade of a trellis of yellow and crimson nasturtium, Annie sat in her chair on the brick walk that wound through the Sweetwater's dooryard garden. June had arrived and with it a profusion of dog's tooth violets and bloodroot, but only a few brief notes from Luke. The time had at least passed more quickly when she'd had a tutor coming each day.

Once she'd had a female tutor who'd lived with them for almost three years. Miss Brimley had been a patient and kindhearted teacher, but a confidante and friend as well. She'd met and married a baker and moved to Oregon, and Annie had missed her for months. She received an occasional letter, but Miss Brimley was a part of her life that was past.

She plucked a white petunia and twirled the coarse velvety stem between her thumb and forefinger, watching the flower spin. Each season she'd entertained herself in the garden for hours.

It seemed she'd lived her whole life in the past or the future, either remembering how good or bad a particular time had been or looking forward to something better. The present was never quite fulfilling—never anything special to try to hold on to.

Except when she was with Luke. When they were together, she would give anything to stop time and live in those moments forever. Too bad life didn't work like that. Too bad she couldn't make the brief moments with him longer than the endless days and long nights, longer than each unendurable week without him, by simply wishing it.

The sound of a rig caught her attention. She couldn't see the street from her position behind the house, but the noise stopped and didn't continue past. After several minutes Charmaine found her.

"Uncle Mort let you come by yourself?" she asked.

"No, Mama came, too. She's inside."

"Oh." Annie wrinkled her nose. "I suppose Mother will expect us to join them for tea."

Charmaine sighed. "I suppose." She pushed Annie toward the stone bench over which a blooming trellis of climbing fern arched and plopped down on the stone bench. "I have something for you."

"What is it?"

Charmaine drew a folded slip of paper from the reticule on her wrist.

"Oh!" Annie pounced upon the missive and her cousin laughed.

She opened the note and read the few heart-warming words: "I can't bear another week. Tonight. Same place."

Annie clutched the note to her breast, anticipation already lifting her spirits.

"What does he say?"

"You didn't read it?"

Charmaine stuck her lower lip out. "Of course not."

"He says he has to see me."

"How positively romantic."

"He wants to marry me."

"How could that ever be? Your parents won't allow it."

Annie shook her head sadly. "I don't know how it's going to happen. I just know it has to. The situation seems hopeless when I talk about it like this or listen to the voice of reason in my head. But when I'm with him . . . oh, Charmaine, when we're together I can believe anything."

"It's positively tragic the way you're not allowed to see him. Just like Romeo and Juliet, don't you think?"

Annie frowned. "Not at all! We're not children. And Luke has no family to feud with mine. And we're certainly not going to drink poison because we can't be together. What a horrible comparison. Take it back."

"Oh, so it's not exactly the same, but it's every bit as dramatically romantic." She clasped her hands together over her breast. "It makes a girl swoon."

Annie chuckled in spite of herself.

Charmaine grabbed her arm. "The Fourth of July is coming before long! All the girls are discussing the plans for the celebration and the dance. We're making a float again this year—just the older girls this time. Janie Dempsey's father is going to loan us his hay wagon and horses. Of course you'll have to come to the Dempseys' to decorate the float with us. We barely have three weeks to get it all done."

"That sounds like fun," Annie told her, thinking it didn't sound nearly as much fun as it used to. But it was a reason to get away. Maybe the excuse would work a few times and she could see Luke during one of them! The idea received added appreciation in her mind suddenly. "That sounds like a *lot* of fun!"

Charmaine's visit made the day pass quickly. Annie endured a late supper with her parents and then wished them a good night. She lit a lamp on her desk and read, checking the time every page or two.

Finally midnight arrived and she wheeled herself silently from the house and along the lane to the spiraea bushes.

He waited for her, his horse grazing along the edge of the neighbor's lawn.

"Luke!" She stood to fling herself against him.

He kissed her long and soundly, a hungry, greedy kiss that tried to make up for time apart. She pressed her face to his chest, inhaled his scent and breathed his strength into her bones. He wove his fingers into her hair and held her head fast against him.

"I've missed you," she said.

"And I've missed you." His voice rumbled beneath her ear.

"You've barely sent me any notes," she said, pulling away to look at him.

"I've been busy. I've been working late every night."

"What's keeping you so busy?"

"I have some news, Annie."

"What? What is it?"

He grasped her shoulders and held her firmly. "I'm building a house."

The words sank in slowly. "A—a house? Where did you get the money for a house?"

"I borrowed it."

A loan? She shook her head. "Daddy loaned you money for a house?"

"No. I borrowed it from the bank in Fort Parker."

"But you asked him?"

He nodded, obviously uncomfortable with the subject.

"My father turned you down. But the other bank loaned money to you? Just like that?"

"No, they came and looked at my business to

155

make sure it was a sound investment. Once they were sure of that, they gave me the money."

"I'm sorry." Her disappointment in her father weighed like a weight in her chest. "It must be a lot of money," she said, trying to comprehend.

"It's not going to be a mansion," he said, sounding almost apologetic. "Not as nice as this house you live in now."

"Where?" she asked, suddenly excited and forgetting everything except what this meant.

"I couldn't afford a lot in town. Besides, your father controls most of the deeds, which I already knew. I found land outside town and I bought enough to keep horses and build a barn and plant a garden. This property's better anyway."

Annie gripped his forearms. "Are you going to take me there?"

"Now?"

"Yes, now! I want to see it! I want to see where we're going to live."

He glanced behind her. "This is dangerous."

"They're asleep," she assured him. "No one will see us."

"I don't know, Annie, I don't think it's wise."

"Oh, please, Luke. The days are so hard to get through." She touched his face and pleaded into his eyes. "If I can see it, I'll have a picture in my mind to get me through the days and nights. Please?"

His hair shone in the silvery glow of the moon.

He dipped his head and took her lips in a crush of damp heat. Annie clung to him. "All right," he said hoarsely. "All right."

After assisting her to Wrangler's back, he mounted behind and urged the horse into a gallop, avoiding houses and heading straight away from Copper Creek.

"Is it far?" she asked over her shoulder.

"No. About five miles."

They'd ridden for several minutes when he guided the horse across a shallow stream. "This is the quickest way," he said.

Wrangler carried them up the bank on the other side and they topped a rise and a slope of pines came into view.

"It's just over here," he said.

The open area he indicated held a stark framework, barely visible in the darkness. "Is that our house?"

"It will be." Luke brought the horse to a stop and slid from his back, then reached up for her. "The ground is uneven here, so watch your step."

She held tightly to his arm, her attention riveted on the wooden skeleton. "I wish it was light out, so I could really see it."

"There's nothing much to see yet."

"This is the door?"

"Yes."

"Only one?"

"I'll build you a bigger house later."

"I wasn't criticizing." She turned and grasped his forearms. "I told you I'd live anywhere with you, and I meant it, but I think this will be the most beautiful house ever."

"You're easy to please," he said with a lazy smile and touched her hair.

Annie grasped his hand for support and made her way to the opening in the framework. "A wood floor? That's good."

"Did you think I'd let you sleep with snakes and bugs?"

"And a fireplace."

"Not brick, the field stones were free."

"I love the stones. Did you do this yourself?"

"No, Gil helped me. And a couple of friends."

"Have you told Gil . . . about us, I mean?"

He shook his head.

"Oh."

"But I think he suspects something. A single man getting a house ready is pretty suspicious."

"So," she glanced around, wishing she could see better. "This is the . . . sitting room?"

"The kitchen is the other end down there—all one long room really."

The space seemed adequate. Another doorway led to a separate room. "The bedroom?"

"Uh-huh."

Annie released his hand and stood in the center of the wooden floor, wrapping her arms around herself. This would be her home soon. She would live here with Luke. They could be alone together, have all the time they wanted to talk and kiss and whatever else they pleased. "No one will monitor my time or my activities here. No one will tell me what I can and cannot do in this house of ours. Oh, it's almost too good to be true."

"It's more than that," he said softly from beside her. "Isn't it?"

She caught his hands. "Of course it is! Oh, yes, Luke, so much more. I'm sorry I sounded selfish just then. I'm excited about us being together. I can't wait until we don't have to leave each other and go our separate ways at night."

Luke caught her against him and hugged her fiercely. Her enthusiasm buoyed his spirits for another week of dawn to dusk work. She was worth every minute, every hour and every day and every aching muscle. He didn't ever want to disappoint her. She deserved so much happiness and love and he wanted to give it to her.

Every swing of the hammer, every stone and nail and peg was one step closer to them being together. He'd worked his whole life toward this goal, though he'd never recognized it until lately. School, ranching, learning his trade, those had all been steps toward winning Annie. Beneath his hands and in his arms she seemed so feminine and fragile. But so real, finally.

He enjoyed the scent of her hair, the glide of her

silky dress against his thighs, the sound of her sigh against his heart. Out of all the men who could have ridden into her life and received her favor, he'd been the one she'd wanted. He would do anything for her, anything to please her, anything to see her smile, hear her laugh, win her kiss.

Bending his knees, he dipped to scoop her into his arms. Beneath the canopy of stars, he spun in a circle, her skirt billowing, her laughter floating toward the mountains. He revolved until it seemed the heavens smeared into streaks of light and Annie placed her head on his chest.

Sinking to the floorboards on his knees, she wrapped her arms around his neck while the world continued to spin, slowing, slowing.

"Thank you, Luke," she whispered.

"Thank you, Annie."

"Let's do this again on our wedding night. And on every anniversary for the rest of our lives. Let's be just this happy."

"Okay," he promised.

She lifted her head. "Maybe you'll get tired of carrying me."

"Never," he denied.

"Maybe I'll grow fat and you'll hurt yourself."

"Look how big I am," he said. "Look how tiny you are. I could carry two of you."

She placed her palm along his cheek. "I'm gonna hold you to that promise."

"You do that."

• • •

In the weeks until the Fourth of July party, Annie only saw Luke on two occasions. Once when her parents rented a rig and took her for a Sunday ride, and the other a night like the last, where she met him and he showed her the progress on their house.

"I should be doing something to help," she'd told him.

"You're giving me the strength," he'd assured her. "Besides, there will be plenty to do when it's finished and needs a woman's touch."

A woman's touch, he'd said, and she'd held that close to her heart since. The only man who'd ever seen her as a woman, and he was the man her parents despised.

She'd helped the girls with their hay wagon float and the decorations for the party, but when time came for the parade and for the girls to perch atop the crepe paper flowers and ride through town, she asked Charmaine to push her to the boardwalk and go on without her.

"Not a chance," her cousin refused. "In fact, look at what the girls came up with!"

Doneta Parker and Mary Chancelor held out an apron of red, white and blue felt roses. "It's for you, Annie," they chorused. "You have the place of honor on our float."

Annie'd never ridden on the float before. She'd always watched and waved from the side of the street as the floats passed. "You're sure?"

"Positive. Up you go!"

She took Charmaine's and Mary's hands and climbed the stack of crates to the back of the bed, which no longer resembled a hay wagon, but a fluttering mass of vivid crepe paper.

She took her seat where instructed. The other girls, chattering and checking their hair and gloves, seated themselves all around her.

The volunteer fire department's three-piece band sounded more like they were warming up than playing a patriotic tune, but they energetically led the gaily decorated procession toward the main street and through town.

Ahead, the floats were cheered by townspeople along the sides of the street, and the girls' anticipation heightened. Annie's heart fluttered nervously, though she was having a grand time. A small black dog barked at the wagon ahead of theirs and a man in a hat picked it up and placed it in an empty flower pot in front of Miss Marples' Ice Cream Emporium.

Annie laughed at the sight, and then their float came into view of the crowd. The onlookers cheered and clapped and Annie waved as hard as the schoolgirls.

She scanned the crowd, seeking one shiny black head and devilish smile, and after straining to find him, finally recognized the smile, but his hair was hidden beneath a straw hat. Grinning,

Annie waved and blew a kiss. He caught it and pressed it to his heart.

The float had moved several feet forward, and Annie let go of the image she'd been seeking and the next person she spotted was Burdy. Will sat on his shoulders, waving like mad, so she waved back. Burdy, however, scowled as dark as a thundercloud. From his side, Diana cast him a wary glance.

Beside her brother's family in the crowd stood her parents, her mother in a cream-colored silk dress and white gloves, her father in a lightweight suit and tie.

Her mother brought her hand to her mouth and fluttered like a cattail in a stiff wind. Eldon immediately reached to support his wife, his angry eyes never leaving Annie.

Had they seen her wave at Luke? Had they seen the kiss she'd blown and his reaction? Would Burdy stomp through the crowd and wallop him? She could say she'd been waving at one of the children—or Lizzy's little sisters, yes, that was it.

A sick sensation rolled in her stomach.

The parade had another few blocks to travel, so she pasted on a smile and endured the ride, waving absently when Charmaine pointed out Uncle Mort and Aunt Vera.

The wagons came to a halt in an open lot at the east end of town, and a few owners came to get their rigs and horses.

"This one goes back to the livery," a woman

from the church Ladies' League's float called. "You girls need a ride back?"

The girls swept Annie along with them, and as long as Charmaine stayed with her, Annie didn't mind. Luke had returned to the livery and met the returning crowd, leading the rigs inside, unhitching horses and turning them into the corral beside the building.

He stayed busy and Annie didn't dare approach him in public, so she took a seat beside her cousin on a bench inside the stable. The others left a few at a time, obviously not thinking that Annie's chair had been left behind at the start of the parade and she would have no way back without help.

Annie hadn't thought of it herself, she'd been so caught up in the excitement of the moment.

"Something wrong?" Charmaine asked.

She shook her head, not wanting to express her worry.

"The Ladies' League's float was beautiful, wasn't it? I hope ours wins, though. We worked harder and longer, we deserve to win."

After several minutes of Charmaine's chatter, Luke appeared, the straw hat shading his eyes.

"You ladies need a ride back now?"

"Why, yes," Charmaine said, jumping up. "Can we ride one of your horses?"

"Charmaine, Mama and Papa would have a fit of apoplexy if I came riding down the street on a horse!"

"Oh." She looked down. "I forgot. Sorry."

"The choir just returned the buggy they borrowed and it's cleared off, so I'll take you in that," Luke offered.

"Okay." Charmaine walked beside Annie out into the sunlight.

"That's sure a pretty dress," Luke said.

"I made it myself," Annie said proudly. "Well, Aunt Vera helped, but I did most of it alone."

"The color makes your eyes as green as new spring grass," he said quietly, and she blushed.

Luke helped them both into the back seat of the buggy and climbed on the front seat to guide the horse. Annie recognized the vehicle as one of the finer rigs her father sometimes rented.

"You must have made a lot today, renting all these rigs," Charmaine said.

"No, I loaned them."

"For free?"

"Yes, it was for the town's celebration, after all."

Charmaine glanced at Annie and raised a brow.

"That was kind of you," Annie said.

"Where we headed?" he asked. The streets were filled with people and makeshift stands selling fudge and popcorn balls and lemonade.

"Annie's chair is at the school where we started," Charmaine replied.

The closer they came to the school, the harder Annie's heart thudded. And there, standing in the sideyard as Luke pulled the buggy to a stop, was Annie's family.

Chapter Nine

"Oh, dear," Annie gasped.

"It's all right," Charmaine said.

"They saw me. They saw me smile and blow him a kiss."

"Easy, Annie," Luke said over his shoulder. "Nothing's going to happen that we can't handle."

Ignoring his assurance, she wobbled to her feet and started down the carriage steps.

Burdell rushed toward her. "What are you doing? Wait for help!"

"Annie!" her mother said, hurrying forward. "What has gotten into you, child?" She stared agape at her daughter. "And where did you get that dress? You left before I could see you this morning."

"He hasn't done anything!" Annie said, rushing to get the words out before trouble started.

"It was me who talked Annie into joining us on the float, Aunt Mildred," Charmaine said, taking the blame. "None of us thought ahead to how we'd get her back to her chair, and Mr. Carpenter was kind enough to give us a ride in his buggy."

Eldon moved forward with Annie's chair. Burdell plucked Annie from the step of the buggy and carried her toward her seat. Diana stood nearby with Will in tow and gave Annie an apologetic shrug.

"Is that correct?" her father asked Annie.

"Yes," she replied quickly. "But it wasn't Charmaine's fault. In all the years I was tutored I sometimes got to help on the school float, but I never got to ride on it. I wanted to, Daddy. It was my decision."

"You could have fallen and been badly hurt," her mother scolded. "I was terrified when I saw you up there. Where's your regard for your parents?"

Diana stepped forward then, just as Luke descended. "Thank you for seeing her safely back here, Mr. Carpenter." She extended a gloved hand and Luke took it briefly. "I know her parents appreciate your attention to their daughter's safety. And I'm sure you went out of your way to bring her here."

"My pleasure, ma'am," he returned politely.

After that, there really wasn't much Burdy or her father could say about Luke bringing Annie home. Charmaine and Diana had made it look like he'd done them a favor. And he had. Suddenly they were obligated to the man they'd detested for so many years.

"Yes, thank you, Mr. Carpenter," Annie added and Charmaine murmured her thanks as well.

Luke tugged the brim of his straw hat politely and turned to leave.

167

"You haven't thanked the man," Diana whispered to her husband and father-in-law.

Annie cringed. It had been enough that they hadn't beaten him flat, couldn't Diana leave well enough alone?

Seated again, Luke shook the reins over the horse's back and the buggy pulled away from the schoolyard.

"We should take her home," Mildred said to her husband.

Her father turned toward her. "Do you want to go home, Annie?"

She almost fell out of her chair.

Her mother placed her hand on her hip and glared at him.

He'd never before asked what Annie wanted. She didn't care why he had this time, she just knew she wasn't going to let the opportunity to express her choice pass. "No. I want to see the contests and the displays and watch the dancing tonight."

"Very well," he said. "But you'll inform us if you get tired."

She nodded. "I will."

"Eldon," her mother said in a disapproving tone.

Charmaine shared a look of astonishment with Annie while Annie's parents had an angrily whispered exchange.

"Glenda entered her pickles in a competition. I

want to go see if she's won a prize yet," Annie said cheerfully.

"I don't think that's wise," her mother objected.

"Annie said she'd let us know when she got tired," Eldon said. Then, more quietly as he stepped behind her chair and pushed, he added, "And I've never seen her tired yet."

Annie twisted to look at her father. His face didn't reveal his thoughts, but he gave her a nod and pushed her toward the activities. When no one was watching, he slipped several dollars into her hand.

Annie had never enjoyed herself more. The only thing that would have given her more pleasure would have been if she could have gotten out of her chair and stood beside the townspeople playing games—or maybe played a few herself. But she'd been allowed to attend, even over her mother's objections, and for that she gave silent thanks.

A crowd gathered around for the sheriff to announce the winning float, and the Ladies' League won again. "We'll beat 'em next time!" Doneta Parker called to Charmaine and Annie.

Glenda invited the Sweetwaters to join her family's picnic at noon. Mildred declined, but Annie asked to stay. Finally, her father left her in Charmaine's care and the rest of her family moved into the crowd.

Glenda's daughters were fair-haired darlings,

Gwen nine and Gerta seven. They wore simple calico dresses that had seen much wear, but were clean and pressed. Annie thought of the wardrobe in her room filled with frilly dresses she detested and wondered if she could figure out how to use the material to make clothing that would fit them.

Annie moved to sit on the quilt beside Charmaine and the girls. Glenda served them lunch, and they ate and visited and laughed.

Glenda's tall, mustached husband, Tim, wasn't the most handsome man Annie'd ever laid eyes on, but he had a genuine smile and a way of making people feel special. His interaction with his wife and daughters touched Annie. She remembered Glenda's tale of how he'd courted her with candy and flowers, and her esteem for him grew even more now that she'd met him.

A pair of lanky young fellows joined them as they finished their lunch. Gwen and Gerta immediately pounced on the youngest, and he hugged them good-naturedly, though he blushed.

"Annie, Charmaine, do you know my brother, Wayne?" Glenda asked. "Wayne, Miss Renlow is Miss Sweetwater's cousin."

Annie had never met Wayne, but Charmaine said, "I remember you from school before you graduated. You work on your ranch now?"

Wayne nodded. "Always did."

"And this is Wayne's friend, Levi Cutter," Glenda said.

The young man she introduced removed his hat, bent to take each of their hands and gave Annie and Charmaine knockout smiles. He wore his fair hair a little too long, but it didn't detract from his compelling good looks. His blue eyes sparkled with humor and seemed to hold intimate secrets.

"Pleased to meet you, Mr. Cutter," Annie said politely.

"You pretty ladies save me a dance tonight," he said with a grin and a wink, then settled his hat back on his head.

The comment embarrassed Annie, and she turned her attention to helping Glenda pack away the dishes and silverware.

The young men wandered back toward the busy street, and Charmaine grabbed Annie's forearm breathlessly. "Isn't he absolutely the handsomest devil?"

She nodded. "Levi's very nice looking."

"No, not Levi. Wayne!"

"Oh—oh, yes, he's handsome, too."

"Levi is a scoundrel and everyone knows it," Charmaine whispered. "He's ruined more than one girl's reputation. They say he lives on a ranch with a brother who is hideously scarred and never comes to town."

"Oh."

"But Glenda's brother is from a nice family, and he hasn't been seen courting anyone. Maybe he'll ask me to dance tonight."

"I'm sure he will," Annie replied. "You'll be the prettiest girl there." She stood and stretched her legs after being seated on the ground for so long, then sat in her chair and waited for Charmaine to push her back to the festivities.

They came upon one of the booths set up in the side yard of the church, and admired the prettily embroidered items for sale. Charmaine examined a pair of pillowslips with bright peacocks stitched in vivid colors and lace crocheted along the hem.

"That's always a popular design," Mrs. Krenshaw said in her loud library whisper from behind the makeshift counter. "They'd be a nice addition to any young lady's trousseau."

"You made these?" Charmaine asked.

Mrs. Krenshaw nodded and turned to answer a question for a woman standing beside Annie.

"Aren't they stunning?" Charmaine asked Annie, running her fingers over the embroidered stitches.

"Yes, they're lovely." She pulled her cousin down close. "I never pictured her sitting and embroidering, did you?"

Shrugging, Charmaine counted change from the coin bag in her reticule and gave it to the librarian.

Annie thought the purchase an odd one for her cousin. "What are you going to do with those? Give them to someone?"

"They're for my hope chest."

"Oh." Annie's gaze flittered across the items on the linen-covered boards. Things for a young lady's trousseau, Mrs. Krenshaw had said. "Do you have much in your hope chest?"

"Mama has sewn me dish towels and my great aunt Elsbeth made me a quilt before she died. Last year Papa bought me a set of dishes from a catalog."

This was the first Annie had considered the notion. Lizzy had mentioned her hope chest, too, but Annie hadn't given it any thought at the time. Now here she was thinking about marrying Luke and she had nothing packed away for married life.

Of course her mother wouldn't have started or encouraged any such collection for Annie, since she didn't believe she'd ever be married. Not much hope there. But Annie's hopes had soared over the past months.

Her interest in the table tripled and she selected two pairs of pillowslips, one embroidered with purple pansies, the other with delicate pale-green ivy, both edged with crocheted lace. She added a set of dish towels and a baby bib to her pile and paid Mrs. Krenshaw.

Charmaine's brows rose into the middle of her forehead, but she only grinned and carried Annie's purchases with her own.

Occasionally throughout the afternoon Annie

glimpsed Luke, watching games, tasting pies, drinking beer with the men. Before the sun started to set behind the mountains, people cleared the street to stand along the sides and horse races commenced.

Annie hadn't expected to see Luke on one of the horses that shot past in a cloud of dust, but when she recognized him, she worked her way to her feet and cheered with the rest of the boisterous crowd.

"Did he win? Did he win?" She jumped up and down in excitement, holding her cousin's arm for support.

"I can't see with you bouncing in front of me," Charmaine replied, and they laughed.

After the races Lizzy and her new husband, Guy Halverson, greeted them. A glowing Lizzy stood beside her young husband with adoration, clinging to his arm and giving him coquettish smiles as they shared talk of the day's fun.

"That's enough to make you sick," Charmaine commented after they'd moved on.

"I thought it was sweet," Annie replied. "You had that same look on your face when Wayne spoke to you."

"I did not."

"Did so. How do you know? I was looking at you. You were making goo-goo eyes at him."

"You're making it up."

"Am not."

"Take it back or I'll push you into a pile of horse dung."

They were still bantering, and Annie had started to edge out of her chair just in case Charmaine got serious, when Luke found them.

"Ladies. Are you having a good time?" He wore the hat again, and Annie wished his eyes weren't shaded.

"Oh, a wonderful time!" She sat back down in her chair. "Did you win the race? There were too many people in the way for me to see."

"Sure did. Georgette is the fastest mount I've ever owned."

"Georgette?"

"She's a mountain pony I bought a couple of summers ago."

"I don't think I've met her yet."

"I'll have to introduce you."

"Now *you* have the look," Charmaine said out the side of her mouth.

Annie ignored her.

"See you at the dance later?" Luke asked.

"We'll be there," Annie replied.

He touched the brim of his hat and moved away in a loose-hipped ramble she couldn't help but admire. His movements were always sure and graceful. She didn't know if she'd ever seen anyone do such simple things with such riveting ease.

"You still have the look, but now a line of drool is hanging from your lip."

Annie took a swat at Charmaine's rump. "It is not!"

"Is so."

"Push me and hush up, or you're going to be the one in the pile of poop!"

Annie couldn't remember a day that she'd had so much fun. She felt almost free, almost unrestricted, almost normal. Almost.

"We don't go home to change or anything?" she asked Charmaine after their parents found them and they all got into Uncle Mort's wagon and headed for the barn where the dance was being held.

"It's not fancy," Charmaine replied. "Just a simple barn dance."

That was fine with Annie, because she'd worn her favorite dress.

The same musicians who had played for Lizzy's wedding were there, as well as a few more. People came from all over the county for this celebration, so the throng packed the Stevensens' barn and flowed out the doors into the deepening twilight.

Tables of food and drinks had been set up along one wall, but the dense crush of attendees prevented Annie from getting anywhere close. Her mother brought her a plate and a drink, and Annie thanked her.

"I had a wonderful time today," she told her.

Mildred looked her over, studying her hair

and face, the green brocade of her now rumpled skirt. "Where *did* you get that dress?"

"Aunt Vera showed me how to cut it out and baste it together. I did the sewing myself." Annie ran a loving hand over the white chiffon bodice, the only ruffle on the entire garment.

"And you're feeling well?"

Annie returned the perusal. It was almost as if she didn't know this woman who'd cared for her her entire life. "I'm just fine."

Mildred raised her chin, but said nothing.

"Did you have a nice day?" Annie asked.

Her mother gave a curt nod.

Glenda's girls found her.

"Mother, do you know Gwen and Gerta?"

"I didn't know their names. Mrs. Harper's daughters, I believe."

The girls told Annie and her mother about a sack race they'd run in that day. Mildred watched them as they spoke, but didn't comment. Later, when they moved off into the throng, Annie studied her mother's face.

"Did you ever feel robbed because you didn't have a healthy, whole daughter?"

"Of course not," her mother replied. "Don't disparage yourself."

"I've thought a thousand times, and berated myself for it, that you liked having me this way so that you could control me. But of course, you would have rather had a normal child.

177

What mother doesn't want a perfect child?"

Her mother's features tightened and she brought her hands together over her chest.

"And isn't that what I've always been?" Annie asked. The music had started, but she paid no attention to it. "All these years, submissive, obedient, staying where I've been placed and wearing what I've been given and not causing any problems? I've been the perfect child."

The idea came as a revelation to Annie. The friction between them had only started when Annie had become dissatisfied with her situation, when her frustration had mounted to an unbearable level and she'd begun expressing it. Now it seemed as though her mother didn't know how to handle the change—how to relate to the more mature, more opinionated Annie.

"I'm sorry if I've been upsetting you, Mother," she said softly. "It's not because I don't love you and Daddy or that I don't appreciate everything you've done for me and how well you've taken care of me. It's just that I've grown up. I've grown up and you haven't let me."

Tears had formed in her mother's eyes, and she blinked them back, keeping her face composed. A few dancers moved in graceful motions on the sawdusted floor several yards away. "Don't be foolish. You need us, Annie."

"I'll always need you. It just might not be in the same way, or to the same extent."

Mildred looked at her daughter as though she didn't recognize her.

Annie handed her the empty plate she'd been holding. "Thank you."

Her mother accepted it, looked at it for a full minute, then gracefully walked away.

Annie watched the dancers, thinking about all the enjoyment in life she'd missed, reflecting on all the times she'd wanted to do things but had kept silent, not wanting to cause a problem, always keeping peace and being acquiescent.

Dozens of imagined scenes flashed in her mind: School. Dances. Parades. Friends. Horseback rides. Will. Luke.

Luke.

The only time she'd ever defied her parents, ever allowed her own wants and wishes to prevail had been to see Luke. And even then she'd done it in secret. As though it was wrong. Or dirty.

Studying the dancers, she spotted Charmaine with Wayne, and she admired her cousin's confidence and polish. Glenda danced with Tim, and she looked ten years younger in his arms. He smiled down at his wife, and Annie wondered how she'd missed his handsome smile.

Levi Cutter took a turn around the dance floor with one young lady after another; right now Doneta Parker was his blushing partner. Doneta's steel-gray-haired father appeared on the side of the floor and watched with stern attention.

Letting her gaze scan the bystanders, Annie found Luke in a cluster of young men, a metal cup in his hand. His piercing blue gaze touched on the dancers, flitted to her, and a moment later one of his friends spoke and he replied, turning his face away.

He was as aware of her at all times as she was of him. They craved being together. They were missing out on something new and wonderful—the beginning of forever—because she was a coward. Because she didn't want to ripple the waters. Because—her heart convulsed—because she feared Burdy doing something harmful to Luke.

He'd told her a dozen times he wasn't afraid of her brother—never had been, and finally the reason dawned on her. Luke had been raised on a ranch, worked in a livery, pounded iron and trained horses for a living. Burdy sat in a bank. Luke could hold his own in a match with just about anybody, she figured, even Burdy. Especially Burdy. Luke was still younger, but now youth was in his favor.

He feared her parents would send her away.

That would never happen. Not now. Not now that she knew what she wanted and had stopped being afraid to voice it.

Annie thought long and hard, the music thumping through her veins. She made a decision and acted on it before she had second thoughts, before she had time to think about people staring at her, before she pictured the horrified look on her mother's face.

Pushing herself up with her arms, she moved her feet in front of the rest on her chair and gathered her balance to stand. That part was easy, she'd done it a hundred times lately.

She brushed the wrinkles from her skirt, confident of how she looked in the new green dress, and took a step toward the dance floor. The next step took a little more convincing, but she ignored the doubts in the back of her mind and moved ahead.

One step. Two steps. Slow, awkward. Her gait was a clumsy kind of step-limp, step-limp that was neither graceful nor agile nor any of the things she imagined it could be. But it got her where she was going—and it got her there on her own.

Her mother had made her so self-conscious of what people thought, that she had to fight the urge to turn and look at faces.

The only face she kept in her line of vision was Luke's. His was the only regard that mattered.

He didn't see her at first, because he'd been engaged in a conversation with two men, but when one of them looked her way, and then the other, he turned his head and spotted her. Conversation died on his lips, and an unfamiliar expression softened his already heart-stopping features.

Annie kept up her steady step-limp, step-limp, discovering the sawdust beneath her shoes, seeing concern on his face turn to a question and then to a welcome and finally to something else —pride. She didn't take her gaze from his eyes for a second.

She became aware that she'd drawn attention; that talk had hushed and that the dancers on the floor barely shifted. She felt every eye in the building focused upon her ungainly approach.

The song changed, but the dancers no longer moved.

Luke didn't take a step toward her; he waited patiently. She drew near, and he smiled, the smile she loved that creased his cheeks and crinkled the corners of his eyes. He handed the tin cup to the man beside him.

She stopped in front of him, breathless not from walking, but from the exhilaration of doing such a bold and daring thing.

"I don't know how to dance," she said, her voice airy with nervous tension. "I don't even know if I can . . . but I'd like to learn."

He didn't answer right away. He studied her eyes, her hair, his blue gaze a sensual caress that made her remember all their private moments together and feel the familiar heat. "I'd like to teach you," he finally replied. "But first I have something for you."

She watched curiously as he reached into his

trouser pocket and withdrew something blue—a ribbon of some sort. He held the ribbon in both hands and placed it over her head, around her neck, let it fall against her breast.

Annie looked down at the ribbon fashioned into a first-prize award, the number one in shiny gold paint.

"You're the winner tonight, Annie," he said softly.

Her gaze rose from his racing prize to the blue sparkle in his eyes, and she smiled hesitantly.

He placed her left hand on his shoulder, took her right one in his and took two small steps toward her. She was forced to move back. He took two small steps to the right. She followed, then turned when he turned, the steps small and easy, but not too graceful.

"Mind trying something?" he asked.

She shook her head.

"Put your right foot on top of my boot."

"Step on your foot?"

"Right on my boot and put your weight onto it if you can."

"I can."

"Okay."

She tried it and he led again, her good leg first, taking the step, then his left leg doing the work of her bad leg for her. She didn't have to lunge to correct her gait this way, and with his agile steps and strong body doing the work, she followed as gracefully as a princess in a fairy tale.

"Is everyone looking?" she asked.

He glanced over her shoulder and nodded.

"Are my parents looking?"

A heartbeat and he nodded again.

"Burdy?"

"He looks like a rabid dog about to attack."

"Can you take him?"

"I think so."

"Then don't stop until someone makes us or until the music ends."

His smile whispered to her heart. "This was a big step."

"I know."

"You're a brave woman, my sweet Annie."

"Not so brave. Just sure of what I want."

"I think I like that stubborn streak."

"We'll see if you say that a year from now."

The smile left his lips. His eyes took on a seriousness she found endearing. "We're talking about a future," he said.

"A future together, right?"

He squeezed her hand. "Oh, yes."

Songs changed, dancers moved around them, and they became part of the celebration.

"How long can you dance with me on your foot?" she asked.

"Until there's a winter in the Rockies with no snow."

With her heart full, she smiled. "Have you always been a poet?"

He gave a half shake of his head and his ebony hair glistened in the light of dozens of lanterns. One corner of his mouth edged up in irony. "Hardly."

To her he was a poet. And a dancer and a lover and a prince. He was everything she'd dreamed of and more than she'd hoped for. When she was with him she could do anything, be anyone. He gave her courage and optimism and made her feel like any other woman of worth. This was the happiest night of her life.

Annie Sweetwater was dancing with the man she loved. The crowd had folded around them, their attention no longer focused on the unlikely couple.

Eventually the warm evening took its toll and Luke asked her if she'd like a drink. He led her to the row of chairs along the wall and she sat gratefully while he went for two cups, then returned and sat close.

Annie sipped tart lemonade, watching his eyes smile at her over the top of his cup. *I love you,* she wanted to say, but she held it to herself for a while longer and touched the ribbon hanging around her neck.

Luke's attention shifted, and she sensed someone beside her. Annie looked up to see Burdell standing over her. Luke stood slowly.

"We're going to talk," Burdell said.

Chapter Ten

"Outside," Burdy added.

Luke stood. "Do you really think now is the time for this?"

"You chose the time, buster, not me," Burdell replied, anger making a vein stick out on his temple. "Walk or I'll drag you."

"Burdy!" Annie struggled to her feet. "Don't do this."

Diana had appeared directly behind Burdell, and she, too, tried to reason with him. "Maybe we could all have coffee at the house and talk this over."

Luke clomped toward the door with Burdell on his heels. Annie grabbed Diana's arm and they followed. Annie had to half run, an awkward stumble with Diana supporting her, to stay behind the men.

"I don't want any trouble with you," Luke said, stopping in the side yard and facing Annie's brother.

"Then you should have left her alone like you've been warned," Burdell replied. "This family has had enough of your interference."

"Burdy, please," Annie called. "Don't do this. This is a big mistake."

"The mistake is his," Burdell hissed.

A few more people came up behind the clinging women, and Annie recognized her father's angry voice. "What did you think you were doing in there, Carpenter? Haven't you caused enough trouble?"

"I don't want a fight with your family," Luke said calmly. "I don't want any hard feelings."

Burdell rolled back his shirtsleeves.

"Don't do this," Luke warned.

"Burdy, don't!" Annie called.

"You're going to leave my sister alone," Burdell threatened.

Luke drew a hand over his mouth, down his chin, then lowered it. "Why don't you let Annie decide what's best for her?"

"She doesn't know what's best for her!"

His words infuriated Annie. "I do so! I know exactly what I want! I'm the one who asked him to teach me to dance, remember? Did you see me, Burdy?" Holding Diana's arm, she spun around and found her mother and father only three feet away. "Did you see me, Mama? I walked over there and I asked him to dance! That was what I wanted!"

Charmaine and her parents had come to stand at the front of the gathering crowd.

"We can work this out without any violence," Uncle Mort said sternly.

Charmaine covered her mouth with her hands and stared.

"He's got a lesson coming." Burdell took an angry step toward Luke.

Luke sidestepped. "Don't do this, Burdell. Think of your sister."

Burdell's face contorted. "Don't you tell me to think of my sister. This is for putting your hands on her, you good for nothing—" He jabbed a fist.

Luke ducked the blow and faced him, looking truly wary now. "Don't do this. You don't want to do this."

"You know what I want now?" Burdell gave a terse laugh.

"You know what Annie wants?" Luke countered.

That angered Burdell more. He swung and Luke raised an arm, warding off the punch.

Overhead a burst of color fell from the night sky and the gathering on the other side of the building made appreciative noises. The fireworks had started.

"You're going to leave her alone," Burdell growled.

"I'm sorry, but I can't do that."

"Why you son of a—" He swung again and this time his fist caught Luke's jaw, snapping his head back. "You'll leave her alone!"

An ache gnawed at Annie's belly. A loud burst of firecrackers startled her.

Eldon edged forward. "Burdell, maybe this isn't the right way to handle this."

Diana released a little sob at Annie's side and Annie put her arm around her.

"I'll handle this," Burdell shouted. "And he'll leave her alone."

"Hit me all you want, but I won't leave her alone," Luke said. "I'm going to marry her."

A collective gasp came from the assembled townspeople.

Tears spilled down Annie's cheeks. "Luke," she whispered, the nightmare of this confrontation erasing the joy she deserved to feel over his words.

Charmaine moved to her side and rubbed her back comfortingly. Overhead, colors radiated from the ongoing fireworks display. The smell of sulfur filled the air.

Luke's declaration had infuriated Burdell even further, and with narrowed eyes, he lunged.

Prepared for the attack, Luke caught Burdell's weight and they wrestled for a moment before toppling to the dirt and rolling while both grappled for dominance.

Luke pulled away and got to his feet. Burdell scrambled up next, breathing hard. He charged at Luke and this time Luke caught him squarely in the chin with a right uppercut, then followed that hit with a blow to Burdell's midsection that crumpled him to the ground.

Luke took several steps back to stand clear of the man.

Holding his stomach, Burdell glared up. "This isn't finished."

Luke beckoned. "Get up and let's finish it then. I'm not gonna fight you every time I dance with her or talk to her. I'm not gonna fight you on the steps of the church when I marry her. Let's get it over right now."

"You sorry son of a—" Burdell staggered to his feet.

"Burdell, stop!" Diana cried. Pulling away from Annie, she rushed forward.

Charmaine wrapped her arm around Annie's waist, lending her support.

"That's enough," Diana said to her husband. "Stop this."

Burdell glanced at his wife, then over at Annie and back to Luke. "All right," he said. "There are other ways."

Annie pulled away from her cousin and limped over to Luke. He didn't really look any worse for the wear, though it was too dark to see if he bore any scrapes or cuts. Impulsively, she moved into his arms and he hugged her.

"I'll get your pretty dress dirty," he said.

Taking his hand, she led him to where her brother stood. "Are you all right?"

He glared past her at Luke. "I'm fine."

Her parents joined them and Mildred took Annie's hand and tried to tug her away. Annie resisted.

"Annie, you've caused enough of a spectacle tonight." Her voice and words, laced with censure and criticism as always, twisted the knife blade of hurt in Annie's chest.

"I'm sorry you're embarrassed, Mother, but if you'll notice, your son was the one who started a fistfight. Luke tried to talk him out of it."

"But you brought it on, Annie, with that exhibition inside."

"Yes." She looked from her mother's pinched expression to her father's sorrowful one, and back. "You've certainly warned me enough about staying in my chair, haven't you? I guess the fact that I can walk and that it makes me happy is beyond the point. The point is, I shouldn't have even a tiny measure of joy if it makes me appear in the least bit clumsy and embarrasses *you*."

"You've been walking?" her mother asked.

Annie nodded. "Everyone has seen me and is happy for me. Everyone except you."

Mildred glanced at Charmaine, at her brother and sister-in-law who nodded reluctantly. Her glare lit upon her husband. *"You?"*

"Daddy didn't know, Mother," Annie assured her.

"They obviously don't understand or care what's best for you," Mildred denied.

"They obviously *do* care," Annie argued. "You are the one who doesn't care about my feelings."

Mildred made a strangled sound and Annie's

father wrapped his arm around his wife's shoulders.

"She's an ungrateful child," she whimpered.

Eldon patted her back and leveled a stare at his daughter.

"Luke and I are going to be married, Daddy," she told him. "It's what I want."

Her brave declaration gave Luke the courage to speak up. "This wasn't the way I wanted it," he told her father. "I would rather have asked your permission and courted her properly. I'm sorry it came to this."

"I think we should speak privately," Eldon said.

Luke nodded. "I agree. But not tonight."

"Monday. In my office."

"No." He'd met the man on his ground before. This discussion needed a neutral location. "Tomorrow after church. We'll stay after and talk then."

Sweetwater seemed to consider the idea only briefly. "Very well."

"I'll be there, too," Burdell said.

"No," his father said, and Luke gave the man credit for some sense. "Not this time. I'll handle it. Now let's all go home and calm down."

Luke steadied Annie as they walked toward the social hall. The last few bursts of fireworks had fizzled out. Surely she didn't want to go back in there and face the remaining people right now. "I can go get your chair for you. Are you tired?"

She nodded. "But don't leave me. Charmaine," she called. "Will you get my chair, please?"

Her cousin hurried inside.

Annie sagged against Luke and he scooped her into his arms, uncaring of who saw them now. She laid her head against his chest, and reverently touched the blue ribbon around her neck.

"People won't forget this Fourth of July celebration, will they?" she asked.

"Not likely."

"May I say it now?"

It took a minute to figure out what she was talking about. What did she want to say? Then he realized, and his heart jumped. "Only if I can say it first."

She raised her head and looked into his eyes. He stood cradling her in the light from the open doorway. "Okay," she said, her lips curving into a seductive smile.

"I love you, Annie."

In the meager light tears formed in her eyes. "I love you, Luke."

He kissed her, but it didn't last because of their smiles. He started walking, carrying her away from the building, toward the wagons.

"Thank you for not killing my brother."

"Thank you for not being ashamed to love me."

"Why would I ever be ashamed of you?"

"Banker's daughter, liveryman, you know."

"No, I don't know. Thank you for not being ashamed to love a clumsy girl."

"You're not clumsy, Annie. You're the most beautiful girl in the state of Colorado."

"And I can dance," she whispered.

He touched his forehead to hers. "You certainly can."

"Thank you for the dance, Luke."

"You're welcome."

"Are you two going to stand there mooning all night, or do you want this chair?" Charmaine had followed them with the wheelchair.

Luke turned with Annie laughing in his arms. "Thank you, Charmaine."

He placed Annie on the seat and she settled her skirts.

Her parents approached wearing their displeasure on their stern faces. Luke wished her a good-night and trudged toward his horse.

The Sweetwaters left in the Renlows' wagon.

Burdell and Diana walked toward their home, Burdell carrying his son on his shoulder.

Luke untethered his horse and mounted, heading for the livery. He'd need to be there when more wagons and horses were returned.

Annie had been right, no one would forget this holiday celebration any time soon, least of all him. He would never forget the image of his beautiful sweet Annie, walking toward him across that dance floor, her chin tilted bravely, her expressive eyes filled with pride and hope and love. He would always remember the dress and the act as a symbol of her maturity and determination. How he loved that courageous stubborn woman.

And now everyone knew it.

Whenever Luke attended church, he arrived late for the service, since he rented rigs to a couple of families for whom he had to deliver the outfit and then ride back, so it was his habit to slip in the back and sit in a rear pew.

This morning he'd entered quietly and sat listening to the music and the preacher's sermon, sometimes letting his mind wander to the upcoming meeting with Annie's father.

Annie wasn't sitting against the wall where she usually sat in her chair, but in her family's pew, and he knew the freedom she must feel without the hindrance of that chair.

Preacher Davidson ended the service and stood on the stoop in the sunshine, greeting the parishioners. Luke observed as Annie stood and made her way to the back of the church, Charmaine at her side, her mother's expression pinched and her cheeks blooming bright pink.

"What do we have here, a miracle?" Preacher Davidson asked, taking Annie's hand.

"I believe so," she replied, and wished him a good day.

Luke followed, shook the preacher's hand, and watched Charmaine get Annie's chair from beside the building and hold it for Annie to sit. Her gaze lifted and she spotted him where he stood on a wooden step. She gave him a tentative smile.

Charmaine pushed the wheelchair and Mildred walked behind them toward their home. None of them looked back.

Luke moved to stand in the shade of the building, waiting for people to disperse, noted when the preacher left and Eldon Sweetwater walked in his direction.

"Want to sit inside out of the sun?" Luke asked.

Eldon shook his head, stuffed his hands into his pockets and paced the hard-packed earth. The only other building nearby was the social hall and no one occupied it today. They didn't have to worry about eavesdroppers.

"I want you to know I never felt right about deceiving you," Luke said honestly, getting this off his chest immediately.

"Deceiving me didn't disturb you enough to leave her alone, did it?"

He winced inwardly. "She's of marrying age, sir. There's no good reason why she shouldn't be courted."

"The good reason was that we forbade it. She's not like other young women."

"No, she's not. I'm glad of it."

"We protected her all her life."

Luke tried to place himself in the man's shoes. He nodded.

"We never wanted her to be disappointed when she couldn't do the things other children did."

"She was disappointed anyway. There are a lot of things she can do that you never let her."

"We felt that was best for her emotional development. You have no idea what it's like to have a child like Annie."

"No. I don't. But I do know what it's like to love a woman like Annie. She's hungry for life, so full of hopes and dreams."

"That's why encouraging her fanciful ideas is harmful," Eldon said, his face rigid with anger.

Luke shook his head. "You smother her. We wired Dr. Mulvaney and he said there was no reason why Annie couldn't walk and exercise and strengthen her leg. He said it might even be beneficial."

The older man stared with a stunned expression. "He said no such thing."

"He did. Annie has the telegram if you don't believe it."

Eldon passed an unsteady hand across his forehead. "Her mother always dealt with the physicians. But she never had any news like this."

"Are you sure?"

Eldon straightened, tugging the lapels of his tailored suit and lifting his chin. "What are you insinuating? That my wife kept vital information like that to herself?"

Luke merely shrugged. He had no idea and wasn't about to make an accusation. "All I know is what this doctor told Annie. And I know what Annie tells me. She wants to live a normal life."

"It's not wise to let her believe she can do that."

"Why not?"

"Look at you. You're a strong, healthy man. Why would you want a girl like Annie, who can't possibly do everything a normal woman can?"

Those words pierced Luke's heart—and lodged anger in his soul. "Annie's limitations are there because you put them there. The few things she can't do aren't even worth mentioning! She can ride, she can sew, she can cook, she can care for a child. If she can't win a footrace at the next Fourth of July picnic, who *cares?*"

"She's never done those things."

"She has. She's ridden with me. She's baked me an apple pie. She made that dress she wore yesterday, and if she hasn't been able to help care for her nephew, it's only because you people won't let her. What more does she have to do to get you to listen? She's been tryin' to tell you for years. She's become a woman. She's capable of so much more. So much."

Maybe some of those words had sunk in. Eldon stared at the ground beneath his polished boots, one eyebrow twitching.

Luke sympathized with the man's confusion. Luke truly believed Sweetwater loved his daughter and wanted the best for her. He let him think in silence for a few more minutes before saying, "I'm afraid you'll only push her away if you try to hang on so tight. She loves you. I know she does. But she wants her own life. And I believe she wants a life with me. I love her. You have to believe I would never do anything to hurt her."

The man raised his head, but he looked off toward the mountains.

"Ever since I first met her, I wanted to see her happy. That's all I want now. I want to make her happy. If I truly thought I was bad for her, I'd have to leave her alone. If I believed walking and doing things was harmful to her, I'd urge her to stop. But I don't. All I've seen is good come from it. She's more assured. She feels good about herself."

Eldon nodded. Finally he cleared his throat and spoke. "I'll give you that. She's been happier lately. Had more confidence."

Luke had said his piece. He waited for Eldon's reaction.

The man looked him in the eye. "I don't want to drive her away. I don't approve. But I won't make her choose between us."

It wasn't exactly a blessing. It was hardly a truce. But it was something. "I intend to court her properly," Luke promised. "We'll set a date."

"For a proper respectable wedding," Eldon added. "Providing you haven't already ruined her." He glared at Luke with a suspicious eye.

His meaning sunk in. "I'll not take offense at what you've just accused me of," he said stiffly. "Not to mention your disregard for your daughter's sense of decency." Truth be told, if Annie'd had her way, she probably *wouldn't* be a virgin, but he'd never tell her father that. "I assure you your daughter's chastity is safe with me until we're married."

Eldon started to walk away, putting an end to their meeting, but he stopped and turned back. "She foolishly—*blindly,* believes she's in love with you. Don't take advantage of that."

Shaking his head, Luke struggled for a reply. "No, sir. I won't," he replied at last.

Eldon walked away.

Annie had been waiting on the porch for nearly an hour when her father walked up the lane. She took the stairs carefully, holding the rail, and met him as he approached the house.

His expression revealed the novelty of having her walk toward him, but she didn't see revulsion or embarrassment like she read on her mother's face.

She reached for his arm and he tucked her

hand into the crook of his elbow and slowed his pace. "You've never met me on the walk before," he said, and his voice shook.

"I always wanted to," she told him softly.

He patted her hand and blinked.

"What happened, Daddy?" she asked, unable to wait another minute.

They had reached the porch stairs and Annie leaned on him to climb them. The screen door opened and shut and Annie looked up to see her mother's disapproving observation.

Annie ignored her. "What did you and Luke discuss?"

"I am not going to fight you," he said finally.

Annie lowered her weight onto a wicker chair. Eldon sat across from her, but her mother stood, her hands folded over her waist.

"He made me see that this is what you want, and that you are old enough to make that decision."

Elation burst through Annie's ambivalent emotions. She blinked back tears.

"You cannot be considering condoning this travesty!" her mother said sharply, then turned to Annie. "You have no idea what you are getting yourself into."

"I believe I do—"

"You're too young to know what you want. This is a passing whim that you will regret. When you're older you'll see that your father and I made the best choices for you."

"I'm not a child. Why can't you see that?"

"Because you're not behaving like an adult," she retorted.

"Mildred, the girl is of age," Annie's father said. "She has a mind of her own. Would you rather she ran off and we never saw her again?"

"I wouldn't do that, Daddy," Annie protested. She'd never even considered the possibility, and didn't know why her father feared she had. "But I *am* going to marry Luke."

"We could *send* her away," Mildred said, her entire posture rigid. "We can keep him from finding her."

"And make our daughter a prisoner?" he asked, opening a palm toward his wife. "Do you really think she would be happy living God knows where with strangers? She would hate us."

"Do you think she will be happy when she realizes she can't do all the things she imagines she can? Do you think she will be happy when that man leaves her for a normal woman?"

"Mildred," Eldon said in censure. "I give the man more credit than that."

A quiver of unease ran through Annie's heart. Hurt and betrayal that her own mother thought so little of her, had such small regard for her feelings, pressed a bruise into her newly gained confidence.

"I will not place my approval on this abomination," she said.

"Annie is going to marry him," Eldon said calmly.

"Not with my blessing. I will not lift a finger to help you make a fool of yourself," she said to Annie. "And he will never be welcome in this house."

Hurt sliced through Annie's chest.

Eldon stood and faced his wife squarely. "Annie is our daughter!"

Mildred turned her face aside. "Not the daughter I know."

He glanced down at Annie. Heart breaking, she struggled to keep her features composed. Why? Why had it come to this? It wasn't even *Luke* who was the problem. It wasn't that her mother considered him not good enough for her—it was that she considered Annie not good enough for anyone! It had always been this way.

"Luke doesn't care that I'm not perfect, Mother," Annie said softly. "He doesn't ask me to be anyone I'm not. He accepts me and loves me just the way I am. Why can't you?"

"You are trying to be someone you're not," her mother returned. "You are trying to be the woman you think he wants. But you're not. You're not capable of being that woman. I don't want to see you regret your impetuousness later, but you will." She turned and stormed into the house.

Eldon seated himself slowly, his expression full of sorrow.

"It's not your fault, Daddy," she assured him softly. "You've done the best you could—always. And I know you care about me—truly about me and what I want."

"I will not let her keep you away from this house," he told her with conviction. "He has to properly court you, and that means calling on you here. And after you're married, we will still have Sunday dinners every other week."

An irrepressible smile spread across her face at the idea of Luke properly courting her, but disappeared at the thought of Sunday dinners. No way could she picture anyone in their right mind handing Luke and Burdell croquet mallets. "We'd better let time work on that."

Her mother's impenetrable mind on the subject didn't give her much hope, either. But there, above the hurt of her mother's lack of acceptance, was the unspeakable joy of knowing once and for all that she and Luke would be together.

No more hiding. No more secrets.

They could be together. The concept was as liberating as being free of her chair.

And now she had real plans to make.

Chapter Eleven

"Luke is calling this evening." Annie read the note Glenda had handed her in front of her mother and made the announcement.

It was cleaning day, and Annie had dressed in one of the work dresses Glenda had given her in exchange for the dresses Annie had cut down and sewn for her daughters.

Mildred said nothing, going about her dusting as though she preferred to pretend Annie didn't intend to go through with this courtship.

Because of his work on the house, he'd visited only once a week for the past few weeks. Each evening that he'd arrived, Mildred had gone upstairs with a headache while Annie entertained him on the porch. Soon it would be fall, and Annie didn't plan to sit outdoors on brisk evenings.

"Did you have much in your hope chest when you married Tim?" Annie asked the young house-keeper.

"Oh, yes, I had tea towels and aprons my grandmother made, and a cast iron skillet my father bought from a traveling salesman. I do love that skillet."

"Does a man expect his bride to have those things?" This trousseau thing had become a worry on her mind. She understood she was supposed to be bringing something to contribute to the household, and so far it didn't look like she had much to offer.

"You'll have wedding gifts," Glenda reminded her.

"Yes, of course." They had set a date, a date her father had frowned at and her mother had met with stony silence because it wasn't a year or two away. Neither Luke nor Annie wanted to wait any longer, so they'd chosen the last Saturday of October.

Her mother rarely spoke to her anymore, as though Annie had done something to deliberately hurt her. It grieved her that the woman could be so cold to her own daughter, that she refused to share in her happiness or simply get past her objections and treat Annie kindly. Annie watched Mildred polishing the brass candlesticks that sat on the mantel.

"Where did those come from, Mother?" she asked, an attempt to spark some communication.

"Your father brought them from a trip East when you were a baby," she replied.

"He's often brought you gifts, hasn't he?"

Mildred's expression took on a faraway look.

"Was he terribly handsome and charming when you first met him?" She'd never asked her mother anything so bold or personal, and she didn't know what kind of response to expect.

The woman rubbed the base of a candlestick vigorously. "He was the man my father preferred."

Annie's parents had moved here with her widowed grandfather only a few years after their marriage. Mother's father had been a banker, too, and had the vision to move to Colorado and invest in real estate during the early days when land was cheap and lumberjacks were free with their pay.

"What do you mean? Didn't you have a say-so in who you married?"

"Young women did what was best for their futures when I was a girl," she said.

Annie looked at her with growing understanding. "Was there someone else you would have preferred to marry?"

"No." Mildred glanced at Glenda, who was occupied with the sooty task of cleaning the fireplace.

"Something you would have preferred to do?"

"I had some talent," she admitted. "I might have liked to study the arts."

"What kind of talent? Acting?"

"Goodness, no. Painting."

"Really? Why didn't you pursue it?"

"Our future was here, in Colorado. I wasn't one to waste frivolous thoughts on things that couldn't be."

"Or things you were told couldn't be."

Mildred's lips pinched shut and the conversation was over.

That evening, sitting beside Luke on the wicker love seat, a warm breeze blowing across the porch, Annie related what she'd learned that day. "She didn't come right out and say it," Annie told him. "But I got the impression that she would have preferred to wait for marriage."

"Plenty of people marry for reasons of economy and politics," Luke told her. "It's been happening for centuries."

"I wonder if my father even knew. I believe he truly loves her."

Luke took her hand. "You can be sure that your husband will love you."

She leaned her shoulder against his. "And you can be sure I'm marrying you because wild horses couldn't stop me."

He grinned. "Are you sure you want to end this courting stuff? We're getting pretty good at it."

Remembering her mother's words, she asked, "We're supposed to be getting to know each other better. Do you think it's working?"

"Sure. I know you can talk about the wedding for thirty minutes straight without a breath. I didn't know that before."

"And I know you must have promised my father something, because we haven't had a moment alone together since he found out about us. I mean *alone,* like we were at your place."

"I did promise him something, and I'm a man of my word."

"Does it have anything to do with my virtue?"

"It does."

She pressed against him and he wrapped his arm around her. "How many weeks until the end of October?"

"I don't know." He kissed her gently. "But it's seventy-three days."

She smiled against his lips.

Sometimes those days crept by, especially when a week passed without seeing Luke, and other weeks it seemed as if the time had flown by and there was always something that needed to be done. Without her mother's assistance, Annie relied on Charmaine and Aunt Vera and Glenda to help with the wedding plans.

After all the ruffled dresses she'd taken apart and remade for Gerta and Gwen, her own wedding dress was a simple piece of work: white satin with lace trim, capped sleeves and a pinaforelike lace flounce in a V-shape with the edge of the lace hanging from the side of her waist like a scarf.

Lizzy's mother showed her how to stitch ruching of the same fabric as the gown along the hem, and Lizzy made her a coronet of crystal-beaded flowers and leaves, to which Annie secured the floor-length sheer veil.

"If this is a dream come true, it might as well be the best dream I can come up with," Annie told Charmaine and Lizzy one afternoon as they made the finishing touches to the dress. A sultry breeze barely fluttered the curtains in Annie's room.

"You could earn a living with your sewing," Charmaine told her. "This is the most beautiful gown I've ever seen."

"Remember I have an account in my father's name at the milliner's and the mercantile," Annie said wryly. "He paid for this gown."

"But you saved him a fortune by making it yourself!" Charmaine touched a satin sleeve reverently.

"I promise to help make yours, too," Annie told her. "When that too-good-to-be-true fellow comes along."

"You will? Oh, Annie, you're a dear!"

"Guy helped at the house the last two evenings, Annie," Lizzy said. "He said it's close to being finished."

"Luke tells me of the progress," Annie replied. "It's terribly frustrating not being able to go see it myself."

"You haven't seen it?" Charmaine asked.

She shook her head. "It's out of the question for me to leave with him without being chaperoned, and neither Mother nor Daddy will accompany me."

"I'll go with you!" Charmaine said. "Why haven't you asked?"

Annie shrugged.

"You know I'm not upset that he wanted you instead of me, don't you? No one could be happier for you than I am."

"I know that. You're a treasure. I suppose I didn't want to be any more of a burden than I've already been."

"Fiddlesticks!" Charmaine said in a huff. "I'll go with you. Plan a date."

Annie gave her a heartfelt smile. "I will."

Charmaine turned to Lizzy. "Shall we show her now?"

Eyes sparkling, Lizzy nodded.

"What?" Annie asked.

"We have something for you." Charmaine left the room and returned with a flat carton.

"What is it?"

"You're going to have to open it."

Annie sat on the bed with the box beside her and lifted the lid. Beneath layers of tissue lay a gauzy white silk gown. She lifted it from the box. "Why, it's beautiful!" The garment unfolded as she raised it. "It's a nightgown."

"Yes," Charmaine said, bouncing on the bed beside her. "We ordered it from a store in Chicago. Lizzy's aunt bought one for her for her wedding night."

"Not exactly like this one," Lizzy said.

"Goodness, you can see right through it!" Annie exclaimed, and her face grew warm.

"That's the idea." Charmaine giggled.

Lizzy added, "He will love it."

Annie stared at the gown and touched a hand to her hot cheek. Her pitifully few encounters with Luke had all seemed so natural and she had welcomed them. But now thinking about her wedding and the nights to follow, her nerves fluttered. Those had been spontaneous heated kisses and touches, but a wedding night was *planned*. Expected. Anticipated.

If Luke was going to see her in this nightgown, he would see that her body wasn't perfect. Whatever was wrong with the joint in her right hip gave it a different proportion than the other. She'd never before thought of him actually seeing that. Seeing her! "Oh, my goodness."

Mildred's steps sounded in the hallway. "I've prepared lemonade, girls."

Annie slammed the lid on the box.

Charmaine giggled, and Annie and Lizzy joined her.

"Thank you, Mother!" Annie called, a whole new worry opened in her mind.

Sunday afternoon had been decided upon. After Luke got his rigs put away and his horses brushed and fed and watered after church he would take Annie and Charmaine to the house.

Annie fidgeted all through church. When the service ended, she pulled on her coat and walked beside Charmaine down the aisle to shake Preacher Davidson's hand. "Only a week left now," he said with a smile.

Her heart fluttered. "I can't believe the wedding's almost here," she replied.

Her parents were directly behind her, and the preacher said nothing to them about the upcoming event, but greeted them politely.

Luke stood at the bottom of the three steps, wearing a dark-navy coat.

Annie's heart lifted when she saw him waiting, his black hair glistening in the autumn sun, and she smiled a warm welcome. Her father gave her his arm and she grasped it to descend the stairs. She looked up at him, his collar turned against the brisk wind, his expression unreadable. "Perhaps you'd like to join us, Daddy? Come see the house Luke has built?"

Eldon met Luke's gaze.

"You're welcome to come along," Luke said with a nod.

A muscle jumped in Eldon's jaw. He turned to his wife, who stood four feet away, her attention deliberately focused on the street, her fingers white on the reticule she gripped with both hands.

Eldon shook his head.

Mildred faced them. "Just where is this house you are building, Mr. Carpenter?"

"It's about five miles northeast of here," Luke replied. "I bought several acres with the protection of the foothills at the back of the house. The landscape is beautiful this time of year."

"And Annie will be expected to live in the middle of nowhere with no protection?"

"It's a short ride to town," he replied. "Closer than the Renlows' place, actually."

"I hardly think an isolated cabin in the woods is an appropriate place for a young lady. She would be better off in town."

"There wasn't any property available in town," Luke told her. "Not that I could buy, anyway." He observed Annie's father deliberately, then looked away. "Besides, this way I have a place for horses."

Annie's parents exchanged an uncomfortable glance.

"Afternoon, son," Uncle Mort greeted Luke, extending his hand. Luke shook it solemnly.

"Good day, Mr. Carpenter," Aunt Vera said.

Luke gave her a smile. "Ma'am."

Eldon turned to join his wife. They walked toward the Renlows' wagon and Annie's aunt and uncle followed.

Annie swallowed the ache in her throat, blinked, and turned her attention away from her unaccepting parents only to find Burdell's gaze locked on them. Diana waved cheerfully from her place at his side. In his father's arms, Will spotted Annie and his face brightened with an adorable grin.

Burdell turned away abruptly and strode toward the street. Will attempted to look back and wave over his shoulder.

Annie waved, then brought her hand up to cover her trembling lips. Luke stretched a palm toward her, and she clung to it.

Charmaine followed, pushing Annie's chair.

Luke had brought his best buggy, and he assisted Annie and Charmaine both to the wide front seat, then placed the wheelchair in the back seat. Annie was delighted to sit in the front and not in her usual place beside her chair, as she did when she rode with her parents. Luke's consideration to place Charmaine at her side, even though the space was tight, pleased her, too.

The crowded seating placed them shoulder to shoulder, and Luke's knee brushed Annie's skirts with each bump and sway.

The vivid shades of flaxen and yellow almost hurt Annie's eyes. They crossed the shallow creek, and even the rivulet of water appeared gold in color. The grass along the banks now lay brown and matted with leaves. A rich glaze shone on the high wooded slopes and the aspen leaves made a brilliant carpet on the dark, damp earth. Hawks sailed in circles above the foothills and a haze hung along the skyline. A small herd of pronghorn grazed in the distance.

They topped a rise, and there on a flat section stood the house and a barn, a corral and a windmill, its shiny new blade turning slowly in the sunlight.

Annie brought her hand to her heart in surprise. "Oh!"

It had been dark last time she'd been here, and the house hadn't been closed in or roofed. Wood siding and shingles testified to a land with readily available lumber.

The house wasn't large, only one story with two windows and a door on the front, but it appeared solid and well-planned with the foothills and the forest at its back. A deer stood drinking from the trough beneath the windmill.

"Look!" Annie cried, pointing. "Isn't he beautiful?"

"She," Luke corrected. "And you won't think so once they start eating your garden."

Luke pulled the buggy to a halt and the deer ran toward the protection of the foliage where it joined another that had been concealed among the trees until it moved. He helped the ladies to the ground and walked behind Annie and Charmaine as they approached the door.

His sudden attack of nerves surprised him. He'd been working for weeks on end to build and prepare this home and now that she was about to see it, he worried that it was small and crude and not at all like the place she was accustomed to living in.

"I plan to add a porch later. We've got lots of land, and we can add on to the house if we need to."

Annie and her cousin stopped in front of the door.

"And I didn't make a ramp, because I didn't think you'd need it. But if you want one, I can add it easily."

Annie smiled at him and shook her head.

"Go ahead," he said. "It's open."

Charmaine reached forward and turned the knob. Annie steadied herself with a hand on the door frame and entered. Luke's belly dipped in anticipation of her reaction. He'd worked so hard and dreamed so many dreams of them together in this place. It wasn't at all the style of life she was accustomed to, and he prepared for her reaction nervously.

The glass-paned windows allowed sun to spill across the hardwood floors he'd spent hours sanding and varnishing. The room they entered held only two plain straight-backed chairs. Guy Halverson had helped him build the mantel over the fireplace as well as the cupboards and shelves in the kitchen area.

"Not much furniture yet," he said. "I thought you'd like to choose it."

She released her cousin's arm and walked toward the other end of the room. He'd purchased a sturdy table and four chairs that a neighbor had been willing to sell.

"I ordered the stove—the newest model with a water reservoir." He was babbling, and she wasn't saying anything. Didn't she like the house? Striding to the cast iron stove, he showed her the covered well at the back.

"I like it," she said simply.

An awkward silence stretched out. Luke glanced from Annie to Charmaine and up at the stove pipe he'd vented through the wall.

"Would you mind if I went out to see if I can spot the deer again?" Charmaine asked, sidling away.

"No," Luke replied. "I wouldn't wander into the woods if I were you."

"No, I'll stay close." She hurried across the room and out the door, plainly giving them time alone.

Annie opened the cupboard doors, inspected the cast iron pump he'd installed.

"You won't have to go out to pump water," he said.

"I see that."

"Want to see the other room?"

She raised those heart-stopping eyes to his, and today, because of the deep-blue dress and matching jacket she wore, they were more gray than green. His heart thumped erratically. They both knew the only other room was the bedroom.

She nodded. "Okay."

He took her hand and led her back across the room to the closed door. He leaned forward and opened it. Annie walked in ahead of him.

The room seemed huge and hollow with no furniture. Guy had helped him place pegs along one wall and build a cabinet in one corner.

"We haven't discussed furnishings," he said. "I didn't want to buy anything we didn't need. What will you be bringing?"

She glanced away, and he realized her cheeks were tinged with color. Lord, he didn't want her uncomfortable with him or this room or anything they'd planned for their life together. With a step, he moved behind her, placing his hands on her shoulders and bending to nuzzle her sweetly scented hair and neck. The uniquely feminine scent of lilacs enfolded him. "I love you, Annie."

She turned her face to bring her warm cheek to his lips and raised her fingertips to his jaw. "Sometimes it seems too good to be true," she said softly.

"I know it's not like the house you live in now," he began.

"No. There's nothing to compare. Don't even think it. I love this house. And I love that you made it with your own hands just for us. I see the caring and . . . and the love that went into it. It's beautiful, Luke. Thank you so much."

Luke closed his eyes, inhaling the presence of this woman he loved and desired.

"I don't have much to bring." He heard the regret that crept into her voice when she spoke those words. "Not much at all. I don't want to ask them for anything."

"It doesn't matter," he replied to reassure her. "I'll get a bed and a chest of drawers for you. I've been bartering carpentry work for shoeing horses and repairing wagons and plows. I can probably strike a bargain with someone for a few pieces of furniture."

She turned in his arms, to face him and raise her hands to his shoulders. "It's really going to happen, isn't it? We're going to stand before Preacher Davidson, say vows that bind us for eternity, and then live here together."

"It's really going to happen."

A silvery tear shimmered on her lashes. "I can forget all the other hurts when I remember that."

"What hurts so bad, Annie?"

"That I have nothing to bring. That my mother won't believe in me. That my family doesn't accept us."

"I wish I could change that for you. If I could I would, you know that."

She touched his lip at the place where he bore a scar. "I know."

Lowering his head, he covered her soft lips with his, testing, tasting, loving her with all his being, wishing he could change the things that saddened her and vowing to give her joy and pleasure at every opportunity from this day on.

Her body curled against his so naturally, her breast pressed to his chest, her fingers kneading the flesh of his neck.

The next instant she pulled away, pressing her palms to her cheeks. "I frighten myself."

Luke breathed a calming breath, ignored the messages of his body, and studied her face. "What do you mean?"

"I mean . . ." She dropped her hands to her sides, studying his face. "I'm so bold with you, when I have no idea what this all means." She turned her body and gazed at the bare window as if avoiding his eyes. "It's natural for me to be a bit frightened, don't you think?"

She meant the physical aspect of marriage, and it tore at him to think she was afraid. "It's a natural thing between a man and a woman," he said. What had she heard? What did young women learn and who told them? He hadn't a clue. "Natural and beautiful."

"I'm sure it is. Do you know this firsthand?"

She turned her head then, damn her, and looked him directly in the eye. Open and candid, his Annie. He doubted many fiancées had the balderdash to question their prospective husbands on the intimate partners in their pasts.

"Well . . ." Nothing to speak but the truth. "The natural part I know about."

One slender eyebrow went up. "Not the beautiful part?" she asked.

"That must be for husbands and wives."

"Oh."

"I was young and—and—well, young men don't always use their heads."

"Prostitutes?" she asked. Straightforward. Honest.

"A couple."

She turned her gaze back to the window. "Any woman you ever loved?"

"You're the only woman I've ever loved."

Her hand went up to her cheek and rapidly brushed beneath her eye. Lord, he'd hurt her. His stomach balled into a knot.

She turned back then. "You will be the first. For me."

He moved to hold her by her upper arms and stare into her eyes. "That didn't have to be said. I knew that without you saying so."

"Because no one ever wanted me before you, you mean."

"No! Because I know you. I know your parents! God, Annie, be a little kinder to yourself." He drew her against his chest and held her fast. "I'm sorry my being with those others hurts you. You have to know that wasn't anything like what you and I have together. No comparison."

She hugged him back and he sensed her trembling against his frame. "At least one of us will know what to do," she said.

He couldn't suppress a chuckle.

She raised her face to his in invitation. Before he could lower his head, she wrapped one hand around his neck and pulled him to her, kissing him fiercely, possessively.

"When did you first know you loved me?" she whispered against his ear.

He squeezed her gently. "I'll have to think on that."

"Well, what are the possibilities?"

"Maybe when I saw you eating peppermint ice cream."

"Maybe?"

"Maybe. Or maybe when you smiled at me across a stack of denims in the mercantile."

She drew back to see his face. "When was that?"

He shrugged. "A long time ago. You were with your Aunt Vera and Charmaine. I remember that because if it had been your mother she'd have dragged you from the store as soon as she saw I was there."

"Maybe then, huh? It must have been a good smile."

He grinned. "It was."

"Or when else?"

He twined a ringlet of her satiny hair around his finger. "Or maybe when you cried because Burdell punched me."

She frowned. "After the Fourth of July dance?"

He shook his head. "No. After I took you for a ride."

Her eyes searched his. "I was only ten years old."

"I was fourteen. Not that much older. I told you I'd have to think about it."

She pulled from his arms and took his hand. "All right. But I'm going to ask you again."

"I'm sure you will."

"Let's go rescue Charmaine from the sun."

"Your cousin is a gem."

"I know. She deserves the next too-good-to-be-true man." Annie hooked her arm through Luke's and he led her through the house to the door.

"I love the house," she said, stopping him before he opened it. "Truly. Thank you."

"I just want you to be happy," he told her with all the sincerity he felt in his heart. "I never want to see you hurt or unhappy again. I want to give you so much."

"You have," she assured him. "Already you have. I don't need much more than your love and acceptance."

He knew she believed that now. But she still needed a nice home and comfortable furnishings and the acceptance of friends and family. He prayed he could give her all she deserved.

The night before the wedding, Annie couldn't sleep. She'd lain awake for hours, staring at the moonlight on the ceiling and telling herself all the reasons why she shouldn't be worried. Finally, she got up, donned her flannel wrapper, and went out to the kitchen to see if any warm water remained.

A sound from the other room startled her, and she limped into the sitting room where a soft light glowed.

Her mother sat in an elegant velvet-upholstered chair, her hair down around her shoulders.

"Mother? Are you all right?"

"I'm fine."

"I wasn't going to bother to make tea just for myself, but if you'll join me I'll kindle the fire in the stove."

"I've already brewed a pot. Help yourself."

"Oh." Annie hadn't noticed the silver service on the low table. Only Mildred Sweetwater would prepare tea in a silver pot in the middle of the night. She poured herself a cup and sat on the divan. "This feels good. It's a chilly night."

Her mother stared at the embers in the fireplace.

"Did you have trouble sleeping, too?" Annie asked.

"I haven't slept a night since this ordeal began."

"I assume you mean since Luke's been courting me."

"Courting," she sniffed. "I haven't seen flowers or gifts."

"He's spending all his money on our house and furnishings, Mother."

"Harrummph."

"Why won't you give us a chance?"

"Because I don't want to be disappointed," she said stiffly. "Like you're going to be disappointed." She raised a hand and flicked her fingers. "When all your fanciful dreams go up in smoke. When you discover he can't take care of you like we can." She arched one brow and delivered a stinging prediction. "When you can't please him."

Chapter Twelve

Annie mulled those words over. Couldn't please him? "What do you mean?"

"Men are carnal creatures, Annie. Their tastes are not as delicate as a woman's. And you—you're just a girl."

Annie's lungs burned when she drew a deep breath. "Are you speaking of passion, Mother? Because I want Luke as badly as he wants me."

"Maybe you do, little girl. But will his supposed love for you last? If a crippled girl can't keep up with a strong man while walking or running, how will you please him intimately?"

Pain twisted in Annie's chest. She set her cup down so hard, liquid splashed over the edge onto her mother's starched and pressed doily. She wanted to cover her ears and refuse to listen to this foolishness and cruelty. "I don't—I don't think that comparison is fair. Yes, he's strong and he's healthy, but he's tender and—and he's loving."

"You're not listening to me," Mildred said, her voice once again low. "You've never wanted to listen to reason. Do what you like, what you're determined to do, but don't cry to me when you learn I was right."

Annie scooted to the edge of the chair. "You're

not right. He loves me. He sees me as a whole person."

"Believe what you must."

Annie stood. In the dim light of the lamp, she stared at her mother for a full minute, but the unrepentant woman met her gaze with icy superiority. "Thank you so much for your gracious help and motherly guidance. A woman always remembers her wedding, and I will remember that you refused to take the smallest measure to support me."

"I'm not going to be responsible when this 'marriage' breaks your heart."

"That would be impossible. *You* have already done that." Annie limped from the room, wishing she could walk gracefully, knowing this was the best her gait would ever be, and praying her mother was wrong about everything else.

She sat on the edge of her bed until dawn crept under the window shades and cast a tangerine glow on the floral carpet. A knock sounded once the sun was up.

Had her mother had a change of heart? "Come in."

Glenda peered around the door. "Morning. Did you sleep?"

"Maybe a wink or two."

"I was the same way, I was so excited."

"You're not usually here on Saturday."

Glenda came toward her. "I heated water for

your bath and I'll help you wash your hair and dry it."

Annie stood, holding the hem of her night-rail and hugged the other woman. "Thank you," she managed to say in a throaty voice.

Glenda led her to the bathing chamber off the kitchen where she had a fire going in the fireplace and hot water steaming in the copper tub. "Here are your bath salts and your lilac water. There's a stack of clean toweling."

Annie smiled her appreciation and Glenda turned away while Annie removed her cotton gown and stepped into the water. The tub had only been filled half-full because Glenda had several buckets of warm water ready for the rinse.

Annie lathered her hair and Glenda poured water over her head. Once she was bathed and wrapped in a warm robe, they sat before the fire and Glenda gently worked the tangles from her hair and helped it dry.

"I wish I could brush some of these curls out for good," Annie said.

"No, no, don't brush them out—let them spring. The charm of your lovely hair is the way it curls around your face and neck. Us ordinary-looking women would give anything for hair like yours." She finger-wove a few spirals into place.

Annie held up her silver-backed hand mirror. "I've always thought this mop was atrocious because it wasn't dark and lovely like Mother's."

"Your mother is beautiful, but you have a beauty all your own. Inside and out."

Their eyes met and neither said any more about Mildred. "Luke thinks I'm beautiful."

"He's right."

The doorbell sounded.

"I'll get that." Glenda hurried from the room and returned with Charmaine.

"Oh, Annie, I'm so excited, I think I'm going to burst! How can you look so calm?"

Annie laughed at her cousin's exuberance. "Lack of sleep perhaps?"

"Let's go get you dressed."

Glenda remained to clean up the bathing chamber while Charmaine led Annie to her room. Charmaine helped her pack her belongings and Glenda went for Tim who took the trunks and boxes to the livery.

Hours later, dressed in her white satin gown and slippers, the beaded headband and veil upon her head, Annie emerged from her room and met her father in the foyer. Dressed in a black frock coat and striped trousers, he made a dashing picture.

Eldon stared at Annie, his expression softening and his eyes misting with unshed tears. "You are so beautiful, my daughter."

"Thank you, Daddy. Thank you for everything." She swept forward in a rustle of silk to give him a careful hug and a peck on the cheek.

"All I want is for you to be happy."

"Luke makes me happy."

Clearing his throat against the tide of emotion, he nodded.

Annie voiced her newest concern. "I don't want to take that dreadful chair, but there is only one doorway—the one at the back of the church. Would I be too cumbersome in this dress for you to carry me up the aisle?"

"Carry you?" His brows shot up in surprise. "Why on earth would I carry you?"

"Well, so I don't have to—to walk down the aisle in front of all those people, of course."

His expression grew stern. "Suddenly you don't want to walk in front of people? Nothing stopped you from walking across the floor at the social hall in front of a hundred eyes. What's different about this?"

"This is my wedding! I don't want everyone to see how clumsy I am." Her mother's criticism had raised her self-consciousness.

"Do you want to appear fragile? Incapable?" He made a clucking sound. "I'm shocked."

She stared, amazed at the challenging words he'd spoken. "Are you telling me to walk down the aisle in front of the whole population of Copper Creek?"

He raised his chin. "With your head held high."

Of course. She wanted to walk down the aisle to her husband. "You're right, Daddy." Tears blurred her vision and he handed her a handkerchief. "Thank you."

He turned and called up the stairwell. "It's time to leave, Mildred!"

Annie'd been wondering all along if her mother would actually attend, but there was no room for argument in her father's authoritative tone.

Mildred appeared at the top of the stairs in a lavender silk taffeta gown that emphasized her slender waist and dark hair. She examined Annie as she descended the stairs, her gaze neither approving nor disapproving. Annie knew she'd chosen well, from her elbow-length gloves to her slippers and veil, but she didn't expect her mother's approval at this late date.

"Your mother and I have something for you." Eldon turned to the cherry table behind him and picked up a small flat box, which he handed to Annie.

Inside the silk-lined jewelry case lay an elegant pearl choker. "It's beautiful!" Annie breathed.

"It was my mother's." Her father placed it around her neck, fastening the clasp, and stepping back to admire the pearls.

"Thank you."

Her mother said nothing, merely picked up her hem and started forward.

Once she was out of hearing, Eldon asked, "Does the chair go at all?"

Annie shook her head. "No. I don't want that chair spoiling anything about this day."

"Very well."

Charmaine was waiting on the porch, and in no time they were in the buggy and on their way in the warm fall sunshine.

Leaves crunched beneath the wheels as Eldon drove the buggy to the steps of the church and got out to assist the women.

Burdell and Diana had been waiting, and Burdy stepped forward. "Oh, Annie, you look beautiful!" Diana said from beside him. "Doesn't she?"

Burdell nodded. "Are you sure, Annie? It's not too late to call this off. I can go send everyone away if you say the word."

"This is what I want, Burdy," she replied. "Thank you for being here. It means more than you know."

He offered his arm until she neared the church building, then left to move the buggy for his father. Diana and Charmaine ushered Annie into the tiny cloakroom where they stood amongst the scents of leather and wool until Burdell returned and the organist began the first notes of the wedding march.

Charmaine nodded to the two young ushers and they opened the polished doors. Annie's father secured her hand in the crook of his arm and gave her a reassuring smile.

He proceeded slowly and Annie raised her chin

and took step after step, feeling every critical eye on her awkward advance. Step-limp. Step-limp.

Luke came into sharp focus, a half-smile slashing his handsome cheek, his blue eyes intent on her approach. From that moment on, no one else mattered, nothing mattered, not even the fact that she would never be graceful, nothing except that from this day forward she would be Luke Carpenter's wife.

He wore the same proud expression he'd worn the night she'd crossed the dance floor and asked him to teach her to dance. Her heart fluttered crazily at the devotion in his eyes.

Eldon took her gloved hand, kissed the back, and placed it in Luke's waiting palm, gave the younger man a cautioning glance, then took his place in the first pew beside his wife. Annie's gaze moved from her parents to her almost-husband.

The rest of the ceremony progressed in a blur of prayers and vows and tears and kisses. Taking Luke's hand, she walked beside him up the aisle to the door and, once outdoors, good-naturedly ducked a shower of rice.

Bending his knees, he swept her into his arms and carried her toward the social hall. Grateful for the rest, she wrapped her arm around his neck and smiled into his face.

"We did it, Annie," he said. "We really did it."

With tears blurring her vision, she nodded, and they shared a moment of silent pleasure. Annie laid her head against his shoulder and sighed.

He carried her into the building and found her a chair.

"The musicians are already setting up," she observed.

He crouched before her and took her hand. "You are so beautiful."

She gazed into his earnest blue eyes. "And your eyes are so blue."

He grinned. "I reckon we'll have beautiful blue-eyed children, won't we?"

Her heart missed a beat. She glanced around at the women busily uncovering food and arranging cups and silverware, at the pile of gifts on a lace-draped table. "All this is really happening to *me* —lame Annie Sweetwater. I had a wedding and a cake and I have a husband just like any normal girl."

Luke raised her hand and his thumb touched the gold ring he'd placed on her finger.

Casting her attention back to the man before her, she corrected her words: "Better than any normal girl—because I've married the handsomest, kindest, bluest-eyed man in all of Copper Creek."

He grinned and she touched his cheek.

"Come on, you have lots of time for that," Charmaine called. "You two have to fill your plates first."

"I'll get yours," Luke said, releasing her hand and standing.

While Luke was gone Burdell approached. He took a seat beside her and watched Luke at the food table. After a minute he said, "If he ever hurts you—"

"He would never hurt me, Burdy."

"I'm just telling you. If he ever does, you come to me. I'll kill him."

Remembering who had pounded who during their last scuffle, Annie held back a smile. "I would come to you," she said somberly.

"Okay." He placed his hands on his knees.

"Okay," Annie agreed.

Burdell sat a moment longer, then got up and strode away.

Later, when the newlyweds opened gifts, Annie exclaimed over the generosity of her neighbors. Of course her father was the local banker and she had to wonder how much effect that had on people's pocketbooks.

Glenda and her girls had sewn aprons and dishtowels. The Renlows gave them a mantel clock, and Burdell and Diana bestowed a set of silverware that Annie knew had been of Diana's choosing. Among the other gifts were blankets and barrels, skillets and dishes, fabric and a rocking chair. Mrs. Krenshaw gave them books, and Lizzy and Guy had purchased them a painted glass lamp.

Annie was overwhelmed at the amount of household items they now had to take to their little house. From time to time she thought about leaving the party tonight and going to that new house with her new husband, and a wave of nerves would make her hands cold.

A tall, handsome man with black hair graying at the temples shook Luke's hand and then gave him a hug, clapping him on the back.

"Annie, this is my Uncle Gil," Luke told her, stepping back.

"Gilbert Chapman," his uncle said with a friendly nod.

Annie extended her hand. "I'm pleased to officially meet you. I do remember seeing you the day you came to my birthday party."

"None of us will ever forget that day, will we?" he said with a wry grin that reminded Annie of Luke's devastating smile.

"I certainly never forgot," Annie said. "Luke takes after you. Were you his father's brother?"

Gil nodded. "He was a few years older. We were close as young'uns, but didn't keep in touch much after we had our own lives. I was sorry about that after he died. But I was glad to have Luke here come to live with me. He was good company for a lot o' years. I guess you're going to find that out."

What a likable man. No wonder Luke thought so highly of him. "I guess I am."

"I'll bring your present by next week," he told Luke. "I couldn't bring it here today."

They visited a while longer until Gil spotted someone he wanted to talk to. She didn't have time to wonder why he couldn't bring their present.

Annie was truly the belle of the ball that afternoon. Everyone wished her well and spoke to her, and when the dancing began she declined a dozen offers, wanting to dance only with Luke, who compensated for her lack of agility and made her feel competent.

"Are you getting tired?" he asked during one of their turns around the floor. "Are your legs holding up?"

"I'm all right," she assured him, not wanting to hold him back from enjoying their wedding celebration.

"You know," he said against her hair, "it's customary for the bride and groom to leave a little early. We can go anytime."

Glancing over his shoulder, she spotted her mother seated between two other wives, but not participating in their conversation. Mildred's attention was focused unhappily on Annie and Luke. Her ominous predictions rang in Annie's head.

Annie blocked them out and concentrated on Luke's suggestion and her joy over this new life for which she'd been so eager. "I guess I'm a little tired," she told him. "I didn't sleep last night."

"Let's start saying our goodbyes, then."

Luke worked them to the edge of the floor and inconspicuously told a few people they were leaving.

"Do you want to come back for your presents tomorrow or shall we bring them to you?" Guy Halverson asked Luke.

"Burt's taking care of the livery tomorrow," Luke replied. "I appreciate the offer, if you don't mind."

"Are you kidding? Lizzy's been dying to see your house."

Luke shook Guy's hand.

Annie caught her father's eye and waved. Eldon strode toward her. He and Luke stared at each other, neither of them speaking. Finally Annie stepped forward and hugged her father.

His arms closed around her convulsively. "You were a beautiful bride, Annie," he said, his voice sounding choked.

She released him, moved back and took Luke's hand, noting that her mother deliberately turned aside and folded a tablecloth.

Charmaine brought their coats and Annie slipped hers on, but carried Luke's. At the door, he picked her up and carried her to the area where the horses and buggies waited and lifted her to the seat. "Want your coat?"

He glanced at the sun still high in the sky. "In a minute."

She arranged her voluminous skirts as he

hitched the horse and climbed up, slipping on his coat and urging the horse forward. He stopped at the livery and loaded the trunks and boxes containing Annie's personal items.

"I told you I didn't have much," she said.

"And I told you all I wanted was you." He leaned to kiss her nose.

She pulled her coat around herself, a chill enveloping the countryside in the shade of the mountains. The beauty of the scenery was lost on her this time, as she thought ahead to the afternoon and evening that lay before them.

It was midafternoon when they reached the house at the bottom of the foothills. Luke carried her to the door and she turned the knob.

"Welcome home, Mrs. Carpenter."

She touched his face, but realized how cold her hand was and pulled it back. He carried her inside and set her down.

Quickly he moved to the fireplace and lit the kindling that had been placed at the ready. Going back out, he made several trips with her belongings, carrying the heavy trunks into the bedroom. He stopped beside her and brushed his palms together. "I have to put up the horse and wagon."

"Go ahead."

"I'll be right back."

She nodded and managed a weak smile. "I'm fine."

He left and she kept her coat on, walking carefully across the bare floor to the empty mantel. They would have a clock, she thought idly. Her gaze drifted to the open door to the bedroom, and she made her way over and peered in.

A bed with an iron headboard had been placed in the room since she'd last see it. A plain wool blanket covered the mattress. Luke's clothing and hats hung on a few of the pegs. A chest of drawers held a lantern, and a shiny bucket and several towels sat on a stack of crates.

He'd done all he could to prepare a home for her. None of it was fancy, none of it was anything like her parents' home. But it was theirs. And he'd done it all himself. For her.

Eyes smarting she turned back to the outer room, hung her coat on a peg inside the door and holding her veil well away, she used a poker to help the fire along. After a few minutes, she added a split log from the stack beside the rock hearth.

The door opened and closed and the draft sucked the flames and sent sparks up the chimney.

Luke removed his coat and hung it. "You got the fire going. You should have waited, you might have gotten your dress dirty."

Annie looked down at the yards and yards of white satin. "I'll never wear it again."

"Our daughter might."

There he went, making her blush again.

He moved to stand before her. "It's a beautiful gown. I still can't believe you made it yourself."

She glanced away and back.

"When I saw you walk into church, my heart just leaped inside my chest."

She laughed nervously. "You were probably wondering if I was going to trip over the hem and fall headlong down the aisle."

He raised a hand to touch her, but drew it back. "No, I didn't think that at all." He looked at his hands. "I have to wash up. I brushed down the horse."

"I don't mind that smell on you, you know."

"It's a good thing, you're going to smell it a lot." He started a fire in the stove. "You know how to do this?"

"Glenda showed me."

Taking a kettle from a back burner, he pumped water and placed it on the stove. "If you bank the coals, so they're just warm, the water will stay warm in the reservoir. I thought that would be nice for you in the mornings."

"It will be."

He removed his dark wool jacket, revealing suspenders crossed over a white shirt with a day's worth of wrinkles. The cotton stuck to his lean ribs and back where moisture from his body had adhered it.

He raised his head and gave her a questioning

look. "I'm going to take off my shirt and wash. Shall I go in the other room?"

Goodness no! She didn't want to miss a moment of this. She shook her head slowly.

His fingers raised to his tie and loosened it, yanking it free of the collar and tossing it over the back of a chair. Next he unbuttoned the top two buttons, but he paused and met her gaze.

Perhaps he was uncomfortable with her staring at him. "Do you mind if I watch?" she asked.

He swallowed, but shook his head, and his fingers continued their journey down the line of buttons until he shrugged out of the suspenders, letting them drop to dangle at his thighs. He tugged the hem of his shirt from his trousers. The shirt gaped open. His chest was covered with hair as black as that on his head.

Annie stared. Her knees trembled. "Do you mind if I sit?"

"No."

She folded onto a chair.

His collar came off separately, and he placed it on the table. With a fluid movement, he tugged one arm from the garment and then the other, and laid the shirt over the chair with his tie.

He was all muscle and sinew, chest, neck, arms, belly, and she could see now that the ebony hair grew in a triangle shape with the widest area across his chest and the narrowest point arrowing into the waistband of his black trousers.

His skin glowed in the sunlight from the curtainless window, dark and supple, nothing like her fair white skin with its dusting of freckles.

Annie swallowed, realizing her throat had gone dry.

He turned and poured hot water into an enamel basin, pulled a cup and bar of soap from a shelf near the stove and scraped soap off with his razor. Stirring with a brush, he made a lather, and, looking in the small square mirror on the wall, he spread it across his cheek, chin and neck.

"What are you doing?" She'd never seen anyone wash their face like that.

"Shaving."

"Oh." Of course.

"Didn't you ever see your father or brother shave?"

"No."

His hand lowered. "Maybe it's ungentlemanly of me to do this here—with you watching. Where does your father shave?"

"I have no idea." But she didn't want him to go somewhere else. "But I like it. Didn't you shave this morning?"

His hand came up with the brush. "My beard grows fast." He finished lathering, tipped his head back and guided the razor up his neck in even strokes.

Annie'd never been so captivated, not even by one of the adventure stories she'd read from the library. What a fascination Luke Carpenter was. Without conscious thought, she stood and moved a little closer, leaning on the back of the chair, his cotton shirt beneath her fingers, the smell of him bringing moisture back to her mouth.

From this close, she could see his eyes in the mirror. He met hers. "I can see that fire in your eyes, Annie," he said hoarsely.

Now he drew the razor down his cheek, across his chin, then down the other cheek and stroked beneath his nose while he made a comical face that gave him access to the whiskers.

Bending forward, he rinsed the remaining streaks of lather from his face while Annie observed the flexing muscles in his back and shoulders, noted the absorbing manner in which his spine separated the corded muscles.

Picking up the basin, he moved past her, opened the door and returned a moment later with it empty. He poured more water in, and taking a cloth, he soaped it and washed his chest and under his arms.

Water splashed as he rinsed. He grabbed a towel to dry his face and arms. Straightening, he turned toward her. A damp wave fell over his forehead. Droplets glistened in the thick curls on his chest where her attention riveted. Annie reached for a length of toweling.

Luke lowered his arms.

Annie took a step forward.

He watched her.

She raised the towel and blotted at the drops on his chest, taking her time, inhaling the scents of soap and man. She wiped his ear, his shoulder, dropped the towel to the floor and stretched a tentative hand to touch the black curls matting his chest, finding them surprisingly soft.

Annie ran her finger across his collarbone, tested the smoothly shaven skin on his throat, then used her palm to test the skin of his shoulder and biceps. His flesh seemed alive beneath her touch. "You are so beautiful," she whispered.

He expelled a breath and raised his eyes to the ceiling.

Annie wanted to press her cheek against that chest. She stared at it hard. Embarrassed by her boldness and the odd quaking in her abdomen, she took a step back.

Luke lowered his gaze. Intense blue heat raked her face and hair, the veil. "You must be uncomfortable after being in that dress all day. Do you need help taking it off?"

Was he thinking fair was fair—time for her to bare herself to him? Her heart hammered up into her throat. She raised her fingers to the pulse there, found the warm pearls.

Watching Luke do anything was like watching a ballet or listening to music. His perfect body moved fluidly and gracefully, each motion a synchronized harmony of muscle and flesh.

She was clumsy and imperfect and would never be called graceful. Luke would never watch her move or see her without her clothes and be able to call her beautiful.

Annie swallowed humiliating self-doubts, knowing he loved her. Never would she be here if he didn't love her.

"Yes," she said, finding her voice, but it sounded as though it came from far away. "I need help unbuttoning my dress."

Chapter Thirteen

"But it's—" her gaze went to the window "—it's not dark yet."

"Not yet," he said, puzzling over her words. "Should it be dark?"

"Well, I just thought, I mean I imagined . . ."

The reason for her hesitation dawned on him. "Annie, we're not gonna do anything at any time that you're not comfortable with. I was only suggesting that you might want to change clothes. If you want to dress in somethin' else until bedtime, that's fine."

Her gaze lifted, and the fire wasn't gone, but other emotions were crowding it. "Luke," she said.

He tossed his toweling aside and took her by her upper arms. "Yes?"

"Could you just kiss me? I'm feeling awkward, but everything feels right when you kiss me."

He smiled and drew her close. "I'd love to kiss you."

Her satin dress was cool against his warm skin as he drew her into his arms and lowered his face to hers. Lace and seed pearls pressed against his aroused flesh. He recalled the ludicrous admission when she'd told him he'd be the first. Annie was as pure and innocent as a newborn babe, but a banked fire glowed deep inside, waiting for fuel and air.

Perhaps it was to his benefit that she'd never been coached in the ways of "womanhood"—that her mother had never expected her to become a wife, because she hadn't been instilled with the foolish ideas of what was ladylike and what wasn't. She'd been thoroughly engrossed by his body and her indulgence aroused him beyond belief. He'd learned already just how sensuous and eager and warm-blooded his new wife could be.

It was his job to show her the beauty and purity of their love. She stroked his bare shoulders, her fingers trembling on his skin, skimming down his arms, kneading his neck. She had no idea of the fire she fueled in him.

Against his lips she parted hers and he sensed her waiting breathlessly for the play of his tongue. He teased her by darting it against her lip.

She made a soft cry in the back of her throat.

This time he drew a line across her lower lip.

Annie held his head still and raised on tiptoe.

"You do it, Annie," he whispered.

She hesitated only a brief moment, then swept her tongue into his mouth, against his teeth, tasting him, drawing him deeper into the kiss.

Her erotic kisses and the glide of her hands over his chest had him aching and burning with want.

She separated their lips by a fraction of an inch to speak. "Can we do it all now?"

His head was a little numb and he had to rethink to make sure he'd heard right. "All?"

"Take off my dress. And the part that comes after that."

"Make love, Annie? You want to make love now?"

She nodded.

As if he would say no? But he wanted her reassured. "There's something you should know," he said.

"What's that?"

"I am yours Annie. My heart." He placed her hand over his chest and her fingers curled deliciously. "My body." He made out her pulse beating rapidly at the base of her throat. "My body is yours. For your pleasure. If you can understand that, then you won't have to be afraid."

"I'm not afraid." Her quavering voice belied those words.

"Has anyone ever told you—that—that it hurts the first time?"

She shook her head. "No."

"It's normal," he offered, hoping to reassure her.

Her body trembled in his arms. "Okay."

"Are you cold?"

"No."

"Then you are afraid."

"Not of you, Luke."

"What are you afraid of?"

She lowered her gaze, encountered his chest, and turned to the window, the picture of innocent beauty in her pristine gown and veil.

He imagined all the things she might fear. "You're not afraid I will hurt you?"

"No."

"You're not afraid to have a baby?"

She blinked. "No."

"Tell me, Annie. You can tell me."

Her cheeks bloomed with bright color. She lowered her eyes to the floor. "It's me," she whispered. "I'm not . . . perfect."

That word stunned him. As well as the fact that she doubted her perfection. "Is this about your leg? Your hip?"

Tears gathered on her lowered lashes.

"It doesn't look the way you'd like it to?"

"No. It doesn't look the way it should."

He raised her face with his knuckle under her chin, forcing her to look at him. "You think I care about perfection? You think after what we've shared and the way I've always treated you that a small thing like outward appearance makes one damn bit of difference to me? You hurt me if that's what you think."

Tears spilled over and ran down her pale cheeks. "I think you're the kindest, most loving person I've ever known."

"Then you know I don't care about a physical difference. I love you. *You.*"

With a sob, she hugged him around the waist and clung.

Luke rubbed her back until she calmed, then pulled away. "I'll help you with your dress and then I'll bring fresh water for you to wash if you'd like."

"Here?"

"No. In the other room. In private."

She nodded and he led her toward the bedroom. She stepped in ahead of him.

Luke's hand trembled on the knob. He closed the door behind him, and self-consciously dropped the betraying hand to his side.

She had moved to stand with her back to the window, haloed in a shimmering silhouette of white lace and seed pearls. Reaching up, she found the combs that secured her veil and drew the headpiece from her hair, then turned to hang the yards of gauzy fabric on a wall peg. Expression serene, she stepped toward him, an action that spoke of trust and courage and strength in itself.

"Luke," she breathed on a rush of air.

He smiled a smile of love that came from a place deep inside, honored beyond belief that she'd taken more than physical steps for him— humbled that she'd stood up to her parents and taken steps of trust, of commitment toward him.

God, how he loved this brave woman. He never wanted to hurt her or disappoint her or tarnish the beauty of what they shared. And he never wanted her to feel less than perfect.

He was in front of her without consciousness of the steps, raising a hand to her temple, to the springy curls that shone like red-gold fire in the sunlight streaming through the windowpane.

The coils sprung back when he released them, nestled against the ivory skin near her eye. He leaned toward her and kissed her there, felt that gentle pulse beneath his lips. He moved his hand to her arm and caressed her through the lace.

She sighed and her warm breath brushed the base of his throat, provoking an internal tremor. He wanted to be calm and strong for her. He wanted to take things nice and slow and show her his devotion in gentle measures. After what had happened in the other room, his body demanded something entirely different, making him feel like a callow young boy.

"Oh, Annie," he said against her hair. "I want this to be good for you. I don't want you afraid."

"I'm not afraid of you," she said, and she placed a palm along his jaw.

He took her in his arms again, looking down into those trusting loving eyes. If love could be seen, then he was looking at it, suddenly over-whelmed by the devotion she lavished with her entire being. "I love you."

Her smile added more sunshine to an already blindingly bright scene, more pleasure to a heart already full to bursting. "Maybe you would want to kiss me again, then," she said.

He loved her playfulness, appreciated her security to feel at ease with him. "Maybe."

She touched his lip with her forefinger, traced the scar that caused her so much concern.

He leaned forward and kissed her, tasting the familiarity of her lips, the newness of their bond, sensing her hesitancy and her need, and loving the heady combination. Her lips were warm and willing, and she leaned into him, her breasts crushed to his chest.

"Oh, Annie," he said against her lips, enfolding her and holding her flush against him and speaking his desire. "I don't want to wait a minute longer."

A multitude of tiny hard seed pearls bit into his flesh where they pressed together, though not nearly enough of a diversion to quell his ardor.

"Do we have to?" she asked, eyes open wide with concern.

"No, no, we don't have to wait, I just thought . . . well, I don't know what I thought . . . that you'd be more comfortable if we waited, I guess." He wanted her to be comfortable, able to enjoy their lovemaking without embarrassment or distractions.

"I think I'm more uncomfortable waiting."

Encouraged, he smiled against her cheek. "Turn around."

She obliged, pulling loose from his embrace and turning her back. With clumsy fingers that shook, he worked on the endless row of pearl buttons that ran from her collar to the base of her spine, revealing creamy flesh and lacy undergarments. He pushed a corkscrew tress from the back of her neck and pressed a kiss to her smooth skin.

Annie shivered and carefully pushed the sleeves down her arms, over her wrists, and let the bodice fall forward. Pulse pounding through his veins, Luke fumbled with the last buttons and helped her push the voluminous white skirts down her hips. He took the dress from her and hung it carefully on a peg beside her veil.

Moving to face her, he ran his palms up the velvety length of her bare arms, smoothed his fingertips across her delicate shoulders to her collarbone, then slid his palm up her neck to cup her face.

She rose to meet his kiss, closer this time, without the yards of fabric between them, without the hard knots of the ornaments on her dress. The fragrance of lilacs and the erotic scent of her skin assailed Luke's senses. She seemed smaller in his arms now, more delicate, more vulnerable.

He found a ribbon at her waist and untied her petticoats. She stepped out of them with his assistance.

He urged her to sit. She lowered herself to the edge of the bed, her willingness an added aphrodisiac he hadn't needed.

He knelt before her and removed her satin slippers, one at a time. Her feet were tiny, her legs slim and curvaceous in white pantaloons and stockings. Her breasts pushed upward over the top of a stiff-looking corset, her nipples visible through the thin white cotton of the garment she wore against her skin. Luke swallowed hard and set the slippers aside.

Never one to run from an adventure, Annie slid her hands across his shoulders, an audible rush of air escaping her lungs. His heart thudded so hard, he wondered if she could hear it.

Her innocent, yet ardent caress of his skin sent a shudder through his body, and he compressed his lips to hold in a carnal groan. They embraced, his chest in the V of her thighs, her mouth against his forehead, her petticoats crushed beneath his knees. He turned his head and nuzzled her neck, her chest, dipped his tongue out to taste her.

She made a sound of surprise, of pleasure.

He cupped her breasts above the corset, rubbed both nipples with his thumbs. "Oh, Luke," she said breathlessly. "Luke, we don't have to stop this time. We don't have to stop ever again. Don't stop."

"My pleasure," he said, and touched his tongue to a hard bud through the cotton.

She gasped.

He found the hooks and eyes and unfastened her corset, the popping sounds loud in the room. He couldn't manage the tiny buttons of her chemise, so she hastily tugged it off over her head.

Her breasts came into view, full and plump, her nipples firm and pink. She moved the garment aside, pausing to untangle a strand of hair from a button.

He managed to help her, then leaned in close to inhale the scent of her skin. She brought her palm to his face, guided him upward until he had to raise off the floor to meet her lips.

They tumbled back upon the bed, and he kissed her leisurely, seductively, calmed now by her reminder that they didn't have to stop. And they didn't have to hurry. She was his now. He had all the time in the world to love her, and nothing and no one could take her away from him.

But when she met his kisses so eagerly, ran her hands over his chest and pressed herself against him as though she couldn't get close enough, urgency sprang up anew. He sat on the edge of the mattress and peeled first one stocking down her thigh, calf, ankle . . . then the other. She didn't help him quite as fluidly with the right as she had the left, and he remembered to be more accommodating.

His hesitation seemed to cause her distraction,

and she rose on one elbow, the fear returning to her features.

"Annie, I told you I don't care. You believe me."

"What if I can't really do this?" she asked, self-conscious now, as if she'd just remembered her limitations.

"Can't make love?"

Her fair skin flushed from her breasts all the way to her cheeks. "I'm not made like other women," she whispered. "I'm afraid I can't be a true wife to you."

Doubly frustrated, not only with physical tension, but with her obvious skepticism, he sat up and thrust a hand through his hair. "Do you have a regular monthly flow?" he asked bluntly.

Crimson, she nodded.

"Then frankly I don't see the problem. You have all the parts you need to make love."

She blinked and he saw the confusion behind her eyes. "But what if it's not good for you? What if I can't—give you pleasure?"

"Annie," he said on an exhale. "Where did that come from?"

She shrugged.

"Why you would worry about not giving me pleasure is beyond me. That would be impossible. If you would be quiet for five minutes, you'd see that this—*ungrounded worry* of yours is the only thing keepin' me from pleasure at the moment."

"I'm sorry."

"You're not the horribly deformed girl you picture in your head. Toss that picture out of there." He thought a moment. "You can ride a horse, can't you?"

"Yes, but—" The denial broke off midsentence.

He gestured with an upraised palm as if to say, *There you have it.*

"Oh." Illumination crossed her features. She raised a tentative smile. "Oh! Take your trousers off, Luke. These, too."

"Remember what I told you?" he said, obeying and sliding his clothing down his legs. "My body is for your pleasure. It belongs to you."

"Oh, my," she breathed, reaching for him.

"Holy—!" He ground his teeth together at the exquisite pleasure of her explorative touches.

"This isn't anything like I imagined."

"I suppose not." Lord, she was a talker. He covered her mouth in a kiss until he couldn't bear her touches another second.

He helped her off with her pantaloons, and she turned one side of her body away from him. "Don't hide from me now. I love all of you, Annie."

She rolled to lie flat on the bed and with an air of solemn apprehension let him look at her. Her hips were not of equal proportions on both sides; one side of her pelvis jutted out a trifle farther than the other. Not caring a bit, he caressed her silken pale skin.

His attention became distracted by the wispy

red-gold curls, the soft curve of her belly, the picture of her as a whole woman, flushed and lovely, with so many vivid emotions lighting her lovely face.

"You are beautiful, Annie," he said, emotion thick in his throat.

"No," she whispered.

"Beautiful." He stroked her from shoulder to hip, knee to toe, kissed the seductive arch of her foot, the curve of her hip, the valley between her breasts, her hot moist lips.

A tiny sob escaped her, hiccuping against his mouth, jutting a breast flat to his chest. He opened his eyes and saw hers, gray-green and luminous with tears. One rolled from the corner of her eye into the hair at her temple. Luke dried the path with his tongue.

A flood followed, a stream of tears that tasted of salt and ate a hole right into his heart. "Don't cry," he said gruffly.

"I'm not crying," she denied.

"What are these then?"

"Sometimes my eyes leak when I'm happy."

"Are you happy?"

She clutched his cheeks fiercely between her palms. "I've never been so happy, Luke. You make me happy. You loving me makes me happy. I have wanted this. Have wished for and dreamed of this. I have loved you since I was ten years old. Don't make me wait any longer, please."

"I wasn't the one holding things up." He touched her then, finding her ready, finding her eager and responsive. Kissing her, he talked to himself, speaking silent reminders of caution and patience.

She would have none of it.

He tried to be gentle; she urged him to boldness. His attempt at preparing her body leisurely was thwarted by her insistence. When he would have paused, she demanded haste. And made a soft cry.

"I didn't want to hurt you," he said.

"It doesn't hurt," she assured him, framing his face with her hands.

"And your hip?"

"I'm perfectly fine. Thank you, Luke, thank you for showing me and loving me."

He groaned and held himself still. He kissed her so she'd know he cherished her.

"I'm not going to break, you know." She moved beneath him, a quivering flex of limbs and muscles that pushed him to the edge.

"I am," he replied. He took a moment to gaze into her lovely eyes, to bask in the need and the love and the fire, collecting himself, but holding back while her muscles tightened and her limbs wrapped his body was like trying to stop a runaway train. The rhythm came from inside his head, the sensations from someplace deep and glittering, and there was no waiting.

Luke shuddered against her.

• • •

She'd fallen asleep. After the sleepless night before and the physical and emotional release of tension, it was no wonder. At the unfamiliar rustle of movement beside her, Annie opened her eyes, disoriented. The first thing she saw was the bare window with the setting sun streaking the sky purple and orange.

"Feel better?"

The deep voice brought a familiar thrill. She turned to see Luke sprawled beside her on top of the covers, dressed in his faded dungarees. Oh, my goodness. She nodded and gratefully noted the crisp white sheet that he'd placed over her. She held it to her breasts. The memory of their eager lovemaking sent a curl of delight all the way to her bare toes.

She had never imagined the wonder of it, the energy and heat of his mouth and body, the sensations of him sliding against her, into her. . . . She closed her eyes.

"Good. I sliced some ham and bread that Glenda sent. Are you hungry?"

Annie examined the freshly painted ceiling a moment, placing her sensual thoughts aside to consider his words and her empty stomach. "A little."

"Want to eat in bed or go out there?"

She studied his vivid blue eyes, let her gaze wander down to that glorious chest. "Read my mind."

His grin inched up. "You wish I'd put my shirt on."

"Nope."

"You can't keep your hands off me, so you want to stay in here."

"Something like that."

He chuckled and kissed her. "Lord, you're fun."

She threaded her fingers into the ebony mat on his chest. "Can I ask you something?"

"Anything."

"Did I—did you . . ."

"What?"

"Did I please you?"

He sighed against her hair. "Any more pleasure and I'd have died of it."

"So I please you as much as those others did?"

He looked at her and frowned. "I wish they had never happened so you didn't have to think about it. There's nothing to compare. Those women were years ago and it wasn't anything like this."

She brushed her fingers over his nipple once. Twice, hoping to distract him from his annoyance.

"I didn't love them, Annie. They didn't love me. Because you love me, what we share is beyond simple physical pleasure. I have never wanted anyone like I want you."

How she needed those words. "Still?"

"Always."

"Did anyone ever watch you shave?"

"Gil. Didn't have the same effect, believe me."

She laughed and snuggled her face against his chest where she'd wanted to place her cheek ever since she'd first seen him without his shirt.

"Do I know any of them?"

"Who?"

"Those women you made love with years ago."

"It wasn't love and Lord, no!"

"Well, I wanted to be sure, just in case I was sitting beside someone in church or shopping at the mercantile or perhaps borrowing a book from the library, that I didn't have to wonder if this woman or that woman had seen your chest—and all the other parts of you."

He was silent a long moment.

"Like that woman who works at the café or one of the girls who takes in laundry. Perhaps Mrs. Krenshaw."

He pulled her head away from his chest and looked her in the eyes, his raised eyebrows creasing his forehead. "You're teasing me!"

She chuckled at his astonishment and loved that she could make him laugh . . . and groan . . . and lose control. Her insides turned to liquid again.

He rolled her to her back and leaned over her to kiss her soundly. "If you have any more questions, ask them now, 'cause I don't intend for this to be a nightly subject. I barely remember anyway."

"I think I know enough," she said, brushing her finger across his lip.

He loved her with his eyes, surveyed her face, her hair, then reached to pull a pin from the tangled mass.

"I must look a fright." Suddenly self-conscious, she reached up to her mangled coiffure and removed the remaining hairpins.

"Oh, yes, a fright. I don't know how I'll stand lookin' at you every morning for the rest of my life."

She placed her hands on his forearm, found the soft hairs there and rubbed. She'd always admired his face, but he was equally incredible all over. So different from her. And so perfect. "Looking at you is such a joy. Can you possibly feel that way about me?"

"Looking at you is like feeling the sun on your face on a mild afternoon. It's like sittin' by a fire and enjoying the heat until your skin feels tight, but you don't want to move away because it feels so good."

She contemplated him in amazement. "Me? Really, you think those things about me? You speak like a poet, do you know that? If you had never touched me, I would have been seduced by your pretty words."

"Someday I'll put that to the test." He ran a finger down her shoulder to the edge of the sheet that covered her breasts and lazily skimmed it back and forth. "Right now touching you is much more fun than talkin'."

"What about the food?"

"Man cannot live by ham and bread alone."

His words were teasing, but the passion in his eyes was real. Annie brushed her fingers along his smoothly shaven jaw, understanding that he'd shaved for her—for this. She caressed his silky thick hair and drew her finger across his brow, down his nose, across his lower lip. "Loving you this much almost hurts," she told him, serious now. "Loving you is fierce and greedy and—and confusing. Sometimes tender, sometimes so desperate I ache inside. I hoped this ache would go away after we were married, but I feel it still."

Luke kissed her tenderly. "Just so you feel me lovin' you back. Feel it?"

She closed her eyes, concentrated on her senses and heard his breath, felt the thud of his heart beneath her palm, smelled his salty skin and the musk of their lovemaking. "I feel it," she whispered.

Chapter Fourteen

They awoke early Sunday morning, and Luke boiled coffee. "I forgot about a teapot and tea," he apologized.

They sat at the table with the sun streaming through the new panes of window glass. The smell of the biscuits he'd showed her how to make lingered in the air. Annie wore her wrapper and a pair of Luke's wool socks. "That's okay," she assured him. "I'll try a cup of your coffee."

He leaned across the table to set down a cup and fill it, and she admired the hair and muscle visible in the open V of his shirt. Her belly quivered at the memories of their afternoon and night together. Embarrassed, she changed the direction of her thoughts. "Are we going to church?"

"Do you want to?" He sat across from her. "Burt is handling the livery today, so I can do anything you'd like." He sipped his coffee.

Anything she'd like was quite tempting. She smiled to herself. Annie couldn't help imagining facing her parents, friends and townspeople, and having them thinking about Luke and Annie's private moments on their wedding night. "Let's not go."

"All right. Guy and Lizzy are bringing our gifts this afternoon. You'll have a lot to do once those things get here. Until then we could make plans. Go over the things we're going to need to make this place a home."

She glanced over his shoulder at the bare window. "Fabric for curtains should be on the list."

Luke got up and found a wrinkled piece of brown paper and a pencil. "Right. A list." He touched the tip of the pencil to his tongue and scratched out a word.

Annie thought of the notes he'd sent her and tenderness washed over her. Astonished that he was truly her husband now, she swallowed welling tears. His strength and agility were tempered by tenderness and compassion. She remembered him walloping Burdy after being provoked, thought of the tasks he performed every day which required power and muscle, and compared that to the poetic words he spoke and the gentle way he touched her.

How had she ever deserved him? What divine quirk of fate had brought this man into her life at an early age and made him fall in love with her?

"Tea. And a kettle," he added, still absorbed in his list. "Sorry about the bucket, you'll need a pitcher and bowl for washing."

"The bucket gets the job done. Can we afford to pay for these things?"

"We have a bank note for the house, but we're not destitute," he assured her. "It'll be tight for a while."

"Maybe I can contribute?" she suggested timidly,

accustomed to any mention of performing tasks being sternly ruled out by her mother.

"How?" he asked without hesitation.

His interest startled her. Now she had to think the idea over. The freedom to actually think about it without fear of censure was exhilarating. Annie straightened in her chair. "The girls and their mothers were largely impressed by my sewing skills. Lizzy's mother said I have a real sense for style and fabrics. I promised to make Charmaine's wedding dress . . . perhaps I could find ladies to sew for."

He didn't say anything, so she hurried to make the idea as plausible as she could. "You'll be gone every day at the livery, and I doubt that the house will take that much time to keep clean. Not that it's too small, I didn't mean that, I only meant that with just the two of us . . ."

Luke tapped the pencil against his cup. "Could you do that here? Or would you need a place to work?"

Annie's jaw dropped. The suggestion hadn't disturbed him in the least! She started to get excited about the idea. "I could do it here. There's plenty of light and I could use the kitchen table for cutting!"

"What would you need?" he asked, the pencil once again hovering over the paper.

"I have scissors and thimbles and just about everything I can think of."

"A comfortable chair," he said. "You'd need a nice place to sit."

Tears smarted behind her eyes. She scooted from her chair and wrapped her arms around him from behind, kissing his ear and his brow. "Oh, Luke! You are the most incredible man!"

He dropped his writing tools and slid his chair back so he could pull her onto his lap.

She framed his face and kissed him. "Thank you, Luke."

"For what?"

"You truly don't know, do you?"

"No."

"For letting me be a real person," she said, her voice hoarse with emotion. "For loving me."

"It's an easy thing loving you." His hands moved up her sides to the swell of her breasts. "You don't have anything on under here, do you?"

"Uh—a nightgown."

He made a face. "One of those flannel contraptions that buttons up to your throat?"

"Not exactly."

He parted her wrapper at the neck. "What, then?"

She flattened her palm over her chest to hold the robe shut. "Something Charmaine and Lizzy gave me. It was the first thing I found when I opened my trunk this morning."

"Well, let's see."

He'd already seen her in the bright light of day and her abnormality hadn't put a damper on his ardor or his desire for her. Feeling scandalous, but also eager to see his reaction, she got to her feet and slowly, watching his face the whole time, opened her wrapper.

His gaze touched every curve of her body through the sheer fabric and he swallowed. "Oh, my."

The list didn't get finished until after lunch.

"Did he like the nightgown?" Lizzy asked in a hushed voice as they washed the few dishes they'd used to eat the casserole and pie she'd brought.

Drying a plate, Annie felt herself blush. "Well, actually, he didn't get to see it until this morning."

"And?"

"And I thought he was going to melt on that chair."

They shared a laugh.

"I told you he'd like it," Lizzy said.

Later, after Guy and Lizzy had gone home, as Annie put away blankets and covered the bed with a brightly colored star quilt, she ruminated over the changes that had evolved in her life over the past months. Besides the miracle of Luke, the newly formed friendships and the acceptance she felt among the townspeople were like a dream come true. Her stifling existence had turned into the full life of a normal woman.

The sadness that her parents couldn't enjoy her newfound abilities and confidence was the only dim spot in a bright future. She could only hope and pray that her mother would come around. Her father had seemed more willing to accept the changes and share in her happiness, but he wouldn't be free to show his approval while his wife still bore such hostility.

The day passed too soon, and the night even more quickly.

On Monday Luke took her to town to order a chair, and while they were there, she posted notices on the walls at the telegraph office and mercantile. That first week she had orders for three dresses.

The work came as a blessing, filling her hands and her mind during the long hours that Luke spent at the livery.

Sunday arrived as a brisk morning with the scent of wood smoke in the air. Since Luke had early-morning work getting rigs ready for the churchgoers, he escorted her to the Renlows' on his way into town.

Aunt Vera hugged her and served a cup of tea and a buttery cinnamon roll. Squealing when she saw Annie in their kitchen, Charmaine pulled a chair beside her to share her latest news about school and the other girls.

"I was beginning to feel as though I'd lost my best friend," she told Annie with a pout.

"She's a bride, Charmaine," her mother scolded. "Newlyweds spend time getting to know each other."

"What more is there to know? Luke's perfect. Right?"

Annie nodded with a grin. That he was. "He said for me to ride along with you and he'll find me in church."

Later, during the hymns, he found her standing beside the Renlows and placed his hand at the small of her back. Annie smiled up, pleased as always to see him, smugly possessive and proud.

This was family-dinner Sunday, and Charmaine had told her that the Renlows would be joining the gathering. Annie hadn't spoken to her parents since the wedding, and the prospect of their unpredictable welcome troubled her.

Her father greeted them after church, but her mother marched toward the Renlows' buggy as though she hadn't seen Annie.

"You're coming for dinner," her father stated.

"We'll be there as soon as I have the livery under control," Luke said with a nod. "After church a few rigs are returned and more are rented."

"I never realized what a consuming occupation you have," Eldon said with a frown.

"It'll be better when I can afford some help,"

Luke replied. "Until then, it's just me. Burt puts in a few hours a week as a favor. He's more of a friend than an employee."

Annie joined Luke as he returned to the livery and handled the customers and the horses with his jacket removed and his shirtsleeves rolled back. She sat on a bench in her plaid shawl and watched him agilely reach and bend to harness animals and hook them to the buggies. He made the tasks look like a work of art, the symmetry and motion pleasing to the eye.

Studying the clean lines of his body and the suspenders that crossed his wide back, she allowed herself to think of the skin and muscle beneath the clothing, and before long she had to remove her shawl. At last he closed the wide double doors, leaving the two of them in shaded seclusion.

"I'll be right back." He returned in a clean shirt, his coat hung over his shoulder on one finger. "Glad I left a few shirts here. I'll have to remember to keep one or two in the back. I'm sure your mother doesn't appreciate the smell of horse the way you do." A grin inched up one corner of his mouth.

Annie got to her feet and stepped forward to kiss him.

"Well," he said when the passionate embrace ended and his eyes had darkened to a sultry blue. "I missed you, too."

She pressed herself against his solid frame, gloried in the masculine feel of his body and his immediate response. Some days the happiness was more than she could contain, more than one person could hold in a lifetime, and she thanked her lucky stars.

Luke tossed his coat on the bench with her shawl, brought his hands up her back, caressed her through her clothing, slid to the front where the hard nubs of her nipples poked against her dress and made an impatient sound low in his throat.

"I wish we were at home," she said, placing her hands over his and closing her eyes. The way he made her feel was like an opiate that made her blood run hot, and she couldn't seem to get enough of that sweet indulgence. She'd discovered something she was graceful at, something that made her feel beautiful. Luke might have to compensate for her lack of agility on a dance floor, might have to carry her across a rutted street and give her balance when she climbed stairs, but there was nothing clumsy about the way she made love with him.

"There's still a bed in the back," he reminded her, his eager lips blazing a path of keen sensation down her neck.

Her skin tingled and her breath caught. "We'll be late."

He touched his tongue to her ear. "They expect us to be late."

She leaned back, gave him a sensual smile, and he swept her into his arms and strode toward the back of the building.

She unbuttoned her dress while he knelt at her feet and removed her shoes and stockings, kissing the bare skin of her revealed limbs. She let her dress fall and he helped her step out of the pool of fabric, then grazed the sensitive backs of her knees and her calves slowly, maddeningly. He ran his palms up, caressing flesh through her pantaloons. She untied the drawers quickly and he stripped them down, then kneaded her bottom.

Annie tugged her chemise over her head. "You still have your clothes on."

He stood behind her and pressed his clothed body against her bare skin, cupped her breasts and teased the crests with his long strong fingers. "Observant of you."

With disturbing slowness he rubbed her nipples while kissing the back of her neck, her shoulders, her ear, whispering love words and letting her feel his arousal through his clothing.

Annie's senses were spiraling in ever mounting tension.

"How did I ever get such a beautiful wife?" he asked, nipping her ear.

Annie shivered and turned in his arms to face him. "I feel beautiful with you."

He lowered his head until his hot moist mouth

found her nipple, and he pulled her against his clothed body. How utterly amazing that she had this effect on a man like him. She slid her knee up between his thighs. Making a sound that sent a frisson of heat down her belly, he stroked her bare back and bottom, pulling her flush against him. He kissed her hard.

Annie pulled away and watched his reaction. His gaze smoldered and his breathing changed, gratifying Annie immeasurably. It was her he desired—her body and her touches that made him whisper her name and shudder with sensation.

She went to work on the buttons on his pants, and he cursed in his frustration to remove them quickly. Peeling open his shirt, she admired the strength and tone of his magnificent body, pressed him back upon the bed and took her fill of admiring and stroking until he clenched his jaw and grabbed her wrists.

With a minimum of words and the gentle coaxing of his work-roughened hands, he showed her she could sit astride him and freely control movement and cadence.

When her limbs trembled, he helped her with strong hands and arms, spoke energy and passion, bracketed her hips firmly and bore the last exerting efforts himself.

Annie lay upon his chest, his heart thudding beneath her breast, feeling as though she had no bones left in her body. The last thing she wanted to do was dress and go see her parents, but the obligation remained.

She sat and pulled together the open front of the shirt he still wore. "I think you'll need another shirt. This one seems to be wrinkled."

"I guess I'll need to keep a larger supply," he chuckled.

They dressed and he escorted her to the buggy he'd left waiting outside, all the while sharing sensual smiles and touches.

Her stomach quivered when they reached the Sweetwater home—her home for as long as she'd been alive, but it had never felt as warm and welcoming as the modest dwelling Luke had built for her.

Mort and Burdell and her father sat on the porch in their wool jackets, Will playing at their feet. When Will saw Annie making her way up the stairs with Luke's assistance, he jumped up to greet her. She bent and scooped him into her arms for a hug.

"I'd better go see if they need help in the kitchen," she said, placing the child on his feet.

"I think it's ready," her father replied. "We were just waiting for you."

"Oh." She turned aside, ignoring Luke's eyes, and stepped into the house before she could blush.

Luke held open the screen and followed. Annie

showed him where to hang his coat on the hall tree beside hers.

"You're here!" Diana called from the dining room. "Just in time. I'll tell Glenda to serve."

Mildred and Aunt Vera's table conversation ceased and Annie's mother gave no indication that she'd noticed their arrival—shockingly poor manners from a woman who prided herself on social graces.

Vera, however, bridged the awkward moment by standing and hurrying forward to hug Annie. She included Luke in her warm welcome, and he seemed caught off guard, his tanned cheeks infused with color.

Charmaine and Glenda came from the kitchen wearing smiles and aprons and greeted them. Before long the family was seated around the table. Glenda served and Eldon carved the beef. Annie caught Luke staring at his arrangement of silverware, and she deliberately picked up a fork, indicating he should select the same one.

He raised a brow and widened his blue eyes comically as he picked up the utensil she'd suggested. She giggled and covered her mouth with her napkin.

Mort included Luke in the conversation, asking about feed prices and the completion of the house. Annie appreciated her uncle's kindness, but then he'd always liked Luke, so his behavior was natural.

"I'd like to see it now that it's finished," Aunt Vera said, her expression animated.

"Oh, me, too!" Charmaine added.

"Well, I'm still making curtains," Annie said. "We need a few rugs, too, I was hoping to find a pattern."

"I can show you how to braid rugs," Vera said.

"Don't buy fabric," Diana added. "I have boxes of scraps that were my mother's in the attic."

"Thank you, both of you!" Annie said, pleased at their generosity.

"Come see the place anytime," Luke said to Mort. "How about next Sunday afternoon? You're all welcome," he said, including Annie's parents and brother.

Charmaine met Annie's gaze, grinned and clapped her hands like a little girl. "I can't wait!"

"I have to meet with one of the Simpson brothers," Burdell said. "And the only time he has to spare is on Sundays."

"You've been putting that off for a month," Diana said. "Another week won't hurt anything." She turned to Luke. "We'll be there. After dinner?"

Luke confirmed the time.

"We don't have chairs yet, but when we do—and when I learn to cook—" Annie began and her words were met by chuckles "—then we'll have you to dinner." She joined in their laughter good-naturedly.

"Tell us where you've placed all your lovely gifts," Charmaine prodded.

Annie eagerly shared her excitement over their wedding gifts, though her mother stood and carried a few dishes to the kitchen instead of listening.

Annie watched her leave, her rejection a returning hurt. Beneath the edge of the linen tablecloth Luke took her hand and squeezed it comfortingly.

Annie noticed Diana giving Burdell a compelling look, and he folded his napkin and placed it beside his plate, then leaned on his elbows and laced his fingers. "We have some exciting news ourselves."

"What is it, Son?" Eldon asked.

"In the spring there will be another Sweetwater in the family," Burdell announced proudly.

Dark eyes bright and her cheeks pink, Diana surveyed the reactions of the family members.

A chorus of congratulations went up around the table.

"Will, you're going to have a baby brother or sister," Annie said to her nephew, and he grinned, simply because she was speaking to him animatedly.

"This calls for a toast," Eldon said and hurried toward the root cellar where he kept a supply of wines for special occasions.

Annie was happy for her brother and sister-in-law. They were wonderful parents and it would be good for Will to have a playmate. She'd always wished she'd had more siblings to keep her company. She tried to gauge her mother's reaction, but the woman seemed indifferent to everything these days.

Sometime later, after the dishes were cleared away and the family members argued their plans for the afternoon, Annie overheard Mort say in a low tone to her father, "Give the boy a chance, Eldon. He's a fine young fella, and he makes your daughter happy. Even you can see that."

Annie paused just inside the doorway to the hall and listened.

"It's going to take some time," her father replied. "I have to live with Mildred the rest of my life, you realize, and she has a blind spot where Annie is concerned."

"I don't understand it," Mort said. "Sometimes she doesn't seem like the same sister I grew up with. Back then she let her hair down once in a while."

"Maybe you could speak with her." Her father's voice sounded hopeful.

"When's the last time you remember her givin' me the time of day? I decided to be a rancher, remember? Not a banker or an attorney or a statesman. As far as she's concerned I threw our father's inheritance away buying land."

"You didn't hesitate to say something to me."

Mort was silent a moment. "You and I are different, Eldon, but we respect each other. Mildred doesn't respect me."

"She loves you, in her own way."

"Maybe."

They moved toward the outer door, and Annie returned to the kitchen. That evening, she told Luke what she'd overheard.

"I'm sorry," he told her. He'd built a fire against the chill wind sweeping down off the mountains and they snuggled on a pile of blankets. "I know you're hurt. But it doesn't bother me. Really."

"It bothers me. Why can't she be happy for me?" she asked, aware of the tremor in her voice. "She just can't see me as a—a normal person—or as a grown-up for that matter."

Her mother's treatment hurt, but as always, Luke's caring touch brought her comfort.

The following Sunday, Annie prepared them a quick lunch after church, then baked two pies from dried fruit Aunt Vera had given her. When their company arrived, Annie scanned the Renlows' wagon and found her mother absent.

"Your mother had a headache," Eldon said, apologetically.

Annie hugged him. "Thank you for coming."

Luke had stoked a blazing fire, and Annie had pulled their few chairs as well as several crates around the hearth. She saw to it that Diana sat in her comfortable chair, then made coffee on the stove and tea in the china pot she'd purchased. Proudly, she served her warm pies on their new blue-and-white china plates.

"You made this?" Her father looked up from his dessert, obviously skeptical. He glanced at Luke.

"Yes," Annie replied. "I can do a lot of things now, Daddy."

"I worry about you being way out here alone while Luke is at the livery."

"There are horses if I needed anything," she replied.

"And you could ride one of them?" Burdell asked, glancing from Annie to Luke.

"Luke's been teaching me how to saddle Wrangler and how to hook him up to the traces on the wagons."

"Is that safe?" Eldon asked, addressing Luke.

"Not knowin' how to do something right is what makes it dangerous," her husband replied. "Annie can do anything she sets her mind to."

Charmaine glanced from Luke to Annie and sighed.

Annie surveyed her father and brother and her husband all eating pie under the same roof and a tide of emotion overcame her. There had been a time when even this much had seemed impossible, and now it had come to pass. There was still hope for friendships to develop, for bonds to strengthen . . . and for her mother to come around.

Over the weeks that followed Annie learned to ride and hitch teams and how to put the animals away properly, how to groom, feed and water them. She learned how much coffee to place in the pot and not to salt bacon gravy. She discovered that a handful of baking soda would put out a fire in a frying pan and that Luke had a fondness for dumplings.

When she made a mistake, Luke laughed and encouraged her to try again. She also learned innumerable ways a man and woman could please each other. Wrapped in his arms each night, she gloried in his soft murmurs, found ways to make him sigh and groan and shudder, as well as ways to elicit laughter. . . . Sometimes they'd barely slept before morning came, crisp and cold, and Luke would start a fire and heat the stove.

Most mornings she cooked him breakfast before he left, but a few times breakfast was forgotten when he returned to bed and snuggled against her beneath the covers, then had to grab his coat and a cold bite of food and run to break the thin layer of ice on the stock tanks, feed the horses and leave for the livery.

Annie sewed beside the fire, comfortably settled in her new upholstered chair, turning out shirt-waists and dresses and dressing gowns ordered by the women of Copper Creek and even several customers from surrounding towns as word spread of her expertise with a needle and thread.

The following month she made enough on her own to pay the bank note and had never experienced such a sense of pride and worth. She rode to Fort Parker with Luke, and he insisted she be the one to enter the bank and present the payment. She returned to him on the boardwalk, the receipt clasped in her gloved hand.

"Thank you, Luke," she choked, the frigid December wind freezing tears on her lashes.

"Don't thank me always," he said, pulling her against the thick wool of his coat. "We're a team, Annie."

She nodded against his neck.

"I have the list we made," he said, pulling a scrap of paper from his pocket. "Shall we make our purchases?"

"I want something special for Diana's baby. And there's something else I want," she told him. "A gift I want to give my mother, and I think I remember where to find it."

"Okay. Let's shop and then have a nice lunch at the hotel."

Luke drove the wagon, laden with packages and supplies, home through swirling flakes of snow. A pristine white layer covered the ground around their house, the cottonwoods blanketed in the sound-absorbing fluff, the aspens still bright yellow in contrast. "Isn't it beautiful?" Annie asked, in awe.

The sound of the horses' hooves and the creak of the wagon seemed loud in the peaceful winter air. The horses blew great gusts of white through their nostrils as they trudged into the yard. "Can you get the fire going while I put up the horses and fork down some hay?"

"Of course. Help me down and I'll carry packages."

She prepared a light supper since they'd eaten a big meal in town. Luke brought harnesses in to repair while they enjoyed the warmth of the fire. In the weeks that followed, Annie used her evenings to work on gifts for Christmas, and had completed something for nearly every member of the family, amazing Luke with her speed and skill.

Something had begun to bother her, and it wasn't until she made a trip into town and called on Glenda while the girls were in school that the puzzle came into place in her mind.

That evening Luke sat at the table with a cup of coffee and the ledger books that held his records of the stock while Annie finished the dishes and started a pot of beans soaking for the next day.

Stomach fluttering, she studied Luke bent over the pages in concentration. She loved watching him, loved spending their evenings together, and appreciated that they didn't have to keep a constant flow of conversation going to be comfortable with each other's company. Annie practiced the words in her mind.

"Luke?" she began.

"Hmm?"

"I have something to tell you."

"Okay."

"You might want to look at me when I say it."

He raised his head and set the pencil down, turning his full attention on her. "Okay."

She brushed her hands over her skirt nervously. "I know we haven't been married very long, barely two months, and we enjoy our time alone together . . ."

He raised a brow in curiosity.

"I hope you're going to be happy about this . . ."

"We won't know until you tell me."

"Yes. Well." She cleared her throat. Thinking better of her position at the side of the table, she stepped closer, right up in front of him.

"Annie, this is very mysterious," he said with a grin. "What is this secret?"

"It's not a secret, really. It's something I only learned today."

"In town? What is it?"

She took a deep breath. "I'm going to have a baby."

Chapter Fifteen

There, she'd said it. Her ears hummed with the rush of nerves, waiting for his reaction.

He stared at her, his blue eyes wide and unblinking.

"I haven't had a monthly since we were married, and I talked to Glenda today, and she asked me a few questions. I went to Dr. Martin's office and he confirmed that there's a baby inside me. Isn't that amazing?"

He laid down his pencil.

"Are you happy?" she asked, hopefully.

"My God, Annie," he said, rising from the chair. He placed his hands on her upper arms and stared into her eyes. A smile broke across his handsome features and he hugged her against him. "Of course, I'm happy!"

He spun her around in a circle, then held her close to his heart. Annie clung to him and allowed her pleasure to flow through her mind and fill her already bursting heart.

Luke pushed her away far enough to gently kiss her lips. "I'm very happy, Annie. I love you. What more could a man ask for?"

"I wonder—do you think I'll be able to take care of him the way he'll need to be taken care of? The doctor didn't seem to think I would have any problems physically. He said I'm healthy and everything's normal. But I suppose I could see a doctor in Fort Parker."

"I have no doubt that you're healthy and normal," Luke assured her firmly. "But if you want to see another doctor, I want you to do whatever you're comfortable with. You'll be able to take care of a baby. Why wouldn't you? What have I told you a hundred times?"

"I know, I know, but this is . . . well it's a little scary."

He hugged her again. "There's nothing to be afraid of. We're together, you and I. It has never mattered to us what people said or thought or that they doubted. We found each other and we've made a marriage and a life together. This is part of that. A very wonderful part of that. Don't let doubts spoil it."

"Oh, Luke, sometimes I don't know how I could be any happier or how my life could be any better, but it just keeps getting more and more full."

"I know," he said, his voice low and husky with emotion. "I know, Annie." He touched her face with tenderness, gazing into her eyes as if she were the most precious thing on earth. He had so much love to give, and he was incredibly generous with himself. He would be a wonderful father. How had she been so fortunate?

Still, she had so many doubts. "I've been remembering all the times I wasn't allowed to hold Will when he was a baby, as though they didn't trust me with him."

"If I've learned anything about your father and brother," Luke said, "it's that *you* are their main concern. If they didn't allow you to hold him it was because they worried for your sake, not the baby's. Just like they don't trust me to care for you properly. It's *you* they care about. Even if their thinkin' has been wrong in the past, they're coming around."

"I've never even held a baby!"

"You'll know how to hold our baby when he gets here. Annie, I'm so proud of you—of both of us." He chuckled. "But you. You are the perfect wife and you'll be a perfect mother."

"I hope so," she said on a sigh. "Are we going to tell my family?"

"About the baby?" He blinked. "Would you let them think you're bakin' too many apple pies? They'll notice eventually."

She laughed. "I'm silly, aren't I?"

"You're silly, but I love you just the way you are."

Annie grew still and silent in his arms, thinking. "Do you suppose that's what's wrong with my mother? She loved me the way I was, and she can't accept me now?" She inspected his expression. "Would you still love me if I changed?"

He stroked her shoulder through her shirtwaist. "You can't always figure everything out," he told her calmly. "Don't upset yourself tryin'."

She knew he was right. She gave too much thought and concern to her mother's rejection. She couldn't go back to being that girl, and if her mother couldn't accept that, Annie would have to build a life without her. But it would hurt.

In the days that followed, she concentrated on thinking about the good things that were happening, loving her husband, planning for their baby.

Annie anticipated Christmas like a little child. She finished two linen shirts for Luke, using his one good shirt as a pattern, and bought him a box of writing stationery and an ink pen. She hid those gifts in the bottom of one of her trunks and wondered if he had something hidden for her.

On Christmas Eve she left a pot of savory stew bubbling on the stove and bundled up, wearing a pair of his boots that she practically walked out of with every step in the foot-high snow, and accompanied him to select a tree from the hillside behind their house.

The tree they selected was too big, because they didn't have any ornaments, but they both loved the size and the shape, so he set it up in the corner of the room and Annie popped popcorn and strung it until her fingers were sore from threading the needle.

They ate the stew and thick slices of buttered

bread on the floor in front of the fire. Annie cleaned up the dishes and rejoined him.

"It smells wonderful." She inhaled the heavy fragrance of their first tree. "Next year we'll have ornaments."

"Next year we'll have a baby," he replied softly.

The wonder of it still amazed her. She leaned against him with a sigh. "What shall we name him? What was your father's name?"

"John."

"John's a good name."

"What if it's a girl?"

"Mmm. Johanna?"

"People might call her Jo."

They discussed names until they agreed they didn't know what they wanted to name their baby and laughed, because they had so much time to think about it.

Annie went to her trunk and returned with her gifts for Luke which she'd wrapped in tissue paper and ribbon. Luke retrieved a small package from his coat pocket and handed it to her. "Mine isn't as pretty," he said.

Annie accepted the gift wrapped in brown paper and string and thought it was beautiful.

Luke opened his shirts and ran his fingers over the delicate stitches in amazement. He got up, slipped out of his flannel shirt and shrugged into his new one. He stroked the sleeve. "I've never had shirts so nice. Thank you."

"You're welcome."

"I'll wear one to dinner tomorrow."

She held up his other package. "Open this one now."

He unwrapped the stationery, ink and pen. "Thank you."

"A businessman should have nice paper on which to write his customers."

"You want me to write their bills on this nice paper?"

She nodded. "It's professional. Soon we'll have letterhead printed for you."

"Sounds pretty fancy," he said with a smile.

He leaned against her and kissed her lips. Annie closed her eyes, but pulled back. "Shall I open mine?"

"Unless you don't wanna know what it is."

"I do!" She pulled the string away and peeled back the brown paper. Inside was a red satin box with gold braid trim and a tassel. Annie opened it to discover a pair of jade earbobs and a matching bracelet on the ivory lining.

"I picked those because you look so pretty in green," he said. "I didn't think you had any."

"I don't, I mean, I didn't." Come to think of it she didn't have more than a simple gold locket besides the pearls her father had given her. "I'll wear my green dress for you tomorrow."

He kissed her again and this time she laid her gifts aside to enjoy his loving attention. No gift could ever be as wonderful as the gift of his love. His accepting, undemanding love.

They fell asleep in their bed that night with the scent of evergreen rich and heavy in the house, the joy of love full in their hearts, and Luke's hand resting protectively over her stomach.

The following morning Luke showed Annie how to warm bricks on the stove. He wrapped them in a horse blanket and placed them on the floor of the buggy for her feet.

A light snow fell as they rode to Copper Creek, the back seat of the buggy filled with packages and Annie's pies.

"Annie, I'd like to stop by my Uncle Gil's, too," Luke told her. "He'll be all alone this year."

"Of course!" she said quickly, wishing things were more comfortable between their families, so that Gil could have been invited to the Sweetwater home.

"Which one of us is going to tell them?" Luke asked.

She didn't have to wonder what he referred to. "I have no idea of the proper etiquette on this subject. It's always been Burdell who has told our family. Maybe that's proper. Or maybe that was just because it's his family. Oh, well, it won't matter. Mother will have a conniption fit in any case." Suddenly, she grabbed his coat sleeve. "They can't do anything, can they? They can't try to take this baby away!"

"Annie, of course not. This is our baby—yours and mine—don't be ridiculous. No one is going to try such a thing."

"You don't know them, Luke. They think I'm helpless!"

"Not any longer. You've shown them differently. Change your thinking, woman."

"You're right. Of course, you're right." She released his arm and rode the rest of the way more calmly.

Luke delivered her and their packages and desserts into her parents' home and took the horse and buggy to the livery where they'd be protected from the weather, then returned on foot.

He knocked and cleaned his boots on the porch. Diana opened the door with a warm smile. "Merry Christmas!" She hung his coat and hat on the hall tree. "Everyone is in here," she said, leading the way to the parlor where the Renlows had already joined the Sweetwaters.

An enormous tree had been decorated with glass ornaments and beads and brightly feathered silk birds. Lit candles balanced on the branches, creating a warm glow in the room. Luke had never seen anything like it, and experienced a twinge of shame over the bare tree in their home.

Mildred seemed in a hospitable mood, serving hot chocolate, and even handing Luke a cup and saucer, though she didn't meet his eyes.

A cherry wood tea cart held a silver service

with steaming tea and orange-glazed cinnamon rolls. "Mmm, did Glenda make these?" Annie asked, biting into one.

"She came and baked yesterday," Mildred replied.

Luke had noted the festive decorations and the elegant furnishings. The gleaming silver and fancy pastries, the talk of Mildred's cook shed an unkind light on all that Annie had given up to marry him. Her sacrifice humbled him. He could never do enough to show her his gratitude.

"I brought pies," Annie said.

The pride in her voice warmed him clear to his soul. Her accomplishments were enormous, and anyone who couldn't see that was a blind, shallow person.

"Apple?" her father asked, one brow raised.

Luke wanted to kiss him for sounding appreciative.

His beautiful wife nodded, her new earrings bobbing. "I haven't figured out pumpkin yet."

"Good for you," Diana said. "I've barely figured out the stove."

Burdell agreed with a nod that earned him a quelling look.

"Do you have help?" Luke asked Diana. Was Annie the only one without a cook and housekeeper?

She nodded. "Not a gem like Glenda, but Mrs. Hopkins is efficient and dependable. She helps with Will, too, and will be ever so beneficial with a new little one."

Luke had cowardly second thoughts about telling her family. If Diana had help, what would they think of Annie having to keep house and mother all on her own—as well as sewing to add to their income? Suddenly, he worried that he wasn't at all the husband Annie had needed, if he couldn't provide as well as she deserved.

The women drifted toward the kitchen and dining room, leaving Luke with Annie's father, uncle, brother and little Will. The child played with a set of carved horses he'd brought from home—a gift that morning. Burdell set up checkers on an inlaid drum table and asked Eldon to play.

Eldon declined, wanting to read a newspaper while the women were gone. Mort declined, as well, closing his eyes where he sat.

Burdell glanced at Luke.

Luke glanced at the board.

Their eyes met.

"Want to play?" Burdell asked finally.

Luke wasn't sure if he did or not, but he wasn't going to decline this first measure of truce. "Sure."

He seated himself across from Annie's brother and Burdell said, "You move first."

The game progressed slowly. Burdell played intensely, and Luke didn't know if the man was always fiercely competitive or if he just couldn't stand to lose to Luke. Having spent many a winter night playing checkers before a fire with his uncle, Luke held his own. The aromatic cooking smells drifted to them, and Luke's mouth watered.

He glanced up to find Burdell studying his face. His gaze went to Luke's mouth and Luke raised a concealing finger to his lip, self-consciously hiding the scar.

"Dinner is served," Charmaine called from the doorway. Annie stood beside her cousin, and her eyebrows shot up at the checker game underway. "Who's winning?" she whispered to Luke, when he took her arm.

"Nobody yet," he replied.

All the food had been placed on the table and the marble-topped buffet, the ham having been sliced before it was carried out, so everyone helped themselves and ate. Luke marveled at the bountiful feast.

"Shall we have our dessert later?" Annie asked.

The men agreed with that suggestion, and Burdell followed Mort and Eldon to the parlor.

Luke stayed to help, scrubbed a roasting pan and a kettle, and went for wood and fresh water as he was accustomed to doing at home, and dried a stack of plates that Annie had washed.

Mildred kept her distance, covertly watching him. Charmaine questioned Luke about the amount of snow in the foothills. Vera handed him a jar of her fudge sauce and asked him to unscrew the lid. Vera was a ranch wife, he realized, accustomed to doing her own cooking and laundry, so perhaps Annie didn't think it was so awful going without.

Mildred appeared to want to dry and sort her silverware herself, so he excused himself.

"Thank you for the help, Luke!" Vera and Charmaine called. Annie gave him a sweet little wave with her dish towel.

"Does he always help you like that?" Charmaine asked as he left the room.

"You wanna finish that game?" Luke asked Burdell, and the man rose to take his place at the game table.

They both had three kings left when the women returned from the kitchen with fresh coffee.

"Shall we save it for later or call it a draw?" Burdell's dark gaze bored into Luke's purposefully.

Luke knew he was referring to more than the checker game. The man's eyes were serious, his expression intense. "Let's call it even," he replied.

Something flickered in Burdell's eyes. He gave a curt nod and placed the game pieces back to their original starting positions.

An old score had been settled here, without so many words, without apology or accusation. Luke thought of the baby, frustrated that his and

Annie's excitement had to be dulled by their fear of this family's reaction. He was averse to opening any new wounds right away.

"Can we open presents now?" Annie asked, and she and Charmaine gave each other wide-eyed looks of excitement. He discovered quickly that Annie's eagerness was over the gifts they'd purchased and that she'd made for her family rather than expectation of what she would receive.

Luke remained astonished that she'd turned out so many handsomely made garments in such short time. Her father opened his gift and examined the shirt she'd sewn for him.

"This is a finely tailored shirt," he said. "Did you find someone out East to make it?"

"I made it myself, Daddy," she told him.

"You what?" He looked at it again.

"I made it myself."

Speechless, he turned it over, examined the cuffs and the collar and the exquisite stitches. "Why didn't I know you could do this?"

"I guess I never had the opportunity before. I've always done needlepoint, but never had a chance to sew. It comes easily for me. Besides, it's fun."

"It's an extraordinary gift," her father said.

Annie's face glowed with his simple praise. Her eyes were shining when she glanced at Luke. He gave her a smile and offered Eldon an appreciative glance. Could the man possibly know how much his approval meant to his daughter?

For Vera she'd chosen a bottle of perfume, for Charmaine a pair of gloves with pearls and lace sewn across the knuckles. Mort received a horse book Luke had selected.

Annie had made Burdell a vest and Diana a lace-edged pillow as well as a baby blanket. They'd chosen a wooden train pull-toy for Will, and he dragged it across the floor making *choo-chooing* noises.

Mildred watched the interaction with mild interest, the package Annie had handed her still on her lap.

"You haven't opened yours, Aunt Mildred," Charmaine said.

Annie cast her mother an openly hopeful look, and Luke took a deep breath.

Annie's mother steadied the heavy gift on her lap. Expressionlessly, she untied the silver bow and let the paper fall back, exposing a flat wooden hinged box.

Unfastening the catch on the front, she raised the lid. Inside lay two rows of small tubes and an array of long slender brushes.

Annie handed her something she'd hidden behind the divan. "These, too, Mother." She lifted brown paper away and showed Mildred the blank canvases.

"A paint set," Charmaine said, and glanced at Annie.

"Your aunt used to paint years ago," Mort told Charmaine.

Annie's mother looked up, her eyes dark and unreadable.

"Do you like it, Mother?" Annie asked. Her vulnerability tore at Luke's heart.

"Why did you buy this?" Mildred asked. "Where did you get the money?"

"Well, I *worked* for the money," Annie explained, as if the fact should have been obvious, and as if the question in itself wasn't rude.

"Worked for it?" Her mother arched one eyebrow.

"Yes, I—I've been sewing. For the ladies in town. I have a lady in Fort Parker now, too."

"When you mentioned sewing, I thought you meant lady's work. Not hiring yourself out as a common seamstress."

"There's nothing shameful about honest work," Luke said. "I'm proud of Annie's sewing."

Annie tried to change the subject by answering her mother's other question. "I bought supplies for you because you told me you liked to paint at one time. I thought you would like to try it again."

Mildred closed the wooden lid. "I'm not living in a fantasy world, Annie. I have learned to accept my life the way it is, and not to foolishly pine for things that cannot be."

Her words brought silence to the room. No one seemed to move or breathe.

"I don't see why you can't still paint," Annie said in a cajoling voice. "Just because you haven't done it for a while, doesn't mean you can't start again."

"A person needs tutoring to be any good," she said. "Techniques must be learned."

Annie's father had grown still. He studied his wife and daughter with a pained expression.

"Well, I think you could still try it for fun," Annie said.

"Not everyone's life revolves around fun," Mildred countered, her words obviously hurting Annie. "Some of us take our responsibilities seriously."

Annie's once gay smile had already faded. She turned luminous eyes to her father, who looked away, and then toward Luke.

"What's really special," he said, "is when your responsibilities seem like fun because you're doing what you want to do." He gave Annie an encouraging smile.

"I'm very impressed with your sewing skills," Charmaine added.

Annie gave her a halfhearted smile.

"There are more gifts to open," Luke said, trying to sound cheerful, and wishing instead he could stuff a wool sock in Mildred Sweetwater's mouth and give her a good shake. "Annie hasn't opened hers."

Annie opened gloves and perfume and a tea set

and books. Luke received a pipe and tobacco from the Renlows, a belt and handkerchiefs from Diana and Burdell. Eldon had purchased them an oval Florentine design gold-framed mirror. Burdell and Diana got one just like it.

Charmaine gave Luke and Annie an unusual dinner-plate-size round picture of two horse heads in a circular ebony frame. "I thought you'd like something for your mantel, and the horses made me think of you."

"That's very thoughtful," Luke told her. "It will look perfect on the mantel."

Annie hugged her cousin.

"And it's a reminder," he heard Charmaine tell her softly, "that the next too-good-to-be-true man is mine."

Eldon made a big production over Annie's pies next, as though he wanted to make up for her mother's cold responses.

They sat about with full stomachs, the scents of coffee and cinnamon and evergreen in the air, and Luke brought up the subject he and Annie had agreed to share this day. Might as well get it out and deal with it. "Annie and I have something exciting to tell you," he said.

Heads turned their way.

"Do you want to?" he asked her. She was seated on the upholstered footstool in front of him.

Her eyes let him know she was still uncertain.

She seemed to think a moment before she nodded and reached back for his hand.

He tried to reassure her with a firm, but gentle grasp.

Without preamble, she spoke the words. "We're going to have a baby."

Poignant silence prevailed.

"We're incredibly happy, and we want this more than anything," she rushed on. "I've been to the doctor and he says there's nothing to prevent me from having a healthy child."

Mildred's hand came up to cover her mouth.

"What doctor did you see?" her father asked, finally speaking out.

"Dr. Martin in town."

"Perhaps you should see a doctor back East—" he began.

"Dr. Martin has always been perfectly capable of caring for me," Diana spoke up. "He delivered Will and he's going to deliver this baby." She placed a hand on her slightly protruding belly.

"Your babies have always been normal," Mildred interrupted. "This is Annie's baby!"

Annie's whole body jerked. "My baby is normal, too!" she cried, sitting up straight and facing her mother. "Don't you say such a cruel thing! Don't you dare spoil this, too!"

Luke leaned forward and placed his arm around Annie's shoulder. She trembled with obvious hurt and anger. "It's all right, Annie, my sweet," he said softly against her hair to calm her.

"Mildred, there's no cause for upsetting Annie," Eldon said logically.

Will, having heard the voices, came to stand at his father's knee. "Nannie cry?" he asked, his brown eyes wide with concern.

"Nannie's just fine," Burdell told his son and pulled him onto his lap. "Nannie's going to give you a cousin to play with."

Annie's head turned toward her brother, and Luke felt the tension ease from her body. Burdell's gaze went from Annie's to Luke's and Luke silently thanked him for this change of heart and support.

Diana touched her husband's arm as though he'd justified her belief in him.

Mildred stood, kicking aside the paint box, straightened her silk skirts and her spine and left the room with her chin high.

The tension seemed to leave with her, especially now that Burdell had become an ally of sorts. Luke wouldn't bet money that the man would spit on him if he caught fire, but at least he'd shown some mercy toward his sister's feelings, and for that Luke was grateful.

Charmaine moved over to Annie and Luke released her so that the two could embrace. Annie surely needed comfort and assurance from the women in her family now more than ever. He was her husband and he would do everything he could to make her happy and protect her, but she needed her family, too.

Charmaine touched Annie's cheek and gave her a watery smile, amazing Luke at the tenderness and love the two shared. He'd never seen a similar display of affection, and had to wonder how Annie's mother could hold herself apart from people who had so much love to give. Since he didn't have much family, he was thankful now that the Renlows would be a good example for his child.

After several minutes, Charmaine got up and helped Diana clear away wrapping and dishes. Burdell knelt in front of Annie. Luke kept his face hidden behind Annie's shoulder, so as not to interfere.

"Your baby is just fine, Annie. We all know that," he said to his sister, his voice softer than Luke had ever heard it. "You will be a wonderful mother. Remember, this is all new, and sometimes new things take some getting used to. I'm seeing a whole different person than the Annie I knew."

"It's still me, Burdy," she said. "Still the same Annie. But I've been able to grow up and live—really live for the first time. Why can't Mother accept that?"

"I don't know. Maybe she thinks you don't need her any more. Maybe she's jealous of your new life without her. You were her whole life for a lot of years."

"Maybe," she said. "But why can't she see that I don't want a life without her? She's the one closing me out."

"I don't know," he said again, and Luke understood his inadequacy to come up with an answer for Annie when she asked those questions that ripped into a man's heart. Annie was still the apple of this family's eye.

Burdell got up, meeting Luke's eyes in a brief exchange, then left the room.

Eldon and Mort had taken seats at the checkerboard, and Will napped on the divan.

"I want to go now," Annie said, turning to face Luke.

He gave her his most encouraging smile. "You okay?"

She nodded. "I just want to go home."

"I'll go get the buggy. I'll need to feed and water the horses, so it will take me a while. You'll be all right?"

"I'll watch their game until you come back. They never call a draw."

Mildred had gone to her room without returning, so Annie hugged and kissed and thanked the rest of her family. Her father put on his coat and carried her out to the buggy and Luke, understanding his need to take care of his daughter once in a while, trudged behind.

"Thank you for the shirt, Annie," he told her, waving from the curb.

"Thank you for the mirror, Daddy!" she called.

Luke prodded the horse forward.

She snuggled against his side, and he wrapped his arm around her for warmth and security. "You sure impressed them with your sewing," he said.

"Yeah. I did, didn't I?"

"Their little Annie can make shirts and pies . . . and a baby. No wonder they need some time to get used to things."

She chuckled. "Let's stop by your Uncle Gil's. I hope his shirt fits him."

Gil's ranch house was obviously a man's domain, furnished for practicality alone. Annie had saved a pie for him, and he thanked her. His astonishment over the shirt she'd made him was a pleasure, and he congratulated them on the news about the baby.

"I don't have any children, so some little Carpenters are mighty welcome around here," he told Annie.

Annie was glad they'd stopped, but eager to get home, so she was grateful when Luke made their goodbyes and helped her into the buggy.

He carried her into the house, brought in all their new gifts and took the rig to the barn. When he returned, Annie had started a fire and placed the round horse picture on the mantel beside the satin box her jewelry had come in. Luke hung his coat and hat and glanced at the plain tree sadly lacking glass balls or candles or beads, thinking again of the material things he hadn't been able to supply.

Annie sat in her chair watching the firelight dance on the tree. "Isn't it beautiful?" she asked.

"It's just a tree," he said. "Your family's is nicer."

"Fancier, maybe, but not nicer," she disagreed. "Glenda probably decorated it as part of the household chores. But nobody *loved* it. Not like we love this one."

He couldn't help but be amazed by her joy in simple things, her pleasure in doing routine tasks and owning the barest minimum of possessions. Annie made all things new and lovely by her pure childlike enjoyment of life and its simple pleasures.

And now with a baby on the way, life would only get better. They had withstood the tests of her family thus far, weathered their disapproval by showing them that their love was greater than the obstacles. Gradually her family was being won over by Annie's enthusiasm and obvious joy. Eldon had softened, and today even Burdell had shown his support.

Nothing could get in the way of their happiness now.

Chapter Sixteen

Luke had lost weight over the winter, she noticed, though she fed him well. He was always working—always cutting wood or shoeing horses or breaking ice from the stock tanks—between the livery and the house he barely rested. Part of his labors was to make things easier for her, and she worried that she was a burden. He grew leaner and more muscled and Annie grew fatter and lazier.

Sometimes she was so tired, she would try to sew and wake up an hour later, the fabric wrinkled in her lap. Other times she'd make up her mind to complete a task and end up beneath her quilt in front of the fire. Luke had made her a thick pallet and instructed her to rest whenever she felt the least bit weary. And that was always. Or so it seemed for most of the winter months.

Spring arrived, and with it a new burst of energy and a renewed vitality. In April, the snow melted and rushed down the mountains, spilling over the creek beds and the riverbanks and turning grass and trees green. Mares foaled and Luke seemed to always be with the horses.

Annie had sewn an entire wardrobe of tiny gowns, hats, blankets and flannels for their baby, lovingly pressed each item and packed all between dried rose petals in a trunk.

Luke bought a cradle and brought it home to her one evening. She sat down in her chair and cried.

"What's wrong?" he asked, concern etching his lean features. He knelt in front of her.

"You're so tired," she said, touching his face. "And I'm so—fat."

He chuckled. "You're not fat. You're carrying a baby, there's a difference."

"But I'm clumsier than ever. You must see that."

"No, I don't," he denied. "You're beautiful."

She smiled at him through her nonsensical tears. "It's been a hard winter, hasn't it?"

He shrugged. "We've paid our bank notes each month. We haven't lost an animal, and we're going to have stock to sell this summer. I knew it wouldn't be easy at first. We both did."

She sighed. "I know. I'm just being a silly woman."

He kissed her. "I need a bath, you silly woman. How about helping me heat some water?"

She did, pouring warm water over him as he sat in the copper tub in the kitchen. She took the soap and cloth and caressed him with the premise of getting him clean. She ended up without her clothes on, shivering as he dried her in front of the fire, his touch creating an internal blaze.

"You're beautiful, Annie," he said, and kissed her round belly, her tender breasts, caressed her with his hands and his tongue and loved her well and splendidly until she had no doubts about his thoughts of her beauty.

She made a simple supper of sliced beef and bread and cheese, and they ate it before the fire, her in her chair, Luke at her feet. He surprised her with oranges a customer had given him that day. No dessert had ever tasted as sweet or as good.

They slept wrapped in each other's arms, the world at bay outside their home.

Spring rains came, pelting the already green and muddy land, and one afternoon the sky grew so dark that Annie lit lanterns and stoked the fire. She had a cookbook open on the table, and worked at rolling noodles as thin as the directions instructed. On some level of consciousness, she noticed that the horses in the corral had been restless for a time. Luke always left the sliding door open so that they could get in out of the weather during the day, so she didn't give the disturbance much thought.

An earsplitting cracking noise startled her so badly she dropped the rolling pin and grabbed the back of a chair for support. Horses whinnied in high-pitched shrieks.

Grabbing a jacket from a peg, Annie opened the door to peer out through the gray rain. One corner of the corral smoldered, dark smoke curling into the heavy air. The horses milled and reared in fright.

Lightning struck again, an enormous jagged arc that hit a tree on the hillside with a crack and disappeared into the heavens in a split second. Annie's heart raced painfully. The terrified horses shied and knocked together, and one of the colts fell and struggled to its feet, covered with mud.

Annie sloshed toward the corral, trying to hurry, but needing to watch her balance in the mud. She reached the gate and let herself in, closing it securely behind her and inching her way along the fence toward the building. If she rolled the door open wider, maybe they'd run into the building instead of trampling each other.

The mud inside the corral was slicker, churned by the animal's hooves and it took all the strength in her legs to pull her feet out with each step. She reached the doorway and balanced herself on the door, then strained against the wood to roll it open wider.

She stood panting, staring at the horses, that still reared and whinnied in panic. From the corner of her eye, Annie caught movement at the edge of the woods, and she squinted at the skinny doglike creatures slinking back and forth in a predatory fashion. Wolves!

If she could get one of the horses inside, perhaps the others would follow. Clinging to the fence for support as well as safety, she slowly edged her way, knowing she should be hurrying. "Here, boy," she said to Wrangler, reaching a hand toward him. His ears pricked back, but he remained where he stood, his flanks trembling.

Wrangler was used to her, and she knew he was docile and would easily follow her lead if she reached him.

Annie released the fence and slogged through the mud across the corral to reach the animal. She grabbed his halter and led him toward the barn. He followed as she knew he would. "Good boy, easy now. Let's get the others inside where it's safe, all right?"

As she neared the doorway, she heard the sucking sounds as the other animals' hooves moved in the mud behind her. A horse shot ahead into the barn. Relieved, Annie hoped the others would follow now. She would get them into stalls and stay in the barn until she was sure the wolves were gone. She had no idea what kind of a threat they were to humans, but she wasn't taking any chances.

A crack of lightning split the air, her surroundings flashed blindingly white, and Annie's ears popped. Horses screamed and bolted. Wrangler sidestepped, and she lost her hold on his halter. In a split second she was smashed painfully against the doorway, and instinctively rolled into a ball.

Hooves flashed and mud flew. Annie covered her head and endured the whirlwind of legs and hooves. Dimly, she noted that the corral was empty, and dragged herself up to roll the heavy door closed, shutting the horses safely inside, closing out the dim light of day. How long would it be before Luke came home?

Pain wracked her abdomen and she bent over with a cry, falling to her knees on the wet straw-covered earth in the darkness. The smell of horse and straw and blood was strong. She closed her eyes and succumbed to darkness.

Luke would never be sure if he'd done the right thing. Perhaps if he'd carried her to the house and warmed her first, the baby would have made it. But when he'd found her there inside the barn in a brackish puddle of blood, his first thought had been to get her to help—to get her to town and to the doctor. He'd hitched a horse to the buggy, laid her gently on a pile of horse blankets on the floor and driven like the devil was on his backside.

"I'm sorry," Dr. Martin said, his glasses on his head, his sleeves rolled back and his face drawn. "The baby didn't make it."

"Annie?" Luke asked first, ignoring his breaking heart to find out about his wife. "How's Annie?"

"She's fine. The bleeding has stopped. She's pretty bruised, but nothing is broken."

"Should I have not moved her?" he asked. "Maybe I should have taken her to the house and tried to stop the bleedin' myself." He jammed his fingers into his scalp painfully.

"We can't know what would've made a difference," the doctor replied. "You saved her life by bringing her here. That much I know. Whatever happened to her, I don't think the baby had much of a chance."

In agony, Luke dropped his head back and stared at the ceiling for a moment. "Can I see her now?"

The doctor nodded. "I've given her something for pain, so she's not too alert. That's for the best, right now."

Luke entered the small room where his wife lay against white sheets, her hair loose and tangled, her face as pale as death. His heart ached at the sight. "Annie," he said, sitting beside her and taking her hand.

Her eyelids fluttered open. She recognized him and a ghost of a smile touched her lips. "Luke," she whispered.

"I'm here." He brought her hand to his mouth, pressed his tear-streaked cheek to the back while regret and heartache seeped through his bones. He wanted to scream and rage aloud at the injustice. His throat ached with unshed tears. He imagined Annie's fear, her pain, and he wondered repeatedly what had happened. He'd seen the singed corral and knew the horses must have been terrified of the storm.

He'd ridden home to check on them, thank goodness, for that's when he'd seen the corral and the closed door and found her inside on the floor.

Annie slept and he thanked God for that small mercy. At least she didn't have to face their loss while her body was weak and bruised.

Annie awoke and stared at the ceiling, unwilling to move because of the pain that shot through her body. Something was different. Something was wrong. She moved her hand to her belly and found only soft flesh beneath the blanket. She knew immediately. Her physical pain was only a degree of the torturous agony slicing through the inside of her—like someone had taken a rusty knife and cut out her heart.

"O-oh!" she wailed aloud, and Luke leaped from a chair beside her to kneel at her side and take her hand away from her belly. He pressed the back against his lips.

Tears coursed down his cheeks and everything inside her went numb in self-preservation. She couldn't look into his red-rimmed eyes. She couldn't endure his pain and hers, too. She couldn't bear to know she'd failed him and brought such suffering and anguish to a man who deserved better.

"Annie, I'm so sorry," he said, his voice ravaged.

She sobbed until her chest hurt and her tears

were exhausted. Dr. Martin came and forced her to drink a powder he'd dissolved in tepid water. She slept again and when she awoke, Luke hadn't moved from her side.

"I saw the corral where lightning struck," he said.

"There were wolves," she told him, her voice oddly calm.

"Wolves, too?"

"I got Wrangler almost inside, but lightning struck again and spooked the herd. I think one of them must have pushed him into me."

"I'm sorry, Annie," he said, his voice raw. "Sorry I wasn't there for you."

"What day is this?"

"The same day," he answered. "You've only slept a few hours."

She wanted to tell him she was sorry, but she was a bigger coward than he was. Admitting her failure was too difficult right now. "What was our baby, Luke?" she had to ask. "Did you see him?"

He nodded. Swallowed. "A boy."

"Where is he?"

"I buried him on our land while you were resting. I wrapped him in one of the blankets you made. I called him John when I said a prayer, is that okay?"

Tears rolled from her eyes and fell back into her hair. "Yes."

"I love you, Annie."

She closed her eyes and heard him breathe.

After what seemed like hours later, voices sounded outside the room. Luke raised his head from the bed and listened.

The door opened and Annie's mother and father entered the room. Her mother covered her mouth with a handkerchief and wept when she saw her. They rushed forward and Luke stood and backed away. Her father took her hand. "Annie," he said hoarsely. "I'm so sorry."

"We're here, darling," her mother said, and stroked her forehead with a soft cool hand.

From the corner of her eye, Annie noticed when Luke left the room. Her gaze went to her mother, found her eyes. "You were right, Mother. I did disappoint him."

After their visit, Annie instructed the doctor that she didn't want to see her husband.

"But he wants to be with you," the man said.

"I don't want to see him."

"He needs you," he told her. "Shutting people out won't do you any good."

"I don't want to see him!" she said, more emphatically.

He studied her for a moment. "All right." He turned and left the room.

She rested listlessly for days, showing no interest in the books her mother brought, only eating because she didn't have the strength to resist. She had never been worthy of Luke's lofty expectations and his idea of her. Losing his baby had proven it.

It was easy to fall back into the familiar routine of being an invalid, of not having to make decisions and letting her mother direct her days. Mildred was kinder and more attentive than ever, seemingly glad to have Annie in her charge, but occasionally Annie caught her looking at her with a sad strange expression.

She didn't want to face Luke. Didn't want to see his disappointment in her or the regret she knew he must feel.

When she was able to be moved, she said to her mother, "I want to go home with you."

Her father came for them in one of Luke's buggies, and Burdell left work to assist him.

Burdell carried her into the Sweetwater house, to her old bedroom and placed her in the bed her mother had prepared. "What are you doing, Annie?" he asked.

"I'm grieving."

"What about Luke?"

"What about him?"

"He needs you. You have us to comfort you, but he has no one."

"Fine thing for you to be thinking about Luke Carpenter's feelings all of a sudden," she stated flatly. "He'll do just fine without me. He's better off without me. I've been a burden to him since the day we met. Just look at him if you don't think so. He's thin and tired and worked half to death because I never carried my share. And now he's lost his son because of me."

"That's not true."

"It is true. I'm tired, please let me rest."

Burdell walked from the room slowly, exchanging a look with his mother at the doorway.

A heavy sense of loss and self-blame wrapped around her like a shroud. Annie glanced at the gaily dressed porcelain dolls lining the window seat, allowed her gaze to find her wheelchair, then closed her eyes against the sting of tears. She was back where she'd started—where she belonged.

Eldon returned the buggy, his face pulled and drawn. "She asked to be taken to our home. She's settled into her bed and quite comfortable."

Luke had spoken to the doctor that morning and had been delivered the crushing news. Annie didn't want to come home with him. He wanted to stomp into her room and confront her, but the doctor had warned him about upsetting her.

So he'd returned to the livery, taken out his fear and frustration over the searing forge, on the glowing iron, pounding . . . pounding.

Luke didn't know what to say to Annie's father. "Thank you," he returned, knowing it was a lame sentiment.

"I'm sure she just needs some time," Eldon said.

"Yes." But why didn't she need him? Did she blame him? Did everyone blame him? "I thought I could take care of her," he said.

"You did."

Luke shook his head. "No, I didn't. The wolves. She would have needed to know how to use a gun, and I never showed her." He stared at the mountains in the distance. "She thought the horses were more important than her own safety."

"Maybe she just needs some time," Eldon said again, as though trying to convince them both.

Luke wanted to believe it. In the days and nights that followed he tried to believe it, tried to understand why she needed time away from him, why her heart didn't ache for him like his did for her.

After several nights of sitting in front of the fire, looking at the pins and needles sticking out of the arm of her chair, touching her clothing and her hairbrush while his guts wrenched, staring at the empty cradle until the wee hours of the morning, he packed his clothing, strung the horses on a tether rope, and moved to the livery where there were fewer memories.

Even here the nights were endless, filled with regrets and worries and dry-eyed mourning.

On Thursday morning, he went to see her and found her on the porch in the sunlight, a shawl draping her shoulders. She sat in her wheelchair and the sight slammed him like a punch in the chest. Had something gone wrong that he hadn't been told about? Why hadn't someone let him know?

"Annie?" he said. "What is it? Was your leg hurt? Something broken that I didn't know about?"

Her head raised. She'd been studying a book in her lap. Her gray-green eyes flickered over him and shuttered quickly.

"You know what's wrong with me."

"No, no, I don't. Tell me."

"Besides losing your son, you mean?"

Her words disturbed him. "He was our son, Annie."

Pain flickered across her delicate features. She composed them. "Yes. You know the extent of my injuries. What are you asking?"

"I guess I'm asking why you're sitting in this damned chair!"

"This is where I belong," she said flatly. She indicated the chair, the porch, the house.

"Have you been walking?" he dared, starting with another approach.

"No."

"You probably need to exercise your legs."

"It doesn't matter."

He studied the delicate slope of her nose, her ivory cheeks, the ringlets at her temple, and craved touching her. He missed her so badly he could taste her and smell her just by thinking. "I've missed you."

She turned away from him and gazed at the horizon. She would be right to blame him. She was more unhappy now than she'd been before they'd started seeing each other. He loved her more than anything, but he'd loved her selfishly, trying to make her more like other people. If he'd left her alone, she wouldn't have to suffer like this now. He was the one who had convinced her to get out of that chair and take on the world.

And because she had—because she'd trusted him—he'd taken her from her safe environment and protective family and let this happen to her. They would all be justified in hating him. He hated himself.

"I'm sorry, Annie," he said softly. "I'll do whatever I can to make it up to you. I'll leave you alone if that's what makes you happy."

She nodded, and he took that as his signal to leave her alone. Maybe she was better off here. Maybe he'd been fooling them both into thinking he could be everything she needed. Obviously, he hadn't been.

Mildred opened the screen door and appeared with a tray holding a teapot and cups. Seeing Luke, she drew up short, then collected herself and moved past him. "Here's your tea, darling," she said to her daughter. "Are you comfortable here in the sun?"

Annie nodded, and Mildred set down the tray and poured a cup full, handing it to Annie.

Annie accepted it. Both of them behaved as though Luke wasn't there. With an ache in his heart and his throat, he backed away from the scene, leaving Mildred to tend to her daughter's comfort, leaving the Sweetwaters to care for his wife.

Mounting the horse he'd left at the gate, he rode away, once again the outsider.

No longer would he have a wife to come home to at night. There would be no son to teach to ride, no children to inherit all he was working for. But work he did, because it was all he had left.

"Do you want to hold her, Annie?" Diana asked. Her sister-in-law approached her with the pink flannel-wrapped bundle. Annie'd been told of Elizabeth's birth the month before, and had asked about Diana's health and recovery. Since Annie hadn't been out of the house for weeks, she hadn't been to Burdell's home or to church for the baby's christening. This was the first time she'd seen their new daughter.

Her niece had wispy dark hair and a delicately round face. She held her tiny hands right up by her face, and squinted her eyes open. Annie wondered what color her baby's hair had been, whether his eyes would have been blue or green.

She could have asked Luke about his hair. "No, I don't want to hold her," she said, her heart pounding too fast at the thought.

Diana held Elizabeth right down beside Annie, where she could smell the infant's milky essence. She felt a painful twinge in her breasts. The child was a miracle, a miniature person, perfect in every way, fair lashes, translucent fingernails, wrinkly knuckles and shell-like ears.

Annie looked up and met Diana's compassionate gaze. Tears of sympathy swam in her sister-in-law's dark eyes. "I am so sorry," she whispered. "We took flowers to your little John's grave. It's in a beautiful spot. Someone had planted forget-me-nots."

Luke, Annie thought. She hadn't even been brave enough to go see the grave.

"You can have more babies," Diana said.

Annie shook her head and looked away, out the parlor window where Burdell played with Will on the lawn. "No."

Two months hadn't been enough time to allow herself to think of that. Two years or two decades wouldn't be enough time.

Charmaine, too, tried to talk to her, tried to pull her from her protective cocoon, but Annie remained withdrawn and silent. She watched through the windowpanes as the family gathered in the newly green side yard and set up the croquet set for the first time that year. Life

328

just went on, she thought dismally. Without her.

After dinner, Burdell ignored her protests and pushed her out onto the porch. He sat on a wicker chair across from her.

"How long are you going to feel sorry for yourself?" he asked.

She ignored his taunt and stared at the hazy mountain peaks.

"The only happy person around here is Mother, because she has her invalid daughter back," he said. "What does that tell you?"

Annie glared at him. "I should have listened to her from the beginning and this wouldn't have happened."

"You think nobody ever lost a baby before?" he asked.

She shook her head against his words.

"You think only helpless crippled people have accidents?"

She shrugged, avoided his face.

"What happened to you could have happened to anybody."

"No. I wasn't fast enough. I wasn't strong enough. I was slow and clumsy and I let him down. He deserves someone with two good legs." She glanced across the yard and caught sight of her cousin running after a wooden ball. "He deserves someone who can be a real help and not a burden—someone like Charmaine."

Burdy was silent for a moment. "He loves *you*."

"Well, I lost his baby, didn't I? How sad for him that he loves *me!* He deserves better. He gave me *everything,* love, kindness, hope . . . he's so good and so pure and wonderful that it hurts." She brought her fist to her heart in proof. "And the first thing he ever trusted me with I lost for him."

"Not the first thing," Burdell denied.

"What do you mean?"

"First, he trusted you with his heart."

Tears blurred her vision. Luke had given her his heart. Completely. Unreservedly. He'd loved her more than she had ever dreamed of being loved. "I just can't bear to face him," she whispered, tears thick in her throat. "I'm so ashamed that I let him down."

"We're to blame for this," her brother said angrily. "Me as much as anyone. I treated you like Mother did for so long that I convinced myself you were helpless. I know I have a hard head, but I saw how happy he made you, how happy and self-confident you were doing things for yourself. I've been wrong. Now I'm sure. This isn't you—not sitting here like an invalid. You are a capable, talented woman. What happened to you and your baby could have happened to anyone— could have happened to Diana in the same situation."

"But it didn't. She wasn't out trying to be a farrier's wife."

"But if she loved a farrier, you can bet she would have. She's just trying to be a banker's wife."

Annie thought long and hard about that statement. If Diana had loved a rancher or a miner or a logger, she undoubtedly would have thrown her whole self into that kind of life—just as Annie had. "Do you believe that Burdy? Do you believe it was an accident that could have happened to anyone?"

"I do. And I think Luke's blaming himself as much as you blame yourself right now. He told our father he accepted the responsibility for taking you away from your safe environment and letting this happen."

"Oh, pooh!" Annie said. "Isn't that just like him to take the blame himself in order to spare me?"

"He's hurting, too, Annie. Think about that."

"I have. And I've decided he's better off without me."

"Right," he said. "Let him hurt alone. Let him grieve for both of you. Poor Annie," he said, getting up. "Poor, helpless Annie." And with that he walked down the stairs and strode across the yard.

His words of mocking pity stung. Annie considered all of Burdell's words in the days that followed. Alone in her room one afternoon, she took a good clear look at her situation. She had been feeling sorry for herself, taking the blame for something that couldn't have been prevented, and in doing so she was throwing away the best thing that had ever happened to her. How could she have let herself fall into this river of self-centered despondency? Luke had lost a son, and she had walked out on him.

Let him hurt alone. Let him grieve for both of you. He had buried their child alone. Had reverently wrapped the tiny lifeless infant in a soft pretty blanket sewn by Annie's hands, dug a grave, said a prayer and cried all by himself.

Annie slid from her chair to her knees beside the window seat and sobbed out her grief and shame and regret. When had she become this spineless traitor who let her husband bear their burdens alone?

Every day after that she got out of her chair and exercised her aching body, strengthening her legs and her resolve. When Charmaine came to call, Annie surprised her by asking her to drive her to the livery.

Charmaine clapped her gloved hands cheerfully. "Oh, you've come to your senses! Are you ready? Do you want your chair?"

"No. Just hold my hand."

Charmaine assisted her into the wagon, climbed up beside her, and guided the horse through the streets. The ring of the hammer met their ears before they ever saw the building. Charmaine stopped the wagon in front of the open double doors. She jumped down and helped Annie to the ground. "Want me to walk with you?"

"No. Wait here, please." Annie gathered her courage and her hem and limped into the shaded building, following the hammering back into the humid depths, toward the forge.

He stood silhouetted against the blaze of the fire, turned without seeing her and held long tongs which gripped a horseshoe into the flames. Reaching up, he pumped the bellows, the muscles across his bare shoulders rippling and shining.

Annie drank in the sight of him. He was leaner than he'd been before last winter, before she'd lost the baby and deserted him. He did everything alone now, with no one to cook for him—to do his laundry—to rub his shoulders at night.

Turning back, he placed the horseshoe against the anvil and pounded. Annie resisted covering her ears, instead let the punishing ring fill her senses. After several blows, Luke inspected his work, then plunged the shoe into a bucket of cold water.

Hissing steam rose around his torso.

Annie let her hand fall from her breast, and the movement must have caught his eye, because he looked up. He seemed startled to see her there, finally setting down the shoe and the tongs and coming forward. "Annie?"

Chapter Seventeen

He grabbed a rag and wiped his hands and face.

"Hello, Luke."

"What are you doing here?"

"I came to see you." Now that she was here, she didn't know quite what to say. He was covered with soot and perspiration, but he looked so good and familiar, she wanted to grab him and hold him. "How have you been?"

"All right."

"And the house?" This felt silly. *I'm sorry! I've been so wrong!* "How are things there?"

"I haven't been there for a while. Several weeks actually."

She hadn't known that. "You've been staying where—here?"

He wiped sweat from his hair, making it stand up in ebony spikes. "It's easier for me."

"Oh. Are you—do you want to live there again?" *With me,* was what she meant. *Can we start over?*

"I think things are probably better this way," he said. "I was away too much. I can't erase anything that happened before . . . but I can make sure you're safe now. I want to help take care of you . . . send money."

"I don't need your money." *I need you!*

He stiffened. "I'll send it anyhow. You're my responsibility."

"Is that all I am now? A responsibility?" *What about wife? What about lover?*

"No."

They stared at each other. The heat from the forge had begun to seep through her clothing.

"It's because of me that you were hurt," he said finally. "Because I was so determined to make things work my way, in my time. I was a fool. I pushed you too hard."

Pushed her too hard? Or expected her to be someone she couldn't be? Did he think he was a fool for ever wanting her in the first place? "So, you're sorry," she said. "Sorry you married me."

She turned and limped from the room, wishing she could run gracefully, wishing she didn't humiliate herself at every turn.

"Annie!"

She kept going, her heart aching with his rejection. Charmaine met her outside the doors. "What's wrong? What did he say? What happened?"

"Nothing," she said, wanting to cry, but not wanting to do it here. "Just help me up and get me away from here."

"Okay." Her cousin obeyed as quickly as she could, assisting Annie and shaking the reins over the horses' backs.

Annie didn't look back.

Nothing was the same as it had been before Luke. No longer was she satisfied to be the doted-upon daughter. Nor was anything the same as it had been since Luke—or since they'd lost their hopes. She couldn't go back to either life, so what was left?

Charmaine helped her down from the wagon and Annie made her own way into the house, through the doorway and to her room. Burdell had told her she was feeling sorry for herself, and she'd taken that to heart and tried to help herself. But now Luke seemed to think she was better off here than with him—how could he think that? Didn't he know? Didn't he care?

She sat abruptly on the window seat, glanced aside and observed the row of angelic-faced porcelain dolls. Here she was back in the bosom of her family, back in this room, back in her chair like a pretty, useless, lifeless doll!

Angry at Luke, angry at life and at her helplessness, she lashed out and swept a doll from its resting place and smashed it against the floorboards. Another followed and another, until only two remained, staring at her as though they knew how crazy and helpless she really was. Turning, she kicked the lifeless broken bodies across the floor.

"Annie!" Her mother appeared in the doorway, Charmaine on her heels.

"Go away!" Annie flung herself on the bed and cried tears of frustration and anger. "Leave me alone!"

Charmaine backed out of the room, but Mildred came to stand beside her bed. "I'll leave you alone after I've had a word with you."

"Oh, Mother, please, what could you say that you haven't said already?"

"Maybe that you need to pick yourself up and decide what you want out of life." She stuffed a scented handkerchief into Annie's fist. "You were happy before, Annie. Don't let anything stop you from getting what you want. Even if it's *him*." Her lip curled a little at the pronoun.

Annie wiped her eyes and nose. "Are you telling me to go after my husband?"

Her back was straight and her eyes didn't quite meet Annie's, but Mildred spoke the words all the same. "I'm telling you to live your dream."

The door closed behind her a moment later.

Annie curled on her side and thought about her dream.

After Charmaine had gone, after Annie heard the sound of the stove lids clanking in the kitchen, she pulled herself together and went to her writing desk. She pulled out a piece of paper and uncorked the ink. She hadn't given up. Not by a long shot.

Dear Luke,

You taught me courage when I was afraid. You showed me I could do things I only dreamed of. You gave me confidence to stand up and walk in front of people without shame. Which one of us is the cripple now? Who was hiding behind their fear today? You are cordially invited to my birthday celebration. I think you know the day—and the place.

With love,
Annie

She found Glenda wiping the kitchen floor. "Glenda, will you please do me a favor?"

"Of course. Are you all right?"

"I am now. Will you please deliver this to my husband at the livery?"

Glenda took the letter with a smile.

"Oh, and these—" she extended the two remaining dolls "—are for Gwen and Gerta."

"They'll love them. Thank you."

Five days later, on the day of Annie's birthday, the sky was a vivid blue. Fleecy white clouds hung above the mountains in the distance, but the air here was clear and clean.

"You surprised me by wanting a birthday party," her father said, tucking her hand in the crook of his arm and leading her across the verdant lawn. "I'm glad you're feeling up to it."

"Actually, it was Mother who convinced me."

"Your mother?" he asked in disbelief.

"Well, not in so many words, of course, but because she got me to thinking about the rest of my life."

Friends and neighbors arrived, Burdell and Diana and their family, the Renlows, Lizzy and Guy, even Dr. Martin and Glenda's family. Annie had invited Luke's Uncle Gil, and he surprised her by showing up wearing the shirt she'd made him, with Mrs. Krenshaw, the librarian, on his arm.

Burdell set up the croquet hoops and Annie tried her hand at the game for the first time. She enjoyed herself, but underneath the surface was the underlying question of whether or not Luke would come. She was working on not worrying when the crowd grew quiet. Turning to observe the source of their attention, she saw the rider stop at the gate and dismount.

Tall and handsome, black hair shining in the sunlight, Luke opened the gate and walked forward. Annie's heart hammered and welcoming joy spread through her like a healing balm. She took a few steps to meet him, then a few more.

She met him halfway, a giddy bubble expanding her chest.

"Happy Birthday, Annie," he said.

"Thank you."

"I have presents for you."

She glanced at his empty hands. "Where are they?"

"Want me to take you to them?"

Wrangler placidly munched grass along the fence. "Go for a ride, you mean?"

"Uh-huh."

"All right."

He took her hand and led her out the way he'd come, out the gate, then walked her all the way to the flower cart at the edge of the yard and helped her on the horse's back. He climbed up behind her.

"Where are we going?"

"Home."

Her heart leaped with joy at the words. She turned and waved at her family who were all watching. They returned the wave, even her mother.

Luke wrapped his strong arms around her and Annie leaned into him, feeling safe and protected within his embrace. The horse moved beneath them, nudging Luke's chin against her hair. Could he forgive her? Could she make it up to him for allowing him to suffer their loss without her?

Their home came into view, a thin curl of smoke trailing from the rock chimney. Instead of leading the horse to the house, Luke led him to a grassy area on the hillside above, tethered him and lifted Annie down. Annie noted something colorful spread on the ground and several items hidden beneath blankets.

"What is this?" she asked.

"A private birthday party," he replied. "Look, I bought you a rug."

What was spread upon the ground was indeed a Brussels carpet in greens, blues, tan and wine with a border and tassel trim. "It's lovely, but why is it out here?"

"Because your other present is definitely an outdoor present and I wanted you to enjoy both at once."

She glanced around, noting the mysterious bundles. "Okay."

He went to one and withdrew a long rifle.

"A gun?" she asked.

"A rifle. And I'm going to show you how to load it and use it. Next time a wolf comes around you won't have to be afraid." He gave her a quick lesson, showed her how to hold the butt against her shoulder and fire. She tried a few practice shots, scaring birds from the underbrush.

"You were right, Annie," he said from behind her.

She lowered the barrel and turned.

"What you said in your note. I was hiding. I expected you to be so brave and overcome your fears, but at my first mistake I turned and ran."

She looked at the weapon in her hands.

"Well, this is definitely the most unusual—and practical—birthday gift I've ever received." She handed him the rifle.

He unloaded it and laid it down.

"You didn't make any mistakes, Luke."

He gestured with an outstretched hand. "There are wolves out here. Bears, too. I knew that. I should have prepared you. Taught you what to do. That was my mistake."

"It's not your fault. I blamed myself for being clumsy, too. What good does blaming ourselves do? I'm the one who left you, remember?"

"You needed your family."

"You're my family," she said firmly. "I needed you. But I ran, because I thought I failed you."

"You could never fail me," he assured her with his eyes as well as his words.

"What about afterward?" she asked, allowing her anguish to push the feelings out into the open. "What about me letting you take care of the baby alone—grieve alone? That was wrong. I'm so sorry."

"Annie, I had to do it. You were too weak, and I didn't mind. You had the whole—physical thing to deal with. I couldn't help with that. I don't even know what you went through really."

"I should have shared it with you. We should have done our crying together."

"I don't think it's too late," he said hoarsely. "I know I have tears left."

"Oh, Luke," she said, rushing forward to wrap her arms around his waist and hug him tightly. "Luke, I'm so sorry."

He held her tightly, his heart beating comfortingly beneath her cheek.

"Luke, can you forgive me?"

"Annie, if we say we forgive each other, then that means there was blame somewhere, and there's no blame. Let's just start over."

"All right," she whispered.

"I have one more present for you."

She released him, and he stepped away, peeled back a blanket to reveal a mahogany box with a horn attached.

Annie had seen one similar on a trip East. "A graphophone! How extravagant!"

"We can dance anytime we like," he said and wound the crank on the side.

Tinny music rang from the horn. Wrangler raised his head and shook it. Annie laughed.

"May I have this dance?" her husband asked, bowing before her like a proper gentleman.

She gave him her hand. He extended one foot. She stepped on it and he guided her across the carpet in time to the music. The music slowed and Annie placed her head against his chest.

"We lost our child together," he said, his voice low against her ear. "We can't let it be something that drives us apart."

She raised her head to look at him. "That day at

the livery you said you pushed me too hard. That's not so. You encouraged me to become who I wanted to be all along. Loving you is what gave me the courage to try."

"We'll have more babies," he promised. "They won't replace the one we lost, but they'll help us get over the sadness."

"Was he very beautiful, our John?" she asked.

The music had stopped, and Luke brought their movements to a halt. "Like a beautiful little man. Perfect in all ways, but too tiny."

"Did he have black hair?"

"Yes. Let me take you to his grave."

He lifted her to Wrangler's back and walked, leading the horse. They made their way down the hill, below the timberline, around knee-high prickly plants and bright patches of buttercups and fireweed. Several feet from the last patch of aspens, with a view of the house below and the horses in the corral lay a small mound of smooth rocks.

Luke helped her down, and they made their way in silence to the tiny grave.

"This is a beautiful spot," she told him after a few minutes of silence.

"I chose it because you can see our house from here."

"Well, it's perfect." She looked at the stones so lovingly selected and placed, and her arms ached for the child she would never hold. She reached for Luke's hand and lowered herself to the ground. "I never thanked you for thinking of the blanket for him."

"Seemed only right. I put him in a pretty box— one I'd saved and stained."

A tear made its way down her cheek. "Didn't have to be very big, I'd guess."

He gripped her fingers hard. "No. He was tiny."

Annie looked up and saw his throat working, his mouth clamped in a hard line. She pulled him down beside her and they wept in each other's arms. Tears of grief and sorrow, but also reviving, cleansing tears. Annie kissed his beautiful face, the scar on his lip, his damp lashes. "I love you . . . more than ever."

"I didn't think I could love you more, but I do," he replied. "I was miserable without you, my sweet Annie."

"I'm home to stay." She turned in his arms and surveyed their land, the foothills, the brilliant sky, and the grave where they knelt. Her attention caught on the delicate blue flowers bordering the stones. "Diana told me about the forget-me-nots. Thank you for planting them."

"I didn't plant them, Annie."

She pulled away to look at him. "Who did then?"

His mouth inched up and those dashing dimples flashed her a smile. "I was curious about that myself," he replied. "Seems a certain woman bought seeds and a spade at the hardware store."

"What woman was that?"

"Your mother."

Her mother? "How did she get here?" she asked in amazement. "How did she find the grave?"

"Burdell and Diana asked about it so that they could come visit. Maybe she heard them talking." He shrugged. "I don't know."

She imagined her mother finding someone to give her a ride to their land—Annie's father?—then traipsing through the mud and undergrowth to find the mound of stones. Annie couldn't have been more shocked—or more pleased. To think that her mother cared enough to make such an extravagant gesture touched her deeply—and gave her hope for the years ahead.

She let the tears fall freely, for herself, for Luke and their baby, for her mother whose dreams had been lost somewhere along life's way but who had encouraged Annie not to lose hers.

When Luke turned her face up to his and kissed her, her tears turned to joy, because her dream was still very much alive. Loving him was what had given her the courage to try in the first place. Loving him would give her the courage to start over. She and Luke faced a bright future—together.

Epilogue

The spring sky was a dazzling shade of blue that contrasted starkly with the fleecy white clouds, the dense pines on the foothills and the faded purple of the distant mountains. Annie studied the bright expanse, reminded as always of her husband's eyes, and filled with unspeakable joy. Once she had wanted to reach out and touch that distant glory. Now she held heaven in her heart, in her arms, in each day and every moment of her life with Luke.

Closing her eyes, she lowered her face to the warm bundle lying against her breast and breathed in life and love and happiness.

"He's a beautiful boy," her mother said softly from beside her.

Annie nodded. Conversation and laughter swelled around them.

"May I hold him for a while?"

Annie smiled and handed Mildred her chubby two-month-old son.

Her mother's face took on a soft adoring expression as she cradled the sleeping baby.

"Watch, Mama! Watch!" an elfin voice called gleefully.

At the call, Annie turned.

Her three-year-old daughter, Rebecca, ran

toward a croquet ball, clumsily wielding a mallet, and managed only to soundly whack her father in the shin.

Wide-eyed, Luke grabbed his injured leg and dropped to the lawn carpet.

Annie rose from her comfortable spot in the shade and hurried toward them, holding back rising laughter.

"I sorry, Daddy," Rebecca said, her round blue eyes serious with concern. "I kiss it better." She leaned over Luke's pant leg.

"Kiss me here," he said, lying on his back and pointing to his lips.

The toddler tripped over her pinafore once, then crawled to lean against his chest and plant a kiss on his mouth. "All better?"

"I think Mama needs to kiss me, too." His gaze twinkling with mischief, he placed a hand beneath his head and casually crossed his ankles.

Annie knelt on the grass, glancing once at Burdy and Diana, who weren't doing a very good job of holding back their amusement.

Leaning forward, she kissed her husband's warm lips.

"Happy birthday, Annie," he said, caressing her face. "Are you happy?"

Tears blurred her vision momentarily, and she blinked until she could see clearly again. She glanced about at the gathering of friends and family on her parents' lawn. Luke's Uncle Gil and Mrs. Krenshaw were making a clover chain for Will. Charmaine was showing a young gentleman friend how to wind the graphophone. Annie's parents sat on the porch admiring their newest grandson.

Annie's precious daughter watched her expectantly. Annie pulled her close and hugged her, her heart full to bursting. Luke sat up. Annie plucked a blade of grass from his hair, then took his hand and placed his palm against her cheek. She gazed into his blue eyes and said with certainty, "This is the best day of my life."

CHERYL ST. JOHN

A peacemaker, a romantic, an idealist and a discouraged perfectionist are words that Cheryl uses to describe herself. The author of both historical and contemporary novels says she's been told that she is painfully honest.

Cheryl admits to being an avid collector who gathers everything, including dolls, depression glass, brass candlesticks, old photographs and—most especially—books. She and her husband love to browse antiques and collectibles shops.

She says that knowing her stories bring hope and pleasure to readers is one of the best parts of being a writer. The other wonderful part is being able to set her own schedule and have time to work around her growing family.

Center Point Large Print
600 Brooks Road / PO Box 1
Thorndike, ME 04986-0001 USA

(207) 568-3717

US & Canada:
1 800 929-9108
www.centerpointlargeprint.com